Dream Daddy

EMILIA BEAUMONT

Copyright © 2017 EMILIA BEAUMONT
All rights reserved.
ISBN: 1544724802
ISBN-13: 978-1544724805

Copyright © 2017 by Emilia Beaumont

All rights reserved.

No part of this book may be reproduced in any form or by any electronic or mechanical means, including information storage and retrieval systems, without written permission from the author, except for the use of brief quotations in a book review.

* * *

Warning: This novel contains adult situations (DD/lg) which may be objectionable to some readers. Not recommended for anyone under the age of 18.

* * *

Want to keep up to date with Emilia's new releases?

Sign up for her newsletter to be the first to know about her new books, promotions and the chance to join her exclusive ebook ARC team!

Newsletter: http://eepurl.com/bODL4L

Facebook: https://www.facebook.com/authoremiliabeaumont

Table of Contents

Chapter One	**1**
Chapter Two	**17**
Chapter Three	**29**
Chapter Four	**41**
Chapter Five	**49**
Chapter Six	**59**
Chapter Seven	**73**
Chapter Eight	**83**
Chapter Nine	**95**
Chapter Ten	**103**
Chapter Eleven	**107**
Chapter Twelve	**117**
Chapter Thirteen	**127**

Chapter Fourteen	**137**
Chapter Fifteen	**147**
Chapter Sixteen	**159**
Chapter Seventeen	**171**
Chapter Eighteen	**183**
Chapter Nineteen	**193**
Chapter Twenty	**205**
Chapter Twenty One	**213**
Chapter Twenty Two	**229**
Chapter Twenty Three	**245**
Chapter Twenty Four	**259**
Chapter Twenty Five	**273**
Chapter Twenty Six	**285**
Chapter Twenty Seven	**297**
Chapter Twenty Eight	**313**
Chapter Twenty Nine	**323**

Chapter Thirty	**333**
Chapter Thirty One	**341**
Chapter Thirty Two	**347**
Chapter Thirty Three	**357**
Epilogue	**365**
All about Emilia	**377**
Also by Emilia	**379**

Chapter One
Lola Ray

The front door slammed. I sat up straighter at my desk and strained to hear the voices below. It couldn't be. He was early. My daddy was speaking, greeting someone, and then I heard him. *Mack was here!*

In a panic I looked down at my clothes. I'd been so busy finishing off a batch of coursework so that I would be ready in time for daddy's best friend, Maddox McClane, arriving that he'd gone and blown my whole plan out of the water. I was still in my nightclothes—a loose T-shirt and pair of shorts—and was nowhere near presentable. Instead of changing that morning I decided to get stuck in to my college assignments so that it would be done and dusted before the Sunday game. But the time had slipped away from me. I had to get ready, dress up for him. Daddy would soon be calling for his chips and dip, too.

Sundays, especially during this football season, were days that I lived for. Not because I liked football, far from it. I could barely stand the sport. But Daddy worshiped the game as most of the men and boys around our small southern town of Weyworth did. The only reason I loved Sundays was because it was the only real time I got to spend with Mack. He would come around each week to watch the game with him. Apparently they used to know each other as kids and when Mack moved into the house behind ours a few months ago, a weekly tradition was born. Mack and Daddy would be glued to the men running around on the field up on the big flat-screen TV in the den, and I would sit quietly out of the way staring in turn at Mack.

Dreaming of him on top of me.

Dreaming of him slipping into me, stealing my virginity away.

Dreaming of him becoming mine.

It didn't matter that he was my daddy's best friend. It didn't matter that he was nearly twice my age. The only thing that mattered was that feeling when, on rare occasions, he glanced over at me and gave me a sneaky smile. That smile made me want to part my legs right in front of him, to let him have a sneak peek at what he was missing out on… on what I wanted to give him. Like the snacks I regularly served him, I wanted to offer up my virginity on a platter to him.

A man like him, there was no doubt he could have any woman he wanted, and probably had. He had the look of experience about him. But I wanted him to want me. To see *me*. He had to realize that my breasts were no longer budding small peaches, but were now real handfuls to grab hold of. To squeeze and nip at whenever he wanted.

I was getting myself all worked up just thinking about him and I closed my textbook with a loud thud and pushed my chair back and headed toward the shower. I had to work quickly. There wasn't a moment to waste. I had less than three hours to bask in his presence and I'd already wasted a small portion of that time daydreaming when I should've been downstairs. *I would pray for overtime to make up the minutes.*

With my hair scooped up into a bun I soaped the suds all over my body and hastily rinsed them off. It was the fastest shower in the history of all showers, a world-record. I resisted the temptation to let my hands skim over my body while fantasizing about Mack... better to fantasize about him where I could see him, in the flesh. Dropping water everywhere, I sprinted back across the hall to my room to towel off and get dressed.

The decision on what to wear was always a difficult task each week. It had to be good enough that I would look hot, but not too hot. Not so slutty that Daddy would notice and send me back upstairs to change. That would be far too embarrassing. Daddy was always pretty strict about what I could and couldn't wear. But I had my ways getting around his scrutiny and disapproval. Not that he paid me very much attention anyway, it was only when he wanted something that he dared to look at me—or when I'd accidentally done something wrong. I'd convinced myself that him ignoring me had to do with me reminding him too much of my mother. The woman who had broken his heart and skipped out of town, ultimately leaving both of us behind.

But really he was just a grade-A dick who resented the fact he had to put a roof over my head ever since my mother split. He treated me like his own personal slave, not his daughter, and for the time being, until I could afford to move out or leave town I had to put up with it.

Keep my head down, get my degree at the local community college, and soon I'd be free. But I didn't want to wait that long, especially not when I thought about Mack… my one true escape.

At my closet I pulled out a few choice items then pursed my lips as I tried to decide between what I'd set out. It was either going to be a pair of tight jeans that would show off my legs, matched with a simple scooped-neck top, or it would be the recent purchase I'd managed to snag in the autumn sale: a strappy, pale yellow sundress. The weather was colder now, but I could still get away with wearing it, especially indoors. It was perfectly respectable with a hem just above my knee. Something that I could wear to church but would still sinfully show off my curves.

I grinned as I thought of what I could do to spice it up, and put the bra I'd originally intended to wear back in the drawer. The fabric of the dress and the paneling at the front would give my breasts enough support, but was also thin enough that I was sure my nipples would be temptingly visible, little nubs for Mack to see. Just the idea of him staring at my body brought a warm flush all over my skin, my nipples already hardening. I hadn't even seen him yet and I was already buzzing with lusty excitement.

With the dress zipped up, I slipped on a cute

pair of flats and quickly dusted a smattering of makeup on my face. Not too much. Daddy hated it when I wore too much. He would tell me I looked like a common whore—like my mother—if I choose the wrong lipstick color or if I coated my lashes with thick mascara. So I kept it simple, sweet, and innocent. Just the look I was going for, if I was being honest with myself. I was far from innocent though. Something had awoken in me recently. A desire, a fire that I believed only Mack could quench.

As I was about to reach for the door handle of my bedroom, ready to run downstairs and make my entrance, I stopped. Before I could talk myself out of it I lifted the skirt of the dress, hooked my fingers around the sides of my white panties and pulled them down and shook them off.

The idea of me being bare in his presence, or of the chance that Mack might sneak a peek under my skirt as I crossed over my legs had me feeling all kinds of naughty and wet. *Maybe I'd even twirl a bit when Daddy wasn't looking, let the hem of the dress flutter upwards for Mack to see*, I thought with a dirty grin, and ran down the stairs.

"Hey! Keep your noise down. We can't hear what they're saying," Daddy shouted as I entered the sitting room that was really more of a den. It was dark, the shades partially drawn so the light didn't land on the TV. Breathless from my little run—I had to admit I had made quite a racket coming down, overly excited to see Mack—I apologized to my father and eased myself into the spare chair off to the side. Knees together. *For the time being.*

"Yeah, well don't make a habit of it. Like a herd of elephants it was," Daddy said and turned his attention back to the screen, where they were playing commercials; trying to sell men like my daddy a new truck. He hadn't missed a damn thing of the actual game, but I resisted shaking my head and talking back; he'd scolded me for much worse in the past, and I didn't want to get banished to my room and away from seeing and spending time with Mack.

Speaking of Mack, I took a deep breath and cautiously elevated my gaze toward where I knew he was sitting. I hadn't yet looked directly at him. I had to be careful not to be too obvious. Daddy was in the Lazy Boy closest to me and I was forced to look past him to the other black leather recliner in order to see Mack. Timing my gazes was crucial. But I was used to this. My daddy never gave up his chair for anyone and Mack was always in the chair farthest away from my own seat. Either way I had to be careful and clever; I was forced to divide my attention.

Sometimes I would pretend to watch the game, feigning an interest, other times I would use my phone as a way to disguise where my attention really lay. And sometimes, when I was feeling really naughty and when they were both so preoccupied with the pigskin on the screen, I would just stare at Mack outright, willing him to look back.

Luckily at that moment Mack was leaning forward, a hand tucked up under his strong chin resting his weight on his knee, and instead of struggling to see his side profile I got a clear view straight away. My insides sighed as I took him in.

Rugged and buff, dirty and hot.

Sexy as sin… with his bulging muscles, typical blue denim jeans, and the tan that caressed his face he could've been mistaken for a cowboy. A pony I wanted to ride. But he was no pony. He was a fucking stallion. One that would buck and thrust. He could saddle me up, whip me, rein me in, and ride me off into the sunset.

For the thousandth time that year I cursed the gods that Mack wasn't younger. I wished he wasn't my daddy's best friend. I wished that he wasn't so completely off limits. Or that better still, I wished that I was older. That my teenage mother had done everyone a favor and spread her legs a bit sooner. If that had happened,

I would've been old enough that it wouldn't have mattered and been able, by now, to make a move. Out from under my daddy's roof and perhaps already in Mack's arms.

Though my birthday was next week, I thought wickedly. I would be a proper woman. Nineteen and ready. I bit my lip as a plan started to form in my mind.

"What the hell are you doing just sitting there?" Daddy asked, rudely interrupting my thoughts. Though he wasn't really asking, and by his tone I knew to keep quiet. "Get! In the kitchen with you. We'll be needing our snacks. And don't forget about the wings. They should've been in ages ago!"

"Yes, Daddy," I muttered and got to my feet, disappointed that I'd be slaving away in the kitchen instead of being able to lazily dream about Mack while he was right there in the room.

"Oh, and bring us two more beers will you?" he said as he lifted his arm and waggled the empty bottle he was holding.

"Sure," I replied and made my way out of the den, closing the wooden door behind me as I'd been taught to do. Had to keep the heat in and not let it escape, Daddy had always warned me; he wasn't made of money… and I certainly wasn't paying anything toward the heating bill, he loved to say. I'd heard it so many times now, it had been beaten into me over the years and it was now second nature to close the doors and shut off lights and electronics when I was no longer in the room. I skirted around the dining table that we barely used and went into the kitchen, heading straight for the fridge. Best not to keep him waiting.

I grabbed two cold long-necks and clinked them down onto the counter, easing their tops off.

I bit my lip looking at the rim of one. *What if I…?*

I knew I was taking a risk, entering dangerous waters. But nothing could've stopped me right then.

Taking the bottle in my grasp I brought it to my lips and kissed the glass opening, imagining Mack's mouth. Becoming bolder I swirled my tongue around, leaving traces of my saliva upon it. *Mack's bottle.*

His lips would connect with the rim as he took a pull, the foamy beer snaking down his throat and along with it he'd take a little bit of me with the malty suds. My nipples stood erect as I contemplated this image. And lower still my pussy pulsed. Little exciting flutterings I had no control over.

Still holding Mack's bottle in my hand I wondered what if I did something more… something a little more naughty.

I lowered the bottle to my thigh, thinking. My heart was racing. Thudding in my chest as the idea of what I was about to do bloomed like a rose, fully forming in my mind. But what if I was caught? What if he realized and said something? It would be his word against mine, though Daddy would most likely side with Mack.

I did it anyway.

I took the neck of the bottle and slipped it under my dress. Breathless I brought it closer to my apex and let the smooth cold glass touch me. I gasped and the bottle almost slipped from my hand. Feeling bolder I increased the pressure and let the top of the bottle skim along the seam of my bare pussy. It felt good. Cold, jolting, and hard. *But it wouldn't feel as good as Mack's cock*, I thought, as I continued to cover the rim with my exquisite juices. I was sorely tempted to take the neck inside me, but I'd never done that before. Never even fingered myself. I was saving myself. Saving it all for when Mack would notice me.

"How's it going in here?"

For the second time in the space of a few seconds the bottle almost slipped from my grasp as the voice boomed around the kitchen. Desperately I whipped the bottle away from myself. The skirt of my dress swayed as if it had been hit by a breeze. My stomach flipped with dread—I'd been caught—and I spun round. I bit my lip and tried to recover. I was blushing like mad, but as Mack came fully into the room, easing up to the central island of the kitchen, I thought perhaps there was a slim chance he hadn't seen what I'd been doing. That maybe the counter had obscured his view from the other side of the room.

He grinned and leaned on the counter as if nothing was untoward, as if he hadn't just caught me touching myself with… *oh god*. I put the bottle I'd been holding down next to the other one on the counter. They both sweated; little beads of perspiration trickling down their glassy exteriors as I waited for Mack to say something, anything.

Mack nodded to the one I'd put down, the one I'd just removed from the seam of my pussy. "Is that one mine?" he asked. He said it with such normality that I breathed a sigh of relief. He hadn't seen. *Thank god.* If he had, he wouldn't be taking the bottle right there in front of me and lifting it to his lips. Would he?

He didn't take a drink. Not yet.

The neck of the bottle merely rested on his lips, under his nose and the dusting of stubble, as he stared at me. His gaze was unwavering. Would he say something if he did notice something strange about his beer? Call me out on what I did?

I couldn't look away from him. I was trapped, my eyes locked on his. We were the only two people in the whole world and he held my life in his hands. What would he do? Would he tell my daddy? Call me out on being the dirty horny daughter I was becoming? But that's what college was for, exploring your body, your desires… Right?

I could barely stand the intensity of his gaze. The side of his mouth twitched. A tiny smile. But I saw it and let out a tiny breath of relief. I'd studied him long enough to know when he was smiling, when he was amused, or when something was bothering him. And that time, in front of me in the kitchen, he was definitely smiling—his pale blue eyes sparkling. He was doing his best to hide it, though.

The tip of his tongue darted out to touch the opening of the bottle. Then his whole mouth locked around the rim and he swallowed down a healthy gulp.

"So sweet, tastes like fresh honey," he said before taking another mouthful, his eyes never leaving mine each time he titled his head back. "Just how I like my beer. Sweet and untouched…"

My mouth was dry as I watched him finish the bottle trying to sort through the meaning of his words. He licked his lips, seeking every last drop.

"Where's my beer?" Daddy yelled from the other room.

I couldn't find my voice and Mack answered for me, "Got 'em."

I pushed the untampered bottle toward him and he took it. "Grab me another, will you?" he said to me, his words low, secretive. I did and handed it over without being able to utter a sound. He gave me a subtle wink and turned to leave the room.

"Hey, Lola Ray?" Mack said as he reached the kitchen door.

"Yes?" I replied, breathless.

"You have a birthday coming up, don't you?"

I nodded.

"Soon, right?"

I nodded again and his eyebrows rose with satisfaction.

"Good. I'm looking forward to it."

DREAM DADDY

Chapter Two
Mack

For a large guy I could be quite stealthy when I wanted to be.

I stood in the doorway to the kitchen after easing the door open and watched Lola Ray at the counter. She was facing away from me, the lines of her sweet young body right there for me to feast on. That dress looked like it was made for her, hugging her tight, like a second skin. Her little waist tapered in, then the outlines of her body rapidly bloomed outwards, her hips swelling, wide and shapely.

And all so very tight. Untouched. Her father was strict about that, I knew. She'd never had a boyfriend and I was damn sure she wasn't allowed to date the local boys at her college either.

I also hadn't failed to notice, before she'd left the den earlier, that she was braless. And so goddamn perky. It was almost enough to make a grown man cry… or excuse himself to go to the bathroom to, well, you know, jerk one off. But I resisted. Instead I wanted to see more, not just the fantasy of her in my head.

Fantasies were all I had though and I allowed myself a few seconds to take the image of her behind in. It would give me something to think about later when I was back home, alone.

From across the room Lola Ray's breath hitched. She hadn't yet turned around—seemingly hadn't heard me come in or noticed that I was standing there—and I wondered what she was doing.

There was a single bottle of beer on the counter. Was she struggling to open the other one? Her head was titled down as if in concentration. That had to be it. I moved closer, silent, not wanting to startle her and saw that her legs were slightly parted. Unusually so. Not a normal stance, and her knees were somewhat bent.

I caught the flutter of her dress, the bottom of the hem rippling. A flash of green; the base of a beer bottle, rising up, beneath her dress.

Then I understood.

Dirty fucking girl, I thought with a devious smile.

She was pleasuring herself, right there in the fucking kitchen, while her dad and I were in the next room. But lucky for me I was no longer in the next room. I was there watching her. Taking in every movement and slight gasp she made. Getting hard. So fucking hard it was becoming uncomfortable. And I wondered if she wanted something thicker to contend with.

She wouldn't know what hit her; I could take her from behind right now, I mused. Replace the neck of the bottle with my cock. Spear her up against the counter, my hand wrapped around her mouth so she wouldn't make a sound. I could be quick, she would be so tight, it would be like it never happened. *Do it.*

Take her.

Don't think about it, I heard a demanding voice cry out. *She wants it. She would love it. March over there, lift up that yellow skirt up and spread her white cheeks before you change your mind.*

Fuck. I wanted to. I needed to have her.

But I had a best friend to think about.

Her father.

My fucking boss. I couldn't lose my job over

one fucking act of insanity with his daughter, no matter how desperate I was to see how tight that little cunt of hers was.

And no doubt it would be tight as a drum.

I startled her and she spun around, her face was a delicious shade of pink. I knew exactly what she was thinking: how much had I seen? If I had seen something, would I say anything? Would I blow up her little world and tell her dad what a naughty girl she was? A little slut doing nasty things in their kitchen who needed to be punished… How she liked to caresses hard objects against her clit?

Fuck, I thought again, regretting my decision to be good, to go against my instincts to take her.

She put the bottle down and stood away from it. Guilty. Caught red-fucking-handed. God she looked even more fuckable now. Innocent. Petrified at what I was going to do. But there was also a mischievous sparkle in her brown doe eyes, daring me to take a sip. She wanted to see if I would do it. She drew her ripe bottom lip into her mouth, clamping it tight between her pearly teeth. A mixture of nerves and anticipation coming off of her in waves.

"Is that one mine?" I asked, concentrating hard on her eyes. They were glossy and wide.

But if I let my own wander I was in danger of ignoring every single sensible warning sign that was going off in my head. Thankfully they were doing a good job of drowning out the cries to just fuck her. But that didn't mean I couldn't have some fun.

Like a scared little rabbit she nodded. Her eyes went gloriously wide again as I surprised her by moving forward, taking the bottle. I brought the beer to my lips and paused. Over the normal sounds of the kitchen, the fridge whirring away, the low buzz of the oven that was on, I could hear Lola Ray struggling to keep her breathing under control. She was breathing fast and low, almost panting.

An image of her on all fours popped into my head and made me smile. Her hands and knees braced up hard against the cold tile of the kitchen floor, and me slipping inside her as she panted harder. She would be a screamer. No doubt about it. But for the time being I would have to do with the little gift she'd inadvertently given me. Though, and I almost chuckled at the thought, was she planning on handing over the sullied bottle anyway? Bring it into the den and let me drink from it, her juices coating the glass, in front of Will, her father? If that had been her plan all along, I had to give her credit for being so bold. She was definitely not the innocent young woman I'd originally had pictured in my mind when I thought of her.

In my hand, the sweet scent of her pussy lingered on the rim of the beer bottle. I let my tongue have the barest of tastes—I couldn't be too greedy, that would only lead to disaster. That *would* lead me to lose control, to fuck her right there and then on the floor, everything be damned.

Her chest swelled as I took my first sip. She was pleased and god so was I. I could see the faint outline of her budding nipples poking through her dress. My cock was straining against my jeans, begging me to let him loose and be done with it. Take her while I still could.

But just like I knew he would, her impatient father yelled from his chair and it was time to back away. To let the fantasy die. There was no way I could have her. Reason and logic, and all that bullshit had to win for now.

However... the little devil on my shoulder turned me back around. She had a birthday coming up. Turning nineteen. A little closer to being acceptable. A birthday that could turn fantasies into reality.

I asked the question and she nodded. It was

almost too good to be true. Now I just had to find out exactly when… and how long I had to hold out before I could claim and devour her pussy for my own.

* * *

The game was dull. We were down, seventeen to ten. It wasn't our best performance at all. And Will wasn't pleased. He never was after a losing game. But there was still time, which was good because it meant I got to stay a little longer at the Saxton's house. It was of course a blessing and a curse. To look but not be able to touch. And sometimes even looking was dangerous. I had to be careful; wait until her father, Will, was fully enthralled in the game on the screen before letting my eyes wander over to where Lola Ray sat.

Each week I'd come and torture myself, over and over. I didn't even really like football, not anymore. Playing in high school and then some in the local college had been enough for me, the expected thing to do. But now I just put up with it, as there was no other legitimate way or excuse for me to be around her. She was like a magnet and I was helpless; a man caught in a siren's cry.

Before that day there'd been no hope. I'd have to be content with my fantasies. But things were changing if the little incident in the kitchen was anything to go by. She was exploring her body, horny, and not afraid—it seemed—of a little pseudo exhibitionism. Granted I was supposed to have been in the den with her father, out of sight, but I couldn't help but think that may not have mattered. She still would've brought me that beer. Still would've let me drink down her cream. She still would've waited for my reaction. She wanted me to know that she liked me. Surely that had been the whole point?

I pondered this as I heard the gentle tap of her nails upon the phone in her hands. The third quarter ended and Will stood up stretching. "Gotta use the john."

I nodded absently, maintaining a casual façade, as he rose out of the recliner and headed for the stairs. We'd been drinking all day, I had a slight buzz, and I was confident that Will would take a while as he drained himself. I sneaked a glance over at Lola Ray. There was a conspiratorial smile on her face as her father left the room, as if she was waiting for just that moment.

Our eyes met.

A rush of need jolted through me. Electrifying me, sparking life into me.

My dick was hard again. The urge to whip it out and let her see how fucking hard she made me was overwhelming.

She tilted her head to the side, an innocent little movement if there ever was one. But this girl—a budding young woman—she may have been innocent but she was also fucking dirty. She knew exactly what she was playing at. She was calculating every move she made, knowing how it affected me. Her coming down braless, in a dress that was practically sheer, was pretty much proof of that. I was surprised Will hadn't said something or told her to put a cardigan on or whatever, but then his mind was on the game, not to mention distracted by the recent difficulties of the construction company he ran and the contract he'd failed to score. Either way I was grateful for finally knowing for sure Lola Ray was all woman now.

She sat quietly in the armchair with her feet flat on the floor, her knees together. The end of the yellow dress was about an inch or so above her knees, nothing much to see. Sadly not riding up her thighs as I wanted it to do. But then she caught my gaze again, smiled and stopped fiddling with her phone and put it down on the arm.

Lola Ray tilted her head, cocking it to the side slightly, watching me as I watched her and started, every so slowly, to open her legs.

No longer were her knees touching.

An inch apart.

Then two.

Oh fuck. I was staring, I knew I was. I couldn't look away. I was in her trap, caught like a squirming fly, sticky in her web. But then I didn't want to get away, I wanted to see.

Three inches. I couldn't wait to catch a glimpse of her panties.

What color was she wearing? Snow-white lacy ones? Or was she more of a minx than I thought she was? Was she bare under there? And if she was naked beneath her dress—she did, after all, conveniently forget her bra—would she be smooth and silky? Or would there be delicate curls waiting for me to see? Wanting to be tugged on?

Five inches. I waited, trying not to drool. Making sure I kept my mouth closed, and my tongue in my mouth, for fear that if I did see her sweet center my tongue would force me to my feet, darting right over there and sink itself into her, my head nestled between her thighs.

Six inches.

Fuck. The shadow was too great. Too dark. I couldn't see a thing. A groan escaped my throat as I heard the sound of water rushing through pipes upstairs. Will would be back soon. Lola Ray's legs snapped shut with a soft smack. Flesh on flesh, the meat of her milky thighs colliding. I wanted to be the cause of that sound again, my hand smacking down on her bottom.

"Do you want another beer?" she asked, startling me to attention, making me move my concentration from her lap to her face.

My throat was dry, but while we had the chance and were alone I wanted to talk to her. I needed to know more…

"So you've got a birthday coming up, huh? When is it?"

"Soon," she replied. Her mouth twitched as she tried not to smile.

"When, Lola Ray?" I demanded. The creak of a worn floorboard sounded upstairs. Will was moving about. Coming back down.

She grinned ignoring my question, as if she knew she had me right where she wanted me. Two could play at that game.

"All right, don't tell me. But you won't get your present."

Lola Ray readjusted herself on the chair, she crossed her legs and sat up a little taller. She contemplated my words, possibly wondering where the trap was. "Will I like it?" she asked sweetly.

"Once you have it, you'll wonder how you ever lived without it."

She took her phone and glanced at it. She was trying to hide the blush that was circling the apples of her cheeks. But she didn't do a good enough job. Was she thinking the same thing that I was? I was almost sure of it.

"Six days," she said, finally relenting, and I was almost taken aback. That wasn't long at all. Six days was a blip in the grand scheme of all things. A tiny moment in one's life when one amassed all the years together. But on the other hand I knew it would be torture. It would be like waiting for Christmas day, knowing exactly what was under the tree but not being able to unwrap it. Counting the days, the hours, the minutes, and even the seconds until I could rush downstairs and tear off the paper and finally enjoy the sweet moment when I could *play* with my present.

But would I be able to last? Would I be able to occupy my thoughts and actions till then?

I would have to, but I didn't hold out much hope. I'd never been a rational man.

Chapter Three
Lola Ray

"So what are you wearing?"

Good question, I thought, as I stood staring into my pitiful closet. I had absolutely nothing to wear. Nothing. At least nothing new. I already spent the last of my money in the sales on that yellow dress, and I couldn't exactly go out to a club in that. I needed something sleeker. There was no way I would've been able to ask my daddy for some spending money to get a new dress, either, he would've grilled me on what I would be spending the money on. If I told him it was for clothes he'd laugh and tell me I had plenty. And I guess in a way I did—he already helped buy me supplies for college. It was just I had nothing sexy enough to go out in for my birthday.

Besides, he wasn't to know about my little birthday adventure. He barely allowed me out of the house as it was. To my college classes and back again. That was the deal.

"Lola Ray?" Robin said into my ear. I was on the phone, discussing outfit choices with my best friend.

"Yeah, I'm still here. I can't decide," I whined and readjusted the towel that was wrapped around my body. I'd only just stepped out of the shower when she'd phoned, eager to discuss our plans for the evening. "What about you? What are you going to wear?"

"Probably my little black number. Can't go wrong with black. Plus it's wickedly short. We better get in after going through all this effort."

"God I hope so. Otherwise this birthday is going to turn out to be a really crappy one."

"Have you told your dad?" Robin said in a hushed whisper as if he might've been able to overhear our conversation.

"Of course not! He'd lock me up if he knew where we were planning on going tonight. Besides, he hasn't even remembered that it's my birthday. Not a word this morning or when he came home before."

"I'm sure he hasn't forgotten," Robin said awkwardly. She was always willing to give my daddy the benefit of the doubt, like everyone in this godforsaken small town. Maybe she thought he needed to be given some slack because he was a single parent.

I turned away from the half-emptied closet to sift through the items that I'd laid out on the bed and attempted to change the subject back to more important things. "Ugh. I seriously have nothing to wear. I need something hot, it is my nineteenth, after all."

"Do you want to borrow something of mine? Ooh, I know the burguncy dress, or my blue one with the sequined shoulder straps? That one has a serious plunging neckline that would look awesome on you."

I thought for a moment as I wandered absently around my room, toward the window that looked out at our back yard… and in on Mack's scruffy bit of land and his house. Robin's blue dress would look good on me, and if Mack should happen to see me in it, his eyes would pop out of his head. Not that there was much chance of him turning up at the club across town. He seemed more like a sports bar kind of guy, though I had to admit I didn't know much about him other than he went to high school and played football with my dad back in the day. He'd only recently come back into town and my dad had given him a job. That was the extent of what I knew. Otherwise he was a complete mystery. One that I wanted to figure out, of course.

My mind meandered at the thought of him and I bit my lip letting the fantasy play out if I did happen to bump into him—the way his eyes would flicker up my body… just like they had done on Sunday. He'd been mesmerized as I'd parted my legs slowly. I'd been cruel but I couldn't help myself; I wanted him to want me and the power from that simple act had been overwhelming. And from the bulge in his pants that he'd tried to hide from me, I knew he was definitely interested in seeing what I had under my dress that day… What would he do if he saw me tonight? Would he try to get another peek? Would I let him?

"You wouldn't mind?" I asked Robin.

"Of course not. Might be better this way anyway, you can come to mine and get dressed and your dad will never suspect a thing."

"I like the way you think," I replied and we giggled.

"Lola Ray! Are you still on the phone?" my Daddy yelled from downstairs. "I'm starving!"

"Just finishing up now, Daddy," I answered back. "Sorry, I have to go, I'll be around soon," I whispered to Robin and hung up the old-fashioned handset.

Out the corner of my eye I thought I saw a light flicker on and off over in Mack's house. Perhaps coming from the kitchen. Turning my attention to the squat brick building I waited to see if the light would flash on again. Was he home? Or had he just left? I saw no movement, but as I stood there at the window, spying on his house, trying to peer through the darkness that was his home my heart started to thud a little harder.

From the back room—was it a den?—he would have the perfect view of my bedroom window. And I wondered if he'd ever watched my window the same way I cautiously glanced at his house, longing to see a glimpse of him. I hadn't seen him since Sunday, six days ago and I was having withdrawal symptoms.

When nothing happened, I thought I must've imagined the light and backed away from the window.

Yet it didn't take me long to step back up to the glass to look again. Like a moth to a flame, I was drawn to it. I let my eyes whisk across the back of Mack's house, wondering where he was right then if not at home.

Feeling bold and naughty—his house was dark and quiet after all—I parted the curtains that dressed my window a little more. As I did the towel wrapped around my body began to slip. It fell, I let it.

Pooled around my feet I stood naked in front of my window, my whole body buzzing from the thought that he could, if he came home, catch a brief, naughty view of me.

My hands automatically found their way onto my breasts, squeezing them as I let the fantasy continue. I shivered a little, the room was cold, but that wasn't the cause—it was the thought of his hands on me, exploring, touching, squeezing, thrusting. *Oh god.*

My hands trailed down my torso, slowly, proceeding with caution… unsure. But with a nibble of my lip I let my fingers slide over my smooth pussy and allowed the pad of my finger to graze across my clit.

I couldn't believe I was doing what I was doing, masturbating at the thought of Mack, right in front of an open window. But the risk seemed minimal, only his house overlooked ours, and it was completely dark.

My breath haltered. My fingers automatically seeking out the entrance to my pussy, but I resisted… I'd never fingered myself. I was saving myself. Saving it all for him. And no matter how much I imagined that my fingers were his cock did I let myself push forward. I gasped a little at the self denial… he could have my tight pussy all to himself. He'd be pleased that I'd saved it all for him. And he wouldn't hesitate to fill me up, to the brim with his cum.

The loud trilling of the phone sounded and I spun around, feeling like I'd just been caught red-handed… but it was just the phone. My heart raced as I waited for my father to pick it up on the downstairs receiver, but the damn thing just kept on ringing. It didn't seem like it had any intention of stopping so I picked it up.

"Hello?"

"Hi," a voice said. Low, gruff, and manly, a little breathless. My eyes widened as I realized who it was. *Mack.* Maddox McClane was calling me?

I stood still in my room, the phone pinned to my ear, not daring to move. Was he calling from his house? Had he seen? Surely not… there were no lights on. My throat went thick with panic.

"Lola Ray are you still there?"

"Yes," I whispered. Why was he calling?

"Good."

"Do you want to speak to my dad?"

"No, I wanted to speak to you actually."

"Why?" I asked cautiously and began to edge away toward the wall. Where I wouldn't be seen if Mack was indeed home.

"Well, I wanted to wish you happy birthday. Someone just ordered the whole bar a round of drinks for everyone, cause it was his birthday, and it reminded me of you."

My shoulders sagged with relief. He wasn't home. He hadn't seen me. But a glow spread through me. He'd remembered. My daddy hadn't, but Mack had. And he'd called to tell me. It also reminded me of something else too.

"Thank you," I replied, smiling, some of my confidence flowing back after the little scare. "I didn't get the present you promised me, though," I said my voice playfully sad. I paced back toward the window to look out at his house again. I'd wondered for days what he might get me. I knew what I wanted but that was just a pipe dream… his cock thrusting into my pussy, filling me up and sparking life within me… his baby growing inside.

My hands wandered over my belly just thinking about it. It could never happen. He was Daddy's best friend. He worked for Daddy.

He'd be fired for just looking at me if he was ever caught. Daddy wouldn't just stop there, either, he would more than likely kill him.

"You will, you'll get your present," he said his voice turning low, breathy. "It's coming."

His last word was drawn out, as if he liked playing with the word, loving having it wrapped around his tongue. My nipples reacted, hardening. I closed my eyes. Coming... cumming... what I wouldn't give to have him cum inside me.

"I'm looking forward to it," I replied trying my best to sound like this was just a normal, everyday conversation. But the more I tried, the more my hands explored my body while talking to him, the more my breath stuttered and hitched.

"What are you wearing?" he asked suddenly. Did he really just say that? I grinned. It seemed like all we'd done was skirt around each other, not even flirting, just looking. Having conversations that could be considered totally innocent... but could be twisted to mean something entirely different depending on one's stance. But now, this was new. He was crossing an invisible line and actually flirting... Or at least I thought he was.

"What?" I asked barely believing it.

"What are you wearing to go out? You are going out to celebrate right?"

"Oh," I replied, dismayed. "Yes, Robin and I are thinking of going out..." I cut myself short not wanting to reveal too much. What if he told Daddy? I didn't know if I could trust Mack... not yet.

"Somewhere fun I hope?"

"Maybe."

"You have to... you only turn nineteen once. Come on you can tell me. You're going to go to Fusion, right?"

"I—"

"It's okay, I won't tell."

"Oh, good. Thanks, Mack."

"Be careful though. Don't let anyone tou—" He went silent, as if he'd gone too far and was regretting it.

"Don't let anyone what?" I questioned. Impatient for him to keep talking.

"Doesn't matter. You just have a good time, okay?"

"I will... will you be there?" The last sentence slipping from my lips without even thinking.

Mack chuckled. "Would you like me to be?"

"You could say happy birthday to me in person."

"That I could… we'll see."

I glanced at the clock on my bedside table and saw the time. "Shit, I have to go. Robin will kill me if I'm late."

"Have fun, Lola Ray," Mack said softly. "But don't let Daddy catch you... or you might get spanked."

DREAM DADDY

Chapter Four
Mack

After coming home from a brutal day at work I let myself in and headed straight for the fridge, bypassing turning the lights on. I was more preoccupied with getting the taste of dry grit out of my mouth after pouring concrete for the best part of five hours. But at least I had a job… and my freedom.

I grabbed the first beer my hand came to and popped its top. As I brought it to my lips I smiled, pausing before taking a swig. *Lola Ray.* God the thought of what she'd done the previous Sunday had me wanting to see what else she was capable off. Beneath that innocent exterior she portrayed for the rest of the world, she'd let me see a tiny sliver of the minx that was ready and waiting to burst free.

I so dearly wanted to be there when she did. To be the one that was the cause of the explosion. I took another swallow of my beer. It could never happen though. It was too complicated. She was my best friend and boss' daughter. He'd have me kicked off the crew, my parole officer alerted too, if he even knew what I wanted to do to his darling baby girl.

I leaned against the counter and glanced out the window to the back of his house. Her light was on. It spilled out into the darkness like a beacon. A tempting light that I had to stay away from for my own good. She was untouchable and off-limits, even if she was legal now.

As I watched her window absently I noticed a shadow moving about her room. The hair on the back of my neck prickled and I stood a little taller, my eyes widening to focus that bit more. I wondered what she was doing in there and prayed she'd pass by the window just so I could catch a precious glimpse of her. I waited for a few seconds before moving over into the den. The place I rented was sparse and there was a battered fabric recliner tucked away in the corner. I pulled it out farther into the room. Not too much though, just a little closer to the window where I had a perfect view of Lola Ray's bedroom.

I sat down heavy with my beer in the darkness—I didn't dare risk turning the light on, not now. I took small sips as I trained my eyes over her bright window. Her shadow bounced too and fro on the painted pink walls of her room.

And then finally I was rewarded for my patience. As if she'd been there all along, framed by the window trim, she stood glowing in the light. If my mouth had been dry before it was imitating a sandy desert now.

Her arms were bare, a towel wrapped around her. Her luscious blonde hair darkened by the shower she'd obviously taken. She was naked under that flimsy bit of terry-toweling and I willed for it to fall, to slip from her perfect, untouched and unblemished body.

Placing my bottle on the floor I eased myself back into the chair. The crotch of my jeans was tight, my cock pulsing for her. I loosened my belt, unzipped and eased the pressure.

When I looked back up Lola Ray was still there but this time her arms were wide, each hand clutched onto the curtains that dressed her window. She was going to do the sensible thing and close them, shut off the little show she didn't know she was giving me. The feeling of disappointment started to sink into my stomach, and a sigh followed swiftly afterward. But then as if I'd been granted a miracle, the grip the towel had on her body slipped, then it from sight. Like a rollercoaster my feelings shot upward, elated, breathless. I was loving what I was seeing and my dick was too. Hard, I wrapped my fist around it, tugging as I witnessed her naked body before me.

Absolutely perfect. Her breasts were two perky swells, and even from the distance between us I could tell her nipples were budding to points. I quickly let my gaze take the rest of her in, knowing it wouldn't be long before she dipped down out of sight to reclaim her fallen towel, and then wrap her body back up. But to my surprise she remained standing there. The light cascading down onto her so I could see everything. Including her soft belly and the smooth mound of her pussy.

My hand started to pump, slow strokes as I imagined what I would do to that body if it were mine. If I was in the room with her.

I'd keep her facing the window, have her legs apart a little so the lips of her pussy could feel the breeze swirling up around her entrance.

Fuck, I thought as she let go of the curtains, her hands moving to her chest. Kneading and touching her breasts. Her head titled upward a fraction as she enjoyed the sensation.

I watched intently, still wanking my cock, as her long fingers explored down her body. Slowly at first but then as if she couldn't resist any more they delved between her legs. She touched herself and I was getting close to cumming. The only thing that would make it better was if I could hear her moan.

Without thinking it through or considering the risks I took my phone out of my pocket and dialed Will's house number. Lola Ray would have to answer it… she had to.

The noise startled her. She froze like a statue at the window, her hand between her legs still. I imagined where her finger might be while the ringing continued in my ear.

Pick up, I dared her.

A few seconds later she bolted into action and though she moved away from sight I still had her in my mind's eye.

"Hello?" she said, soft and full of caution. God she sounded so innocent. Corruptible.

With my hand still on my cock, tightening my grip, I tried to gain control of myself so I could speak.

"Hi," I said. Two letters, one syllable and yet it was hard to even say that without groaning and cumming right then. I hoped she didn't pick up on the breathlessness of my voice and wonder why I sounded like I was in the middle of running a marathon. Or maybe I did want her to notice… anything seemed possible in that moment.

I risked opening my eyes to look back up at her window, but she was gone and had not returned. She'd also gone quiet and I asked her if she was still there. She was still there in my mind, naked and now she was parting her legs open for me wider. Maybe even bending over a little, so I could see her perfect, plump pussy lips from behind. I wanted to lick her up then sink myself into her.

"Yes," she whispered. She sounded a little out of breath too, or was I imagining the rush of her words? Maybe she was touching herself again and I stifled a groan at the thought.

"Do you want to speak to my dad?" she asked. I couldn't tell if she actually wanted that to be the case, but either way I said I didn't. Then realizing I didn't actually have an excuse for calling her out of the blue my mind scrambled to think of a reason. I just wanted her to keep talking, the sound of her voice tickling my ear as I stroked my cock up and down, imagining that the tip of it would soon breach her tight pussy.

I controlled myself enough to reply, and controlled myself further in order to not just blurt out the truth. The truth that I was right there wanking off while thinking of her and what I wanted to do her. But she was old enough now…

"Well, I wanted to wish you happy birthday. Someone just ordered the whole bar a round of drinks for everyone cause it was his birthday, and it reminded me of you," I said partially lying. I did want to wish her a happy birthday, but not just over the phone—in person, our naked bodies writhing up against each other as I devoured her and stripped her of her innocence.

My toes made fists in my boots as I edged toward the brink of no return. Lola Ray mentioned the gift I'd promised her but failed to give her. By god it was a promise I wanted to keep even with the forbidden nature that surrounded us. *One day soon*, I thought. The moment when all my resolve and restraint would disappear would be the day she got her present.

"You will, you'll get your present," I said trying to keep my voice even. Trying so desperately not to groan as lights began to spark in front of my eyes, as I imagined thrusting into her… my cock pulsing, spurting cum everywhere. "It's coming."

DREAM DADDY

Chapter Five
Lola Ray

"I told you that you'd look good in that dress, didn't I?" Robin said as we stood in line. We both had our arms wrapped around our middles to try and keep warm as we waited to get to the front of the line of the club.

I glanced down at the dress she'd let me borrow and smiled. It did look pretty fucking good on me. Robin was a fraction smaller than I was and a little taller so the short blue dress was a little tight. It was plain in places but while it lacked a pattern it made up for it with the stylish cut. It pinned in my waist and with it being tighter across my chest it let my cleavage spill out that bit more. It would've been a lot shorter on Robin had she chosen to wear it that night but the hem still ended at least five inches above my knee. The blue sequined shoulders drew the eye too, and led one's glance to the plunging neckline. It was a good effect, it was just a shame that Mack probably wouldn't ever see me in it.

Mack, I thought, loving how playing his name on a loop in my head would get me all hot and bothered. I still couldn't believe he'd phoned to wish me happy birthday. But I tried not to read too much into it. He was my dad's best friend… he was probably doing it to be nice, and nothing more. And all those little looks he'd given me were in my head… fantasies that would never play out. That breathy groan he'd tried to hide on the phone, too, was nothing… it couldn't be. I didn't want to get my hopes up, but there I was wondering, *what if?*

What if he does like me?

What if I told him what I wanted him to do to me?

What if I told him I wanted to have his baby?

"There you go again," Robin said as she waved an impatient hand in front of my face. "What on earth are you thinking about? You should be excited it's your birthday!"

I shook myself out of my reverie and focused back upon the face of my best friend.

"I am excited. I promise. Just nervous," I said trying to cover my tracks. "I'm worried that the fake IDs your brother got us won't get us in."

Robin arched an eyebrow and looked at me in that serious playful way she tended to overuse. "You're kidding me right? Crosby is, like, the master of these things."

I nodded, knowing she was right. Her big brother was in art school for a reason; he was wicked talented, and could whip up anything official-looking on his computer and did so regularly. He had a little side business selling fake IDs, which Robin helped facilitate with the kids from our school. And not one of them had ever complained that his new paid-for ID had failed him.

But as I glanced to the head of the line to where the muscled security guys stood, my stomach twisted. It was different when I was the one under the microscope, yet Robin seemed to be taking it in her stride. I needed to be cool and follow her lead.

Ten minutes later we were at the head of the line, a thick red rope between us and the bulging bouncer. He gave us appreciative glances as we waited for it to be our turn. There was a nod from another guy by the door and the big guy stepped forward to unhook the rope.

He towered over us but then thought better of letting us pass unquestioned.

"Good evening, ladies," he said, his voice incredibly low and gravelly. Like he smoked ten packs a day and had no intention of ever quitting.

Robin preemptively stepped forward full of confidence and smiled at him but stopped when the rope wasn't taken away.

He raked his eyes over our faces, debating. "Aren't you going to let us in?" Robin asked him sweetly. Then she nodded to me, "We have a birthday to celebrate."

"Oh really?" he replied. He stared at me and I could feel the nerves getting the best of me. What if we were caught and the cops were called? My dad would find out and then I'd be in for it. He hated it when I lied to him or disobeyed him. It was his number-one rule.

I swallowed and urged myself to speak. "My twenty-first," I spluttered out, finishing the sentence off with an uneasy smile.

"Happy Birthday," he said and I could tell he wasn't buying it… even though our lie was only a partial one. It was my birthday, just not my twenty-first.

"Want to see our IDs?" Robin asked impatiently and began to dig around in her clutch purse.

A beat passed as the security guy studied her. "Nah, that won't be necessary. You ladies go on in and have a good time."

We linked arms and gave him a last smile as we skirted by him and entered the club.

A wall of noise greeted us. "That was close," I said loudly in her ear, but I knew she could barely hear me over the pounding dance music. She nodded anyway then turned to me.

"It's time to get you wasted, birthday girl!" she shouted back, and eagerly dragged me deeper inside the packed club.

* * *

We came back from dancing and were almost immediately approached by two guys. We were at the bar waiting to be served when Robin leaned over to me. "Don't look now but we got two cuties incoming." I began to turn my head. "Don't look!" she squealed. "Ooh, they look older. I love college boys."

We'd been getting looks all evening as we stayed together, dancing up close, eyes burning into the backs of our necks, so it was really only a matter of time until someone plucked up the courage to try and join us.

"Oh he's delicious," Robin said her eyes pinned on someone over my shoulder.

The thought that maybe it was Mack spun a web in my mind. I hadn't told Robin anything about Mack even though I so desperately wanted to share what was going on in my head with someone, but I knew she'd crinkle her nose at the idea of getting it on with an older guy. Her type was muscle-bound football players, preferably ones in college.

But of course it wasn't Mack, it was silly to get my hopes up. A jock sidled up to Robin. I smiled for her; he was good looking and big—his shirt stretching across his broad chest—she grinned back at me.

"Can we buy you girls a drink?" he said. Robin nodded coolly and the guy bent his head down to her so she could whisper to him. I knew right then I'd lost her for the rest of the evening.

I felt a presence next to me and glanced up.

"Hey," the jock's wingman said to me. He was cute too, maybe one too many dimples for my liking, but strong, tall, with dark hair, and moody blue eyes. He seemed a lot less confident than Robin's catch or maybe his indifference was on purpose… trying to play it cool. Politely I said hi back and wondered if I was meant to make small talk while Robin got cozy with her guy.

"What's your name? Mine's Jason," he said

and inched in closer beside me, making use of the spaces between the fixed stools. My thigh was pressed up against his leg and I had to force myself to keep it there.

"Lola Ray," I said back but he shook his head as if he couldn't hear then bent down so I had to repeat it.

He stayed close and turned his head to my ear this time, "You're the prettiest girl in here you know, Lola Ray."

I was fully intent on keeping my distance from any guy that night—what with Mack running around in my head—but I had to admit I did smile when Jason started to flirt. He ordered us some drinks and even though it was difficult to hold a conversation we managed for the most part. I learned he was a senior in college, his buddy Nick was too, and he was majoring in psychology, which surprised me. He looked more like the type to study business or politics instead. But he just shrugged it off when I mentioned it. He tried to pry into my life, where I lived, what I was studying; he clearly thought I was a willing participant in the conversation. In the end I went with the wise choice and said I hadn't decided yet and was light on the details. That was another of Daddy's rules: keep your secrets, secret.

"How about I get you another and then we can head out on the dance floor? We need to show off that body of yours," Jason said and flagged down the bartender before I could agree. But I didn't object, it was fun to have this kind of attention. While Jason was getting the drinks I turned to find the seat next to me occupied by a woman who wasn't Robin. For a quick moment I panicked and looked around, searching, but soon spotted her in the arms of Nick, dancing to the beat of the music.

A figure off to one side caught my attention as I turned to Jason, but when I looked back the figure was gone. I could've sworn I'd seen Mack. Mack in his leather jacket, sporting a day-old beard. Either that or I was becoming obsessed. I scanned the crowd again. Hope and butterflies filled my belly, an excited swarm.

If he's here, I thought, *I have to make a move.* I could blame it on the alcohol… *Don't let Daddy catch you… or you might get spanked.* Mack's words echoed in my head. Did he mean that *he* would spank me? The idea thrilled me.

"Here you go," Jason said interrupting. He frowned when I didn't take it straight away, still searching the crowd.

"Thanks."

"Come on, knock that back. Let's party!"

I swallowed the shot in one go and regretted it almost immediately. Whatever it was felt like it was burning its way down. But there was a warm glow that soon replaced the nasty taste.

I took Jason's offered hand and he led the way, squeezing between hot bodies until finally he stopped on the edge of the dance floor and pushed himself up against me. His arms wrapped around me tightly so that I couldn't escape even if I wanted to, and we began to dance.

It felt like we'd danced for hours, the minutes blurring into the next as I knocked back drink after drink that Jason gave me. The never-ending music was so loud and everyone, not just Jason, closed in on us, pressing against me as the beat continued. I was so hot and the alcohol was soon making my head fuzzy.

"Do you need some fresh air?" Jason asked his face concerned.

I nodded and he smiled, "Let's get you out of here."

I should've known right there that I was in trouble, but I didn't see his predator-like smile for what it was. I thought he was just being nice.

DREAM DADDY

Chapter Six
Mack

For the second time that night I saw her naked.

For the most part I kept myself hidden, on the outskirts of the club, my back pressed up against a wall as I watched her from a distance. She couldn't know that I was there spying on her. *Practically stalking her*, I thought.

The baseline of the dance music beat an accusatory pulse inside my head. I had no idea what I was doing there. A few weeks ago I wouldn't have even contemplated doing anything like I was thinking about. Keeping my nose clean was my priority and yet there I was, keeping my eye on her instead.

I kept trying to tell myself that she was my

best friend's daughter, off-limits, way too young for me, and yet after speaking to her on the phone and finding out where she'd be partying that night I grabbed my jacket and followed her.

I told myself I was there only to keep a protective eye on her. To make sure she got home okay. But I knew that was only the partial truth. I wanted her.

I longed for her to scan the room and find me over in the dark corner, my eyes only on her. The fantasy was too tempting but it was also far too dangerous. I was an idiot… thinking only with my dick. But Lola Ray had cast an unknowing spell on me. I had no control over my actions.

And that dress she was wearing wasn't helping. Tight and clingy, it showed off every sensual curve of her young body. It left little to the imagination, especially considering I already knew what lay underneath.

Lola Ray and her friend moved onto the dance floor, wide, excited smiles on their faces. And by god when they started to move, together, I thought I would need to head into the bathrooms and give in to the release I needed. If Lola Ray could move like that on the dance floor, her hips swaying seductively, her butt bobbing up and down as she danced around her friend, I knew she would be amazing in bed. Sat on my cock wiggling, swirling her body around. The thought of what I wanted to do to her wouldn't go away. But that's all they were, just thoughts. I couldn't act on them, even if she was old enough now.

Watching would have to be enough.

But then the evening turned sour. I had to know that eventually some hulking jocks would approach the two girls. They were too irresistible to ignore.

From my position it was hard to see Lola Ray and her new tall male friend, so I edged closer, out of the shadows. His hands were on her. Lightly touching her shoulder as he bent to whisper into her ear. I wondered what he was saying, what was he suggesting? I knew what he was trying to get... but a protective fury boiled up inside me. She was mine. No one else's.

She smiled at him. She looked happy. But was she just being polite because her friend had paired off with the other guy? Or was she into it? By the way they were positioned at the bar, close together, her head tilted up toward him, it was anyone's guess. But she wouldn't, would she? Not after that little peep show she'd given me... even if she hadn't been aware that I was watching.

What happened on Sunday could've been a fluke. Even though she'd acted promiscuously when I was around, I couldn't quite know for sure if I was reading it all correctly. It may have just been my own mind playing tricks on me—making me see what I wanted to see.

What the fuck am I doing here?

I was being an idiot, practically crashing her nineteenth birthday, being overly protective. But just as I was about to turn away and leave her to her fun the guy she was with did something that made me stand still and pay attention. While Lola Ray's head was turned I could've sworn the little shit put something in her drink. I tried to replay what I saw again in my mind. His hand moving over the shot glass to pick it up, but there was a tiny ripple as if he'd dropped or let something splash into it.

He handed the glass to Lola Ray and encouraged her to drink the whole thing. She looked from the shot glass in her hand to him. He nodded and smiled. A wolfish smile… a dangerous smile. And I knew right then I hadn't imagined what I'd seen.

The only problem was what was I going to do about it? I couldn't leave, not now. Not after I knew she was in trouble.

The guy, who was soon to be a dead guy, pulled Lola Ray to the centre of the club to dance.

The way he wrapped himself around her, his arms touching where mine should be, I wanted to kill him.

But I couldn't in good conscience wade through the crowd and drag her away. I couldn't smash his face in before the mass of people that pressed up against us. Security would have me in no time if a fight broke out. The cops would be called, she would see me, and there would be too many questions. I would never see her again. And somehow Will would get wind of it. Then not only would I lose my job, but also my best friend. He'd been there for me since I'd moved back to my hometown. Gave me a second chance and a job when I was down to my last dollar. And while our friendship was mostly built upon our time as kids on the football field—we didn't have much in common as adults—it was still a relationship I valued. And yet there I was, scum, the worst friend imaginable… thinking about his daughter, wanting her, and needing to rescue her.

"You want to buy me a drink?" a loud but sweet voice crooned into my ear. A girl who couldn't be much older than Lola Ray placed a manicured hand onto my upper arm. She gave me a smile that implied if I did buy her a drink that anything was possible. For good measure her eyes flickered up and down my body, stopping momentarily at my crotch. I knew she was a guaranteed lay.

Sure I could bend her over and make her call me daddy, but she wasn't Lola Ray. She wasn't what I needed.

I shook my head at the girl. "I'm too old for you," I said simply, lying, hoping she'd take the hint.

A frown crossed her face but she wasn't put off. "Age is just a number."

I pulled my arm out of her grasp trying to keep track of where Lola Ray had been the last time I'd seen her on the dance floor. "I'm not interested."

"Ugh, creep!" I heard being shouted at my back as I walked away from her, moving closer to the center of the club.

My eyes scanned the heads of the dancers, moving and swaying to the music, but I couldn't see her. Her blonde locks were nowhere to be found. Beams of color arced over the space, highlighting the faces of the people. But not one was Lola Ray or the man she'd been with.

Fuck. I'd lost her. And god only knows what he was going to do with her now. But I wasn't going to give up. I pushed through swarms of happy drunk people searching for any sight of her or her friend. I must've searched for ten minutes before realizing they weren't inside anymore.

He must've taken her out of the club.

I rushed to the exit, panic and regret beating a tune within me. I couldn't let this happen. But it was happening. I could've stopped it. But I hadn't. I'd thought of myself and what would happen to me instead of thinking of her safety.

The heavy metal door of the club's entrance clanged open as I pushed through it, letting my rage spill out.

"Hey, watch it!" a man yelled but I ignored him and started to scan the street for any sign of her. *Fuck!*

As I paced further away from the club and the waiting line, peering into closed-up shop doorways, I pulled out my phone and stared at it. Luckily, I had her cell programmed into it. Will had asked me to pick her up from college a few months ago when he had to go out of town, and had given me her number. He'd given it to me in case I got stuck and couldn't make it so I could let her know. I hadn't had to use it then. *But I could use it now*, I thought.

"Fuck it," I muttered and tapped at the contact and started the call. Maybe she would pick up, maybe she'd be able to tell me where she was and I'd go get her.

But as I waited, the ringing, an irritating jingle

in my head, I heard the clatter of metal and a muffled moan a few yards from my position. Then I began to hear the echo of a cellphone ringtone… I chased after the sound and slowed as it grew louder. It had to be her phone. I still hadn't ended the call. I edged closer to the alleyway from where it was coming from and eased my head around.

The guy stomped down hard onto Lola Ray's phone, cutting off the sound abruptly. The alley was silent now. Then I shook my head, it wasn't silent. There was a confused moan emanating from the shadows. *Lola Ray.*

The guy turned away from the end of the alley and back to her. She was slumped down in the darkness. He picked her up and propped her against a pile of discarded crates. Using his body to keep her pinned he began to strip her.

It took me a moment to realize what the fuck he was doing. He ripped the shoulders of her dress letting the front fall slightly forward. But the dress was too tight and he had to yank it down in order to reveal her breasts. God, even in that state she was stunning. Beautiful and precious. But this guy had dared to touch what was mine, or at least was going to be mine. He was going to pay.

He was too preoccupied to hear me advance up behind him. His hands reached for the bottom of her dress, now pulling it in the opposite direction, up to get access.

Her head lolled from side to side. Completely out of it. But her eyes seemed to focus a little as she witnessed me come from behind her would-be assaulter, widening slightly in response.

Did she recognize me?

It didn't matter. I wasn't going to let this happen to her.

I crunched forward not seeing the shards of glass under my feet and the guy swung his head around. It was almost perfect, even though I hadn't intended for it to happen that way. As soon as he turned his head my arm went up, I ratcheted it back then let it loose. My fist smashed straight into his nose.

He went down. Lola Ray's legs started to buckle. I caught her with one arm and eased her down to the ground. "I'll be right back," I told her. "You're safe now."

I wasn't done with that fucker yet. I was going to make sure he never walked again.

* * *

She lay slumped on the passenger seat of my truck. I'd wrapped her up in my jacket, lifted her body into my arms and taken her away from that alley. The guy I left face down in a pool of his own blood. If he drowned I wouldn't lose a moment of sleep over it. He deserved what he got and I hoped he rotted where he lay.

It had taken every fucking part of me to resist touching her while she was in that state. With her chest exposed and perfect tits hanging out the thought of just taking one taste of her was so tempting. I warred with myself.

When would I ever have the chance again?

When would I, after this evening, have the chance to wrap my lips around her nipple, swirl my tongue around her hard little nub, and see what she tasted like? Cause surely after that night, she'd shy away from me. She'd stop her attempts at flirting.

But then as I got her into my truck and eased the door closed I knew if I did anything of the sort then I would just be as disgusting as the man I'd beat bloody in the alleyway.

The moment when I touched her, for real—if that time ever came—would be when she wanted me too. When she was lucid and awake to know what she wanted.

Seeing her reaction when I licked at her body or teased her open would be an even greater pleasure than just taking her right then without her never knowing it.

A small groan slipped from her lips as I drove the truck away from downtown. I had no idea what I was going to do with her yet. Take her home where he father would confront me and ask countless questions? Or back to mine? *Fuck.*

In her state, with her dress ripped, almost torn apart—it was barely clinging onto her body—he'd look at me with accusatory eyes. He'd imagine the worst. And even if I told him the truth, about the guy, about the alleyway, I was sure he wouldn't believe me. Or maybe he would, but then he'd turn his focus onto Lola Ray. He'd be ashamed of her, even though it wasn't her fault. Sure she'd sneaked out and gone to a club but she didn't ask to be date-raped. But in a small town like this, Will with his equally small mind and reputation for being a good old boy, would still blame her. And I didn't want that. I needed to protect her.

"Mack? Is that you?" Lola Ray whimpered from the seat. Her voice was croaky yet soft and full of confusion, as if she'd just woken up and had no idea where she was. Which in a way she had.

I took my eyes off the road and looked at her. She was so vulnerable and small, her hands clutching the edges of my jacket around her. Eyes wide with a million questions.

"Shh, I'm here. You're safe."

She nodded, her eyelids fluttering closed a few times. "Your hands? What happened to your hands?"

I loosened my grip upon the wheel and wiped the back of each of my fists on the fronts of my jeans, trying to get rid of the blood that coated them. But it was too late, she'd already seen, and most of it had already started to dry hard on my skin.

"I'm okay. Don't worry about me," I said softly.

She was still completely out of it and that was the last time she spoke that evening. Out of the corner of my eye I saw her curl up a little bit tighter, into a protective bundle, before she rested her head against the window and fell asleep.

I pulled the truck to a stop at the crossroads. Ahead would lead to her house. Left and around would lead to mine. I had to make a decision.

Staring down her street I tried to figure out a way I could get her into her bed without Will hearing me enter and creep through the house with her in my arms. I knew there was just no way it was going to work, even if I did know where the hidden spare key was.

A horn behind me tooted with authoritative impatience. I glanced in the mirror.

"Oh shit," I muttered as the telltale outline of a cop car became clear. I swallowed and hoped to god he wouldn't find a cause to pull me over. If he did, I was going to jail. No two ways about it. A half-naked, drugged-out chick in my truck at this time of night meant I was up to no good to an uninformed observer. Not to mention the state of my hands that clearly indicated I'd just been in a fight. Two and two would be put together with that kid back in the alleyway and I'd be fucked. Don't collect $200, go straight back to fucking jail.

I quickly put my hand up in apology and put the truck in gear and turned left. But the moment I was through the turn my stomach sank as I realized I'd forgot to turn on my signal.

DREAM DADDY

Chapter Seven
Lola Ray

I woke with a pounding headache. It felt like the inside of my skull had been scooped out and replaced with a dozen rattling marbles. And they were bouncing around, ricocheting against the inside of my head. But as I slowly opened my eyes, breathing in long deep breaths, a new scent registered in my mind. A different smell, not unpleasant, enveloped me—warm, musky, safe. I pulled the covers to me. They weren't my sheets. They were a dark blue plaid, while mine at home were a rosy blush with barely visible grey damask pattern printed on them.

The thought that I wasn't in my own bed scared me momentarily and I stayed curled up frozen while I tried to retrace the events of the previous night. My birthday… and I could barely remember it. Had I gotten so drunk that I'd passed out somewhere, at someone's house? But I couldn't remember going to an after-party. And where was Robin?

The last thing I recalled was my hand being held tightly. Then a face presented itself in my mind's eye. A grinning eager smile as he handed me a shot, then another one, and another… pulling me onto the dance floor, his breath on my neck, his hands trying to find their way up my dress to my underwear.

Oh god.

But then another face danced around the edges of my fuzzy mind.

Mack? Surely not.

He hadn't been there. *I'd merely dreamed of him*, I told myself.

I tried harder to remember what the dream had been about. Images of his truck flickered behind my eyelids. I was in his truck and he was driving me somewhere. In the dream his hands were swollen, bloodied. That part I could see quite clearly. I'd been so worried about him, if he was hurt… I didn't like the idea of him hurting. *But my dream was the last thing I should've been thinking about*, I told myself as I lay in a stranger's bed.

I scanned the room trying to pick out any distinguishing objects or clothing. It didn't seem like a typical college guy's bedroom. The wood was dark, the room plain and tidy, no textbooks or trophies or electronic gadgets. My eyes wandered over to a solitary wooden chair. It was doing a good imitation of a clothes horse. A blue dress hung over the back. *My dress.* It was torn, that was evident even from my position on the bed. The blue sequined shoulders were in tatters and the seams up the side were ragged. Robin was going to kill me. But then I started to question what I was wearing instead.

Fuck, no.

I didn't have to look under the covers to know that I was practically nude. Only my black panties remained on my body. Perhaps that was a good sign.

I hoped to god it was. Losing my virginity on my birthday to some random-ass guy was not the plan. I wanted to give it to Mack and if that had been taken away from me I didn't know what I was going to do.

A creak outside the room startled me upright and I pulled the covers closer to my body as if they could protect me.

"Can I come in?" a voice said. It was low, cautious, but it had a hint of familiarity to it.

Was it best to answer? Or to stay quiet?

The door pushed inward; seemed I wasn't going to get a choice in the matter.

"Lola Ray? Are you awake?"

The moment I heard my name, even through the fogginess of my head, I knew I was safe. *Mack.*

Mack emerged through the doorway, tall and ruggedly handsome as ever. He was dressed in a dark grey T-shirt and jeans and his eyes were softened with kindness.

"I'm awake," I replied, a little breathless. I was in Mack's bed. I'd dreamed of slipping beneath his sheets so many times that when it was actually happening I couldn't believe it. But I still couldn't figure how I'd gone from being in the club to his bed. Maybe the dream of being in his truck had been real?

"I brought you something to eat. And some aspirin. I bet your head is pounding?"

He took another step into the room, staying close to the edge as if he was in danger and needed to keep far from me. He put a tray laden with breakfast items down onto a nearby chest of drawers then took a quick step back, near the door. Was he afraid of me? Or what he wanted to do to me?

"Thank you," I mumbled and looked up questioningly at him. He would be able to fill in the pieces of the night I was missing. But would he want to? I looked around searching for my phone but couldn't find it. "What time is it?"

"Early. It's just turned seven," he replied, not giving anything else away. The air in the room seemed to have closed in around us. Both of us not sure of what to say or how to react.

But I had to know what happened. "Mack?"

"Yes?"

"What happened... how am I—" I stopped, unable to say the word. I knew I would blush like mad.

"In my bed?" He swallowed. He was even cuter when he was nervous.

"Yes."

"It's a long story." He shook his head as if trying to summon the right words. We both knew me being there was a huge risk and I had to think he was trying to find the right ones and figure a way to tell me that wouldn't send me flying from the room and back into my daddy's arms... telling him where I'd just come from. In the end after I let him pace at the foot of the bed for a few moments. "Just tell me."

That seemed to encourage him and he sat perched on the wooden chair staring at me. "You were in the club." I nodded, I knew that bit. "I was there. Watching you."

"You were watching me?" I tried to say it with a blank face, trying not to react. *He'd come, it had been him I'd seen for a brief moment in the crowd.* He'd come because of me, he wanted me. I was sure of it.

He hurried to correct what I was thinking, but he wasn't fooling anyone. "To make sure you were safe, of course. I didn't want you to get in trouble. Young girls in clubs, you hear all sorts of shit going on." I let him ramble, his words only making me feel more sure. He wanted to protect me. He might've convinced himself it was out of some duty to my father, but we both knew better.

"And I'm so glad I did. There was this creep... I think he slipped you something, in your drink," Mack explained. "Then I found you with him... he was about to—"

I nodded, my mood turning somber. That sounded about right, but I still couldn't remember the event with the clarity I'd wanted to. Probably best I didn't though, I thought.

"So I stopped him."

It was then I looked down at his hands. They were swollen. Traces of dried blood upon them. Bruised and battered. He'd gone to war for me. He'd done more than protect me.

"Thank you, Mack," I said and nodded toward his hands. He followed my gaze. His hands flexed on his lap then he dropped them to his side as if he was trying to hide what he'd done. I wanted to somehow repay him, to give him what I'd been dreaming about for a long time… to let the covers slip and let him see me right there and then in his bedroom. But the moment didn't feel right. As tough as he looked Mack was a sensitive soul and I believed if I did what my shoulder devil was screaming for me to do then he would walk out of the room and never give me a second glance ever again. And I definitely didn't want that.

"Anytime," he finally said. "I couldn't let you get hurt. Not like that, not when…" his words trailed off and I was forced to fill in the blanks. *Not when I wanted to be the one?*

I decided to change the subject. "Do you think I could borrow a T-shirt and pants? Anything? I don't think I can go home like this." *Home.* My father was going to kill me if he caught me sneaking in, but I prayed he wasn't up yet.

He'd probably gone to bed after draining a six-pack and not thought twice about where I was because I told him I might stay over at Robin's.

Mack stood abruptly. "Sure. Of course. Let me see what I can find." He left the room and after a few moments he returned holding out a small pink T-shirt and a pair of ladies' grey sweatpants. I looked at him, wondering how on earth—

"My sister's," he explained. "She sometimes visits and leaves a few bits behind in the wash."

I nodded trying to believe him. They probably belonged to an ex who he didn't want to admit to... but if that was true, then that meant he *was* worried about what I thought if there was someone in his life.

I reached for the clothing and our fingertips skimmed each other's as he handed them over. He paused, staring at me so intently that I thought he was going to lean down and kiss me. I wouldn't have objected if he had, but I was even more disappointed when he seemed to catch himself and retreated back to safety.

"I'll leave you to it," he said and was about to pull the door closed.

"Mack?"

He stopped and drew his eyes back up to mine as I sat in the middle of his bed.

"Thank you, again," I said, not wanting him to leave but not able to come up with anything else to keep him there.

"Anything for you, Lola Ray." He paused. "Do me a favor?"

I tilted my head and smiled back at him and repeated his words. "*Anything* for you, Mack."

"Don't tell your father about this… about you being here, I mean."

"You mean I shouldn't tell him how I went out to a club and got drunk and nearly got taken advantage of? Or how you undressed me, saw me naked, and that I spent all night in your bed?"

His face paled, his eyes widened, and I almost laughed.

"No, Mack. I won't tell him. I like our little secrets."

DREAM DADDY

Chapter Eight
Mack

Two separate yet very loud and insistent thoughts ran through my mind that morning. Both were equal in my head, vying for attention, as I stood in the doorway looking down at her in my bed. *Naked in my bed*. And for a moment I was stuck with indecision. With her ruffled locks and sleepy eyes looking back at me, I couldn't decide.

Get her out of the house as fast as possible before her father noticed she was missing? Or keep her there? In my bedroom. Forever. And do what I'd been dreaming about. Tie her up and never let her leave.

Could I do it?

She had to want it...

Thankfully the cop from the night before hadn't pulled me over and caught me with a half-naked young girl in my car, and I'd managed to get her back to my house without anyone seeing. I'd scooped her up, still out of it, her eyes fluttering open a couple times as I climbed up the stairs to the bedroom, wishing it was under different circumstances.

Once in the room I laid her down on top of the sheets and began to strip the tattered dress from her perfect body. Even then I'd had to resist leaning down and stealing a kiss, or letting my hands skim over her skin any longer than was appropriate. But I knew that wasn't the way to make her mine. She had to want me to do it. She would have to give herself to me willingly. Only then would I touch her and explore her fully.

She moaned my name as I draped the sheets over her, covering her body. And by god did I want to slip in beside her. Lock her up and keep her forever.

"Not yet, baby girl," I whispered and left the room hard as a rock. Before I could contemplate what I was doing I jumped in the shower, only a wall separating us, thinking of her and stroked my cock furiously. Thinking about how her lips would feel wrapped around my shaft, pumping into her, deep and hard. I closed my eyes convincing myself that the fantasy was just as good… but I knew it would pale in comparison from marching into the next room and claiming her.

I drained myself of the temptation and removed myself from the upstairs, choosing instead to sleep on the couch instead of the small guest room that was far too close to Lola Ray.

The next morning of course the temptation was at the forefront of my mind as soon as I woke. As soon as my eyes sprang open. My heartbeat pulsed rapidly as I remembered who was upstairs. She had to go… or I had to take her for my own. They were the only two choices I had.

She didn't help with her teasing… but with the mention of her father and the thought of what he might do to me if he found out she was at my house I backed off. Though Lola Ray seemed disappointed with that. I went back downstairs into the kitchen and listened to her move around above, getting dressed in my sister's clothes and then slowly, apprehensively, she came down the stairs.

She found me in the kitchen leaning against the counter and I told myself I wasn't going to move an inch. She was just going to say goodbye and then leave.

"Thanks for the food, my head is feeling better," she said as she placed the tray onto the table in front of her.

"No problem."

We stood staring at each other for what felt like an eternity. Neither of us knowing what to say. Or how to act in what seemed like a most ridiculous and awkward situation.

"Well, I better go," she finally said.

I nodded my goodbye and clamped my teeth down upon my teeth. Preventing me from telling her she was welcome to stay a little bit longer. Even just a few minutes more.

She moved to the back door and looked back at me, a smile playing on her lips, her eyes bright and seemingly unaffected by what had happened to her the night before.

"I'll see you later, Mack, my knight in scruffy armor."

"That you will," I said surprising myself.

Lola Ray grinned and returned her smile. I winked at her as she pulled the door open and left.

From the kitchen window I watched as she hurriedly made her way through the yard and up to the short fence that ran along the border of the two properties. She vaulted herself over effortlessly and ducked down and ran to her own house, my heart in my mouth the whole time thinking it would just be our luck that Will would make an appearance right then at the wrong moment. But thankfully he didn't, and she made it inside.

* * *

Less than six hours later I saw her again in her yard, wearing as little as possible. Enough fabric covering herself to make it seem decent, but I knew by the way she caught my eye it was all carefully calculated and done on purpose. The bikini was tiny, small triangles positioned over her nipples and pussy, held in place by shoestring straps.

"Hey, Mack, where do you want this?" Will asked as he came into the yard carrying bags of cement. My head whipped around, shocked he was suddenly there. Had he caught me staring at his daughter? I prayed not. But why on earth was he here? Then I remembered, as I noticed what he had in his arms. He'd offered to help me clean up my mess of yard and build the brick barbecue I'd told him about.

"Oh, hey. Anywhere will do for now."

Will put the sack down and turned to survey the area. "We got our work cut out for us today," he said.

I nodded and agreed that it was indeed going to be a tough one… especially with his daughter just on the other side of the fence practically naked. I wouldn't be able to keep my eyes off of her.

Forcing myself to turn the other way I gestured to the cement. "How much do I owe you for that lot?"

"Nothing, we had some left over from the last site and thought you could use it. There's more in my truck."

Grateful for an excuse to leave the yard—I could feel Lola Ray's gaze penetrating the back of my skull, even with those huge round sunglasses of hers—I followed Will eagerly back to the front. I hoped to god she didn't plan on staying out there all damn day.

We made several trips back to Will's truck, grabbing tools and equipment and with Lola Ray on my mind I wondered if she'd said anything to him about her little adventure the night before. I guessed if she had, she probably didn't say anything about my involvement, otherwise Will certainly wouldn't have been helping me out in my yard.

Unless, a dark thought crossed my mind, he was playing it cool, biding his time, planning on digging me a grave in my own backyard—instead of the foundation I had planned—and then when I least expected it, shoving me into it, and pouring fresh quick-setting concrete on top of me.

I glanced at Will out the corner of my eye trying to figure out if I was overreacting. He seemed calm enough, though he was his usual quiet self. Nah, I decided, he wasn't about to kill me. At least not yet anyway.

Once we got everything gathered we started clearing out a bunch of weeds at the bottom of the back fence. Will made idle conversation, talking about the last football game, asking how my sister was, and telling me about the bid he'd put in for a big contract. Which was good. It meant I didn't have to look at her. I could stay hunkered down on my knees, and she was out of sight.

"What the fuck are you wearing?" I heard Will yell beside me.

I popped up and swallowed a thick thump in my throat as I followed Will's gaze.

He'd spotted her. Draped upon the sun bed, skin exposed, making sure she wasn't going to get any tan lines.

"Daddy?" she asked and pushed down her sunglasses.

That innocent way she replied made me want to chuckle. And okay, it also made me want to spank her. She wasn't fooling me, that was for sure, but maybe Will would believe it.

"You heard me!"

"I'm wearing a bikini, Daddy. Don't you like it? Mack, do you like it?"

My heart stopped and I couldn't help but blush. I felt Will's eyes on me, daring me to answer in any way that would be considered inappropriate. But fuck, she did look good in it. She would've looked cock-teasingly good in anything.

"Can't say I noticed," I replied, my tone surprisingly even.

"It's too small, go cover yourself. Now!" Will shouted.

Lola Ray rolled her eyes when Will ducked out of view and swiveled herself around on the sun bed, her feet planting down before slowly and seductively getting up. I had to look away.

"And while you're in the house get us two beers. Do something useful today, huh? Instead of lazing about! I don't know what I'm going to do with that girl... she's turning into her slut of a mother.

I shouldn't have agreed to her going to college, it's giving her all these ideas."

I kept my mouth shut. Lola Ray's mom was a sore subject with Will. Best not to say anything.

We went back to work and Lola Ray still hadn't reappeared. Probably too pissed off at her dad. Sick of having to do his every bidding. But with her constantly on my mind I thought I was going to trip up and say something wrong. Instead I tried to act casual. Not bringing her up would be just as weird.

"So, did Lola Ray have a nice birthday?" I asked, like any best friend would, asking after his family.

"Huh?" Will looked over his shoulder at me a deep frown on his face.

"Her birthday?" I elaborated. "Her nineteenth? It was yesterday, wasn't it?"

"Ah, fuck." Will ran his hand through his scraggly hair. "Was that this weekend?"

Unsure of how to respond I just shrugged as an irrational impulse to smack him in his mouth came over me. Had Will really missed and forgotten his own daughter's birthday? How fucking heartless could he be? I knew he was hard on her, basically treated Lola Ray like a slave, making her do all the housework and cook him meals and the like… but actually missing her special day? That was unforgivable. Did he not care for her at all? Then I glanced over to where Lola Ray lay, back on a weathered sun bed, her head angled toward the sun. How must she have felt to have been forgotten? It made me want to wrap my arms around her even more. To protect her from everything she had to put up with.

"Ah well. She'll have another next year," Will said as if it were no big deal. My fists clenched up tightly and I had to turn away from him. Hitting him wasn't the answer.

"Maybe you should get her something? There's still time."

"Get her what? She has everything she needs. I give her a roof over her head, clothes on her back, and food in her belly. Not that she eats much. Besides it's just another year."

I shook my head. "You're pretty heartless, you know that," unable to stop my tongue from flapping.

"What?"

"You heard me."

Will straightened and I thought he was going to get in my face, start the fight I so eagerly wanted to have—at least then I'd have the excuse to hit him. "Maybe you're right, but fuck, what do you get a girl like her? She's useless, like her mother was, and I have no idea what she's into."

I suppressed a smile. *I have an idea what she's into*, I thought, and remembered the present I'd got for her and sent in the mail earlier… anonymously of course. I couldn't wait when she got it, opened it… and put it on. It was the first step to getting what I wanted.

Will stood seemingly waiting for an answer. "You're asking me? I have no idea. Maybe jewelry, a nice necklace?" I shrugged. I imagined her wearing nothing but a locket around her neck, it twinkling away as she sashayed her way toward me, every part of her bare and wanting.

With his hands stuck on his hips, I could see the wheels of Will's head turning. Thinking over my suggestion. He shook his head as if he couldn't believe what he was considering. The fucker didn't want to spend a single cent on his kid. The selfish asshole.

"Fine. Whatever. I'll get her something. But she doesn't deserve anything fancy."

I shrugged again as if it was no skin off my nose, but I knew he'd felt shamed into doing something nice for her. Always thinking about how he looked to others… he hadn't changed one bit since high school.

Will looked at his watch. "I'll be back later then. Means you don't get my help for a few hours, though."

"That's fine with me. Hey, Will," I said before he could turn away and leave, "get her something worth more than pocket change. I'm sure she'd appreciate it."

"Yeah, she better."

Chapter Nine
Lola Ray

"Where did my father go?" I asked as I moved closer to the fence. I'd seen him leave down the side partition of Mack's house, but Mack hadn't followed him. And I wondered if they'd had some sort of fight. The look on my daddy's face when he was leaving was irritable—the same look he got if I ever pissed him off.

Mack shot up from the ground. He'd been bent over dealing with scraggly thick weeds on his side of the fence, sweat practically dripping from his rippling body. I let my eyes linger on his torso, tight abs, and tanned skin for a moment longer than I should've. But I didn't care anymore. I was nineteen now and after being in his bed, well I felt like I was owed. He'd seen mine, I wanted to see his. Besides I wanted a repeat performance of making it into his bed, but the next time would be with him in it too. Maybe with me on top.

"What?" he replied. I'd scared him sneaking up on him like that and smiled sweetly at him.

"My daddy, is he gone? He's not just in your house is he?"

"No, he left."

"Where did he go?"

"Does it matter?" Mack asked and took a cautious step closer to the fence. I caught him looking at me. From his tall frame he had a perfect angle to look down at my body, the whole length of it, from top to bottom even with the half-panel fence in the way. He liked what he saw, I knew that. I watched as his Adam's apple moved distinctly in his thick throat. But with a response like that, he wasn't as coy as I thought he was going to be.

"No, I guess it doesn't matter where he's gone. Just that he's gone and we can finally be alone again."

"Lola Ray," Mack said, his tone edged with a warning. I knew what he was trying to say. That *we* could never be. But that didn't mean I wasn't going to stop trying, or give up, or never tease him.

"What?" I asked innocently and batted my eyes at him. I leaned my arms on the fence, pressing myself up against it, letting my cleavage bulge a little.

"You know damn well what. Besides, your father told you to go get covered up."

"I don't take orders from him anymore," I said absently. "*Besides,* I don't think you want me to cover myself up, now do you?"

"It doesn't matter what I think."

"Oh but I think it does. I think you want to see more of me. I think you got a look at me last night and you're dying to see more. In fact I think you're barely keeping it together right now."

He was silent and stared at me. A dark gaze that had my skin rippling with pleasure.

"You know what?" I said with a small sweet smile, "I've decided I don't want any tan lines at all." I stepped away from the fence so he could see all of me again. "Mack, would you mind ever so if I went topless?"

He shook his head, but not in answer, in helpless frustration. He was ready to explode and I was pushing all the right buttons. By god I wanted him to explode, to forget about why he shouldn't do what he wanted to do and just do it.

I wanted him to drag me over the fence, bend me over, and thrust deep inside me. I needed him to be in me, explode in me.

I placed a hand behind my neck finding the right strand. If I pulled the knot would untie and my bikini top would fall away. He would see everything, right there in my backyard. He wouldn't be able to look away and I couldn't wait to see his reaction. My eyes dipped from his face to his crotch and back again. He already had a semi just thinking about it.

"Lola Ray," he warned again, "don't."

"Why not? There's no one here but us."

Before he could object again I tugged on the strand and the whole thing came away from my body. My breasts were deliciously exposed, full and perky, my nipples dusky and hardening with every moment that he continued to look at me.

He moaned. Guttural, primal.

I stepped forward an inch and whispered, "You want to touch them, don't you? I want you to. I want you to lick them."

I could feel my pussy pulsing, my bikini bottoms becoming wet with my arousal. *Please, touch me.* I wanted to scream and beg. But he took a step back.

I gave him a little shrug as if the whole thing had been no big deal and turned away. Hiding my disappointment. But I wasn't going to give up that easily. I walked back into the kitchen, grabbed what I needed and slowly, so I knew he would notice me again, made my way down to the fence. He watched my every move and I kept my eyes trained on him. A few times the muscles in his huge pecs twitched. But when I finally made it to within a few meters of him, still topless, it was like he was angry with me for making him feel that way.

"What now?" he asked with impatience. "Can't you see I'm busy? I don't have time for your games, Lola Ray. If your dad comes back and sees you like that, where I can see, he's not only going to kill you, he's going to kill me."

"I don't care," I said. "I'm sick of hiding what I want."

"And what do you want?"

"I want you... I want to suck on your cock."

He put his shovel down with a harsh clang and closed the distance. For a second I thought he was charging at me and was going to leap over the fence and give me exactly what I'd requested. But he stopped short.

"You couldn't handle me, little girl."

"Oh really? You don't think so?"

He shook his head.

"I brought you something," I quickly interjected and showed him the cold long-necked beer I'd grabbed from the refrigerator. "Something to quench your thirst…"

He hesitated as I offered it to him over the fence. But when his hand came up to claim it I snatched it back.

"Wait I forgot something. You like them sweet, right?" I asked and dropped my hand.

"What are you doing?"

"Watch," I said breathlessly. Like the last time it felt so good, I put the top of the bottle against my pussy, letting it hit and rub against my clit through my bikini bottoms.

Then I hooked a finger onto the side of the fabric and pulled the bottoms aside. He could see all of me now. I let the cold bottle softly hit the flesh of my sex and bit my lip as I looked back up at Mack.

"This could be your cock, Mack. Right here… I want you… inside me."

"Stop," he breathed, barely audible.

"You don't want me to stop, you want me to

fuck this bottle, don't you? You want to see it slip inside me and imagine it's you doing it instead. Oh god, it feels so good. You would feel better, wouldn't you? But I'm not going to do that. You want to know why?"

I tilted my head up to look at him. He was licking his lips.

"Why?"

"Because I want you to be my first, Mack."

"Shit," he breathed.

"I've saved myself for you. I've never even slipped a finger inside myself. I want to, but I want you to do it first."

"Jesus Christ, this can't be happening."

I stopped rubbing myself against the bottle and lifted it back up for him to take it.

"Taste me, and tell me you don't want me."

He took the bottle from my hand and I could see his jaw working, pulsing from effort, from indecision.

"I never said I didn't want you…"

I smiled; a small victory.

"But?" I encouraged.

"You have no idea what you would be getting

yourself in for. No idea whatsoever, baby girl."

"Tell me. I want you and you want me. It's simple."

"It's not fucking simple. I would fucking break you."

I tilted my head to the side. "What if I'm already broken?"

Chapter Ten
Mack

She was pushing my limits, baring herself to me like that. Every single cell in my body wanted to lean on the fence and pick her up, put her over my shoulder and take her inside. She had no clue what would happen if I gave in to that temptation. She'd probably think that I take her upstairs, and fuck her on the bed. Perhaps a little rough, she seemed eager to want it rough, but she knew nothing about what would happen to her. She was too young, too fucking inexperienced.

Shit, she was a fucking virgin. I'd imagined that she was, but there she was admitting it. She was every man's wet dream and she was offering it to me on a platter.

This was far from dangerous territory, this was insanity.

"You're not broken," I said and looked at her body again. She was perfect, and I would ruin her, that was for sure. One night with me and she'd go running into the night.

"You think because I look like this that I'm not fucked up?" she said her voice on a razor's edge, harder than I'd ever heard it.

"We can't, Lola Ray," I said for what seemed like the millionth time. She didn't know it but I'd been chanting that in my head for days, weeks, months. *We cant, I can't... I can't fuck her. I can't fuck my best friend's daughter.*

"Your dad..." I added as if in a way of an explanation.

"Fuck my dad. Maybe I want a new daddy..."

I stood stock-still letting her words sink in. If any words were going to tip the balance and allow me to give in to my desires it were those. *I want a new daddy.*

But she had no idea what she was saying. She was a kid, play-acting, throwing a tantrum, saying anything she could to get what she wanted. She didn't know what those words meant to me.

"Mack?"

There was only one way to find out if she was truly willing, truly ready to submit to me.

"Listen to me right now."

Her eyes widened a little, her smile faltered. "I'm listening," she responded, as if on cue. Maybe she did know what she was doing.

"You're going to do exactly what I say. Do you understand? It doesn't matter what I tell you to do, you're going to do it. If you can do that, then and only then, will I ever consider touching you. Do you understand?"

She nodded, obediently. "What do you want me to do?" she asked, her voice all breathy and eager. She was never going to expect what I was going to ask and I couldn't wait to see her reaction. She was going to be pissed.

"I want you to put your top back on, and go back into the house."

Her eyes narrowed and her juicy lips pursed into a tiny pout. Sooner or later I'd part that mouth with my cock… but not yet. Not unless she could follow orders.

"I don't understand—"

"It's simple. Top back on and go back inside. I don't want to see you again until Monday."

"Why Monday?"

"That's not how this works, Lola Ray. You don't get to ask questions. You either do this or don't. But if you don't, you'll never get what you want."

She nodded. Then a second later she bent down to retrieve her discarded bikini top. She started to retie it around herself as I brought the beer I'd nearly forgotten about to my lips.

Lola Ray noticed and watched me drink. I swallowed every last drop then handed the bottle back to her. A little bit of her bravado had disappeared only to be replaced with uncertainty… her innocence returning. She was unsure. And that was just how I wanted her. She thought by coming on to me like that she was wielding all the power… but now the tables had turned.

"Go on, inside like a good girl. Do what your new Daddy tells you. Or you'll never get spanked."

Chapter Eleven
Lola Ray

I should've been furious with him.

Almost every part of me wanted to go against what he was saying and leave my top off, and even maybe strip myself completely bare. Defiant and disobedient. Who was he to think he could tell me what to do?

But there was something in his voice that made me think twice. The rough quality of it suggesting that there was more to come if I was a good girl and did what he said.

His eyes had turned stern, a steely grey, like he wouldn't tolerate anymore of my nonsense, but perhaps also wanting me to push back a little too… so that I could be punished. And though the thought of what he might to do me— spanking, his skin on my skin—I also wanted to please him too. So I did what went against every fiber of my being and put on my bikini top, covering myself back up.

The corner of his lips twitched. He was pleased. Pleased that I could follow orders, perhaps. Like I was his puppet to direct... and he was my master.

My nipples hardened in anticipation. What else would he make me do? And why on earth did doing nothing except obeying him feel so damn exhilarating? Like we had a special secret between us. It was like I was experiencing a new sensation, stroking me from the inside out, making me quiver with need. The need to do more, needing for him to tell me what else to do so that I could obey. It came to me that I would probably do anything he asked me to.

I went back into the house, turning my back on him and not looking behind—as much as I wanted to, I knew I shouldn't... there would be consequences, and I couldn't risk the promise of whatever Monday was going to bring.

He'd promised he'd see me again on Monday... but what exactly was going to happen on that day? Would he fuck me then? Make love to me? Would he let me crawl into his bed and thrust his cock inside me like I almost begged him to do? Or would he continue to tease me? Either way I smiled, my hand going to cover my mouth as soon as I was inside. All this meant one thing; I hadn't imagined any of it. Mack wanted me. And I was going to do everything and anything I could to make him mine… including whatever he told me to do. I would do it, so help me god, even if it killed me.

The whole of Sunday was torturous. Time dragged by like molasses being poured out of a tin. And then when Mack didn't show up to spend the afternoon with my dad I was like a cat on a hot tin roof. I couldn't sit still; I kept wandering around the house, glancing out of the windows wondering where the hell he was. Perhaps by saying he'd see me on Monday that meant he wouldn't see me at all in between then either. Or perhaps he just couldn't risk it. In a way the seal had been broken. We'd crossed a barrier of sorts when I'd been so blatantly obvious about what I wanted. And by admitting that he wanted me too, in one way or another, he'd crossed that line as well. So coming over as usual, spending time with my father while Mack was probably thinking about fucking me, was a step too far in his mind. Or at least that's the excuse I was able to come up with.

Otherwise, why stay away? Was he doing it on purpose? Making me insane with need?

I wanted nothing more to see him again and slip him sweet treats all day long… or even better corner him in the kitchen while my dad was in the next room. I could've showed Mack exactly what I wanted to do for him. He could've bent me over the counter and ran his fingers up my wet seam… my father barely left his chair during a game, his eyes glued to the flatscreen. Mack and I would've had plenty of time to do what we wanted.

But no, if my last encounter with Mack was anything to go by, I knew that wasn't going to happen. He was too cautious, too calculated. He would have me only when he would allow himself to, and not a moment before.

I stayed awake for most of the night, the anticipation of Monday morning far too exciting. I tossed and turned in my bed needing for the new day to begin so I could find out what on earth Mack was planning. I was desperate to see him again. But the night seemed to take twice as long to end.

Finally, dawn peeked through my curtains and said hello and I bounced out of bed eager for the day to start.

"You're up early," my father grunted as I joined him in the kitchen. He was sat on his usual stool eating a huge bowl of cereal and drinking coffee.

"Didn't sleep much, and thought I'd get a head start on the day," I replied trying to keep the excitement out of my voice. I grabbed myself a cup and poured some coffee into it and joined him at the counter. By the untouched, rolled-up newspaper was a long but small box with no markings on it, and next to that a bigger cardboard box.

My father didn't like me touching the mail before he'd had a chance to inspect it but I had a feeling something in one of those boxes was not for his eyes.

Cautiously I nodded to the packages. "What are they?"

He shrugged. "Addressed to you. The small one is from me, though."

My eyes widened. Did I hear him correctly? A gift for me from him? This from the man who didn't believe in gifts, and who hadn't given me a Christmas present, let alone a birthday gift, in years.

I gave him a cautious smile and took the small box into my hands, studying it for a moment before opening it. I'd mistakenly thought it had come in the mail, but it was just a simple and plain cardboard box, which was wrapped around another box inside. I slipped the cover off to reveal a jewelry box, soft blue velvet covering it. With an uneasy glance at my father I began to open the box. He'd never given me anything like jewelry before, was this some sort of trap? Was there going to be nothing inside and he'd start laughing hysterically? It wouldn't be the first time he'd given me "nothing". A box of fresh air one Christmas, the year after my mom left, to demonstrate the point that he'd given me everything I deserved already that year.

Inside, sparkled a gold chain with a small heart pendant, also in gold. It was pretty, but I knew it hadn't cost him the earth. But it was the thought that counted right? He hadn't forgotten.

"For my birthday?" I asked.

He nodded.

"Thanks." I shut the box with a snap and was about to get up from my stool and go give him a hug before putting it on, when his words stopped me.

"I want to see you wearing it, though. I didn't buy it so it could just sit in a drawer, you hear?"

I shrank back and nodded. For a tiny moment I'd been happy that he'd done something nice. But now he was putting limitations and demands on his gift and that wasn't sitting well with me. I opened up the box, as if I was being forced to, his gaze upon me telling me if I did anything but would be the wrong move. I lifted the flimsy chain around my neck and fiddled with the clasp. It was clunky but I eventually got it on. My father grunted as if he was pleased and I forced a smile upon my lips. I was feeling anything but happy. I wanted to be nowhere near him right then, and the chain around my neck—if it didn't end up turning my skin green—felt like a noose. A tether to a man I hated.

Before I could stop myself and while my father had turned his attention back to his cereal, I took my cup of coffee, tucked the other package under my arm and silently left the kitchen.

And it was a good thing that I did.

I sat on my bed as I ran the edge of a pair of scissors down the middle of the tape holding the parcel closed. Carefully I pulled back the flaps. On top of a sprinkle of white packing peanuts was a plain white envelope. I resisted digging further down to explore what lay beneath and turned my attention to the envelope instead.

Printed in neat blocky handwriting on the front was "Baby Girl."

The grin that exploded on my face the moment I saw those two words was immense. This had to be from Mack. It just had to be, I thought.

And in one swift moment he'd washed away all the negativity that had been building up inside me from dealing with my father.

My own words played in my head again… *I had a new daddy now.* And he'd sent me a gift. Which would no doubt be better than the cheap metal around my neck.

Inside the envelope was a plain white card with more writing on it. There was a bulleted list. Instructions, I thought with excitement.

1. Do not let anyone else see what's inside.

2. Do not put them on until I tell you.

3. If you do, there will be consequences.

4. Something extra… To replace the one that was lost.

Beneath the list it was signed with a single letter: M.

I read the list over and over again trying to decipher its meaning. The first was obvious, of course. The second, I would find out as soon as I looked deeper within the box. And the third, well, it was vague probably for a reason. But I was beginning to want to know what the consequences of defying him would be.

Unable to resist any more, I placed the card back in its envelope and started to rustle around in the box. First my fingertips touched nothing but the peanuts and then they hit a hard object, and then another. I grasped it and pulled it out, not caring when a bunch of the packing material came flying out too, scattering all over my bedspread.

My jaw dropped as I looked at the box. An iPhone. Before I started to play with it I dug my hand back in and fished for the second item my hand had connected with.

"Oh my god," I breathed as I stared at the other gift.

Then I took the card back out of the envelope. I could hear Mack's voice in my head. *Do not put them on.*

I ripped the box open and disobeyed him, the phone forgotten. I had another toy to play with.

But as if I'd summoned him by my disobedience, like he was coming to punish me, the doorbell rang, and I heard Mack's voice below.

DREAM DADDY

Chapter Twelve
Mack

As I stood in Will's entranceway I wondered if the mail had already arrived. Had Lola Ray received my little gift? Had she read my note and fully explored the box yet? *She could be upstairs right now*, I thought, *getting ready for her classes, thinking about whether or not to ignore my instructions*. If she knew what was good for her she would leave them off until I told her to put them on. But I knew Lola Ray was going to be a challenge, and it wouldn't have been that much of a surprise if she defied me.

"Won't be a minute, just gotta grab my tools. Fucking truck wouldn't start. Last thing I need."

"No problem," I replied as Will disappeared to gather his things. I hadn't planned on making an appearance at his house that day—I was going to make her wait a little bit longer, tease her, make her beg to see me again—but I couldn't say no to my boss and friend when he rang to ask for a ride. Saying no would've only raised his suspicions and put everything I had planned in jeopardy.

Above me I heard the creak of floorboards as Lola Ray made her way to the stairs. I knew she wouldn't have been able to resist coming down if she'd heard me and I looked up waiting for her to appear.

My eyes locked onto hers as she made her way down the stairs, taking each one slowly and purposefully, never letting our gaze from each other break.

She was smiling, biting her lip, and I could tell right away she'd been a very naughty girl. She'd broken one of the rules already.

"You look happy," I said, risking starting a conversation that Will could overhear. I cautioned myself to choose my words very carefully. Act normal. Don't let the fact I want to punish his daughter override the control and façade I was trying to maintain.

"I am. Very happy," she replied and licked her plump lips. She was wearing the shade of innocence, a light soft pink that shined slightly upon her tempting mouth.

"And why are you happy?"

She stopped just over halfway down the stairs, so I was forced to continue to look up at her. A position I did not like.

"Because my *daddy* got me a birthday present." The way she wrapped her lips around the word "daddy" I knew she didn't mean Will. That pleased me. She was already eager to use the word, and I wondered what else I could make her say.

Though I could also tell that Will did make good after our conversation the other day. Lola Ray was tugging on a chain around her neck, one I hadn't seen her wear before. Must be the gift he bought for her. It looked like he didn't go to too much of an effort—a thin chain, no doubt picked up from a pawn shop.

If I had my way Lola Ray would be draped in nothing but the finest—diamonds, pearls, glittering gems. But she wasn't mine yet.

"Did you like your present?" I said hoping she caught my meaning. She nodded and nibbled on her bottom lip again.

She let go of the chain and her hand skimmed over her tight shirt and down to her skirt.

Right there in front of me, over the material of her short skirt, she palmed her pussy, holding it tight, then let out the smallest of whimpers.

"But it didn't have the controller," she breathed, her voice full of disappointment. "It wasn't in the box."

I stepped forward, closer to the banister and lowered my voice.

"It's a good thing I didn't include it then. You've already broken one of my instructions... You've got them on right now, haven't you?" I say it all with a harsh undercurrent. Telling her that she will be punished for going against what I wanted.

"Maybe," she said, as she cast her eyes away from me, caught red-handed. If Will wasn't in the house I would've launched myself at her, brought her over my knee, stripped the pair of vibrating panties off of her bottom, and spanked her hard. I would've left my handprint on her ass, stinging, sore and red, as a reminder to never ignore my wishes ever again. But I had to stand there and glare at her. Even though she had been caught, she was pleased and that just made me want to slap her ass even more.

And yet I could feel my cock thicken just thinking about her with them on in front of me. The controller I'd kept for myself, attaching it to my keyring. The keyring was in my jeans pocket just begging to be taken out, to be used. I wanted to see her face when I was in control of her pleasure. But it was too risky to use. Instead I thought of something else.

"Come here," I said, keeping my face as deadpan as possible. My eyes flickered down the hallway that led to the internal garage door. Will could come through at any moment. But he would first have to open the door and then look around it before we were caught. I had time to play with.

Obediently, Lola Ray stepped down a few times until our eyes were level. *She thinks I'm going to lean in and kiss her*, I thought to myself, her eyes dipping to my mouth in anticipation… wanting me too. But while she was distracted I reached out and cupped her breast in my hand, my fingers soon finding her little nub, and I squeezed.

Her eyes widened and her mouth dropped open. I could see her tongue, glistening and wet. But she didn't know what to do. I pinched her nipple with my thumb and forefinger, harder this time, and her chest rose and fell.

"You've been a naughty girl, haven't you?"

She nodded and watched as I squeezed again.

"Say the words. Do it now."

She's breathless, her eyes searching mine, asking why. "I've been a naughty girl," she whispered.

"Good." I praised her. "...And you need to be punished, don't you?"

She nodded again but still I gave her another squeeze, seeing if she would catch on. I smiled when she did. "And I need to be punished. I want my daddy to punish me."

I dropped my hand and let her free just as the door to the garage creaked open.

Lola Ray's face was flushed, so pink and lovely, and even her eyes were shiny, a little wet. *I did warn her*, I told myself. She had no clue what she was doing when she pursued me. And now with her father coming down the hallway, she was either going to run to tell him and cause my whole world to come crashing in or she was going to a good little girl... one with potential.

"What's going on?" Will asked, presumably noticing the silence between us.

I waited to see if she was going to say something. Then just as I was about to open my mouth Lola Ray interrupted.

"Just showing Mack the necklace you got me.

I do love my present, *daddy*. It's the best present I think I've ever been given."

I gritted my teeth to prevent myself from smiling like a fool. *Good girl,* I thought, and risked a glance at her. She met my gaze. And if there was ever anyone with hungry eyes, it was her. She wanted more of what I had to give her.

"You ready, Will?" I asked and looked back to her father.

"Yep, got everything. Here, hold this, will you? I can't carry it all." I took the metal toolbox and though it was filled to the brim, I lifted it with ease.

"Do you need a ride to class, Lola Ray?" I asked because it didn't seem like Will was going to, but he interrupted anyway.

"We don't have time to drop her off. We have to get to the site. She can get the bus… or walk. She's got legs," Will replied with a slight snarl. As if giving his own daughter a ride to school was the worst thing imaginable.

"It's okay, I'll walk, *Daddy*." It's a good thing that Will wasn't looking at me when she said that because I couldn't help but wink at her.

Will skirted around me and he went to leave. "Be good," I called over my shoulder to Lola Ray as I followed Will out.

My mind was still on her as I drove Will and I to the construction site. I couldn't get her out of my head. She was stuck in there like glue, and I was beyond distracted. A couple of times Will tried to start a conversation and I only managed to reply in grunts, effectively ending the conversation before it even began.

I thought about how her tit felt good in my hand, how it felt even better when I rolled her hardening nipple between my finger and thumb. But more importantly I loved how she reacted. The flush on her face, her heart beating faster than it ever had beneath my touch, and lastly her enjoyment. She hadn't pulled away, in fact at one point I could've sworn she'd leaned into my grasp. Wanting me to twist and squeeze hander.

And god those vibrating panties, she was so eager to use them. The hours I could spend torturing her to the brink of pleasure was exhilarating. But while her father was in my truck, beside me, I had to at least keep my thoughts in check. I couldn't get hard while he sat there.

In fact the whole thing was insane. Where did I really see this all leading? Disaster was where.

"Jesus! Watch out!" Will yelled and reached for the wheel. He yanked it and we narrowly missed a mailbox. I'd been so in my head I'd almost run us off the road, into a line of mailboxes and into the ditch that lined the side.

"Shit."

"What the hell is wrong with you?"

I shook my head, slowed down but kept on driving.

"Seriously, you've not been the same for a few weeks now. And then you nearly get us killed. Anything I should know about?"

"It's nothing," I said, trying to reassure him. *Fuck.* She was really getting under my skin, making it almost impossible to concentrate and function normally.

There were only two ways to make it stop, to get my sanity back. Either I took her for everything she had. Use her up, get her out of my system, fuck her, and that would be that. Stop stringing it out and just do it. She wanted me to, that was for sure. That little innocent act wasn't fooling me. She craved what I could give her, what I could teach her.

But all that was a huge risk. Yes she hadn't screamed when I grabbed her that morning, but could I trust her to keep her mouth shut? Could I control her enough for our relationship—fuck it wasn't a relationship, it was nothing yet—but could I control her enough to make it so normality could be resumed?

I should just end it, I thought. Throw away the controller… the evidence linking those panties to me. If Will ever found them he'd want to know where she'd got them. Who had given them to her… She would probably crumble and tell him.

Fuck.

Though, I was fucked either way. I had to have her but did I dare risk the consequences?

It had already gone too far. I'd crossed the line and yet the thought of her in my arms, protecting her, giving her everything she could ever want, wouldn't go away. I knew I wanted to fuck her, that was blatantly obvious. But there was more to it.

An image of Lola Ray swollen with child flashed in my head… on all fours, tied up, her pussy wet and wanting.

I had to stop this, I thought. The vibrating panties had been a silly, dangerous mistake. A slippery slope. I was going to throw the controller away, into the first trash bin I saw.

Chapter Thirteen
Lola Ray

I pulled the baking dish of hot lasagna out of the oven and set it on the protective heat mat on the counter, nearly burning myself in the process. I'd almost burned myself twice already while I wasn't paying attention to what I was doing. I was far too distracted hoping that I'd see Mack again. Sometimes my father would invite him around for a meal after their shift seeing how Mack lived by himself, nearby, and what with Mack giving him a ride I almost bet that he'd ask him in. And I was going to be prepared.

After a mind-numbing day in class, wanting the time to move faster, I practically sprinted home to start on the meal. My father expected that I made dinner each night anyway, so it wasn't like it was a big thing, but with the possibility of seeing Mack again I wanted to make it special, put that little extra effort in. Get changed, too, into something a bit more enticing.

Maybe he would touch me again, I thought, biting my lip. All day I'd gone over every detail of the morning. Coming down the stairs and seeing him for the first time, his eyes on me, never leaving my body. The way he spoke to me, stern and serious, but with an undercurrent of playfulness too. And then the way he claimed me with just one simple action. His large rough hand on my breast, finger on my nipple. Simultaneously he'd made me freeze, all the while my insides were ready to explode. I was too shocked to do anything except give in to the sensations. Through the material of my shirt I felt his warmth, his urgency, his commanding presence. By squeezing the way he did he told me he was in charge. And right then I was ready to obey… to do anything he wanted me to. If he'd asked me to get naked right there and then, with my father still in the house, who could catch us at any moment, I would have.

I wanted to please him and have him all for my own.

But I would have to be good, I knew. I had to do what he said before he would ever touch me again, that seemed obvious. And I couldn't wait. Perhaps when he turned up for dinner we'd be able to sneak a few moments alone. What would he make me do? Would he make me do anything? Or would he keep me waiting? I was buzzing with nervous energy when I heard a truck pull up outside.

It had to be Mack's. I rushed to the front and peeked out of the window. Mack's dark grey truck with a weird yellow trim stood idling by the curb. Through the dark windows I couldn't see any movement inside.

My father got out first and started to walk up the driveway.

Disappointment settled deep inside me when the truck pulled away and picked up speed down the road. Mack wasn't going to be joining us.

The front door slammed shut and my father's footsteps, loud and clunky, travelled down to the kitchen. "Lola Ray, dinner better be ready, I'm starving!"

I left my post in the living room and followed his trail down the hallway back to the kitchen. "It's just cooling," I replied and busied myself back around the counters, pulling out the salad I'd prepared earlier. I tried not to let it hurt me that my father hadn't said hello to me. Instead he'd just come in and demanded that his food was ready. If I didn't know better I would've thought that I was his wife not his daughter. But a tiny plan had begun to form in my head by that time, which would change all that. I hadn't been lying when I told Mack that I wanted a new daddy… someone to take care of me, for a change.

I grabbed a plate and quickly served up a generous portion of the food and took it to him. "Here it is. How come Mack didn't want to come in?" I risked asking.

"How the hell should I know?"

I shrugged trying to make out it was a non-issue. "He knows I make plenty…"

"Stop pouting like that. He's probably got better things to do that hang around here all the time."

With that seed planted in my head I wondered if Mack would be heading straight home or instead going to a bar where he could meet women his own age… ones who didn't bring a boatload of complications with them. Jealously swirled an angry storm inside me and I darted from the kitchen and ran upstairs.

"Stop running! I'm trying to eat in fucking peace here! And where the hell is your necklace?" my father yelled as I ran up the stairs, but I ignored it all. Even the subsequent request. "And where's my beer?" *He could get his own beer tonight*, I thought wickedly.

There was one way for sure to know if Mack had gone home but I needed to be in my room, looking out my window, to find out. I eased my bedroom door closed and made a beeline straight for it. My eyes darted across the back of Mack's house. It was dark and in shadow. There were no lights on inside. *It wasn't far from our house to his by car, so he should've been home by now*, I thought. There should've been some sign that he was in.

I waited. For too long. But just as I was about to turn away a light flickered on. The dusky yellow light cast shadows all around Mack's den-like space on the ground floor. I gasped as I saw Mack sitting in a recliner facing the window. Facing me?

Could he see me? I wasn't sure. Surely if I could see him from this angle, he could see me? I hesitated, but then lifted my hand in a small wave. He didn't respond, he just sat there. Then the light went off.

Behind me my new phone buzzed twice telling me I had a text message. I turned to look at it on my desk. Was it from Mack? Was I hoping too much? But only he knew my new number. Reluctant to leave the window I glanced back to where I'd seen him only moments before. But there was only darkness.

My phone buzzed again.

This time I left the window to pick it up.

Daddy > You're going to do exactly what I tell you to do

Daddy > You've been a bad girl and you need to be punished

My hand went to my mouth as I read the messages. Breathless and smiling I wondered if I had to reply back. What on earth could I say? What did he want to hear? I was excited at what this all meant and quickly typed my reply.

Lola Ray > I'm ready for my punishment

Simple. Direct. Willing to please. *God, I wanted to please him so much.* It felt like an age before another message came through. I almost thought I'd responded with the wrong thing. But finally my phone vibrated in my hand.

Daddy > Strip for me

A rush of excitement tickled me from inside. My body felt like it was on fire and I hadn't even done anything yet. He hadn't even touched me. All it had taken was three words to make me feel so alive.

I began to kick my shoes off when my phone buzzed again.

Daddy > In front of the window

I blushed. Of course. I shook my head, I was so eager to follow his command that I hadn't thought that he couldn't see me where I stood. With my phone in my hand I eased back in front of the window. This was totally different from the other time when I stood there naked; he hadn't been able to see me then, had he? Maybe he had been there all along…

I rested the phone down on the window ledge and crossed my arms while grabbing the edge of my tight shirt. *I would pull it off slow*, I thought, he would like that. He'd want me to take my time.

I revealed my stomach, then my bra, and finally pulled the shirt over my head and let it drop down on the floor. My skin was alive, I could almost feel his penetrating gaze on me.

Without wanting to stop, I eased my skirt down to around my ankles so that I was only now wearing my bra and panties. After Mack and my dad had left that morning, I'd gone and changed and took off the present Mack had given me. I thought he would be pleased by that, that I was doing what he wanted without even really saying it.

Turning my back on the window I reached for the clasp of my bra, then discarded it. I glanced over my shoulder to where I imagined Mack was sitting. My phone buzzed.

Daddy > Turn around.

I did, slowly, and let him see me.

Daddy > Take them off. I want to see it all. I want to see what's mine.

I swallowed. *Mine*. He'd laid claim to me. I certainly wasn't going to object. He could have me, I would bend for him and give him anything he wanted.

With a blush rising on my cheeks—I'd never stripped on purpose for a boy or a boyfriend, let alone a man who was nearly twice my age—I peeled off my panties and stood, resisting the temptation to wrap my arms around my body to shield myself from view.

I stood for a moment. Was I supposed to touch myself? Did he want me to? I thought best of it and kept my hands at my sides. He would tell me what he wanted. So far he hadn't been shy about doing that.

Daddy > You are so goddamn beautiful.

I nibbled my lip at his response, then looked down again as a second message came through.

Daddy > And I'm going to ruin you.

My heart thumped wildly within my chest.

I thought I was going to pass out. My pussy pulsed in equal measure. What did he mean? *It didn't matter*, I told myself, if he was able to give me pleasure without even touching me that meant something.

Daddy > Now, be a good girl and put on your present

Oh god. Ever since I'd seen the package that morning I'd fantasized about how or when or even if I'd ever get to experience them... and now he was telling me to put them on. I rushed to find the vibrating panties, tucked away at the back of a drawer, hidden—not that my father ever did any laundry, but I didn't want to take the chance of him finding my new dirty secret. With them in my hand I went back to the window and slipped them on.

I glanced up at the dark space across the yards to where Mack had to be sitting and waited. The missing controller. He had to have it. Or was he going to tell me where it was hidden? I'd checked the box thoroughly, it was nowhere to be found... but perhaps that morning he'd left it behind. Excitement buzzed through my veins as I waited... waited for anything to happen.

But when nothing did I picked up my phone and quickly typed:

Lola Ray > What now? What do you want me to do? I will do anything.

Then my whole world flipped over.

An intense buzz, vibrations that I'd never ever experienced in my whole entire life shook my world. The vibrating panties came to life, my clit was pulsing, being pummeled over and over again by an unrelenting wave of serious flutterings. I dropped my phone and screamed.

Chapter Fourteen
Mack

At my instruction she stood naked before me. Granted it was through two panes of glass and there were two yards separating us as well. But I could still see her, clear as day. It was a glorious sight. One that made me hard as a rock. I wanted to sit there and wank at her image all night, and think about how her sweet little mouth would suck me off at my command. But I didn't. Instead I just stared.

She was beautiful and she was all mine.

I already knew she was mine, that it was inevitable. I'd finally admitted it to myself. There was no point denying it anymore. Every inch of her body I'd silently claimed as my own. And eventually I'd do more than silently claim it.

I'd make it real. She'd give herself over to me completely, without hesitation, and she'd love it.

Her body longed to be touched, and I was desperate to please her. Would give my left nut to feel her again, beneath my skin, writhing and squirming as I let my fingers go to work. Making her body sing with pleasure… and pain. I wanted to see the color rise on her bottom as I spanked her, or the look on her face when she was over my lap and my finger caressed her slit. Would she beg for it like a good little girl? Wanting Daddy's cock? Or would she endure the torture? I didn't know which would please me more, but just having her all to myself was probably enough.

My cock thickened, demanding attention. But I ignored it. If I couldn't touch her, then I wouldn't let myself cum. I'd save it all for her. I knew denying myself was pushing me toward becoming a crazed man… sooner or later I would explode. *But it would all be worth it*, I told myself. I thought how much better it would be when she was right in front of me, in the same room, preferably tied up, close enough to touch and unable to escape. I let myself hope that I'd finally found someone, even if she was as young as Lola Ray was, who wanted what I could give her. Wasn't afraid to embrace it… and would let me take control.

She'd proven she could do what Daddy wanted. And this little exercise though a partial fantasy was a good way to see how well she behaved for me. Could she submit to me fully?

So far she made me very proud. It was only baby steps at that moment, but she had demonstrated her willingness to follow my instructions. A fast learner. I couldn't expect perfection all the time, but the consequences of her resisting would be just as pleasurable as watching her obey my every command. She seemed almost primed for this life by my side, with me as master and her as my everything.

She stood idle. Waiting for further instructions and I couldn't help but just let her stand there—her breasts out, her pussy encased with a device I was going to have fun with. It's as if her body was made purely for me. A gift, a prize for being able to resist this far. Since I'd arrived back in Weyworth, I'd had my eye on her, watching in the last few months when she'd transformed, a stunning butterfly spreading her wings, testing her boundaries. I could tell she was eager to experiment… and all that had been confirmed the moment I caught her in the kitchen that fateful Sunday. The moment when everything changed and I knew I had to have her… I just had to wait a little bit longer until I got my reward.

My eyes raked her body again, studying every curve and dip. Her long arms by her side. Perfection. She was on view like a piece of artwork, a statue created just for me, all for my benefit. All at my direction and insistence.

Ah she was young—*but malleable*, I thought—with slight disappointment as she bent at the waist, her glorious tits dangling away from her body, as she picked up her phone. I almost couldn't wait to wrap her breasts up with rope, see them bulge… her hands would be tied too, behind her back on her knees. Legs parted open, a rigid bar between them, unable to close.

She'd learn to wait longer.

I picked up the controller and held it ready. I'd made sure to get the most expensive item, the one with the longest range. I wasn't quite sure if it would work and reach across the distance that was between us, but there was only one way to find out.

A reply appeared on the screen of my phone.

It was time to punish her for her impatience. I couldn't wait to see the look on her sweet face. Would she bite her lip? Close and scrunch up her eyes? Would she rip the garment from her body? *If she did the last thing*, I thought, *then she would really be in trouble.*

I pushed the button.

I took a sharp breath as the electronic device sent the signal. How long would it take to reach her? What would happen? Would there be a feeble buzz and her face would fall, disappointed?

It felt like an age before a reaction manifested on her face. A glorious one. I couldn't have asked for more.

Her lower half jolted as if she'd just been zapped by a lightening strike from the side. Her mouth dropped open, an expression of fear, pleasure, and everything in between slid across her face. For a moment her eyes were so wide. So shiny. Were they glistening with tears?

She didn't know what to do except scream.

I heard it from all the way across the yard, over the fence, through my yard and through the cracked open window in the room. One long shriek, a desperate cry, surprise and excitement and panic all rolled into one. I'd never heard such bliss before in my whole entire life.

I held the button down.

I wanted to listen to her cry, moan, and scream all day.

Her hands went to her crotch, as if to try and stop the sensation from tickling her clit, but I kept on pressing the little controller in my hand. She would probably cum… all at my doing. I wanted to join her, my cock struggled in my jeans begging for a release.

Only a second or so had passed but somehow I came to my senses. What if Will heard her scream—surely he would've if he was in the house? And I'd only just dropped him off not so long ago. *Fuck. I was an idiot.*

I let the button go and waited, holding my breath. Would Will investigate the scream? If she was my daughter I'd be up the stairs like a shot, needing to see if she was okay. But Will wasn't parent of the year.

I kept my gaze pinned to the bedroom window and Lola Ray. Her face transformed into a calm smile, relieved that the vibrator had stopped torturing her. Her eyes lifted to across the way, to me, though I knew she couldn't see me in the shadows. She smiled again then bit her lip. Maybe she wasn't ready for the high setting just yet. She'd soon get used to it, if that's what I wanted.

Suddenly her head whipped round, her hair swishing with the movement. She dropped out of view then reappeared, pulling items of clothing onto her body as quickly as she could. That meant only one thing: Will was coming.

The last thing I ever expected happened and in a few moments the whole situation had turned into a nightmare. Will charged into the room and I could see Lola Ray, now dressed at least, back away from him. She was moving closer to the window. Will came into view. It was blatantly obvious that he was shouting at her. Maybe the scream had been the last straw… I had no idea what went on in that house, but anyone could tell that if they spent longer than five minutes with Lola Ray inside that home, that it wasn't a happy household. At least not for her. On the outside Will was a businessman, respected, admired. But as someone who had secrets, I knew he was hiding something. I had my suspicions of course, but I'd never seen him do anything untoward while I'd been there. It was one of the reasons I made the excuse to go around each Sunday or go around whenever I could… just to make sure. To keep an eye on what I wished could be mine. And though Will was never really on his best behavior while I was there—he was snippy and hard with her, demanding her to wait on him hand and foot—he'd never hit her in front of me.

Not until now.

I leapt from my chair as the blow landed. Will's hand swinging then going across her face. I couldn't see it exactly but from the whip of her head I knew he'd hit her hard. She wobbled to the side. More shouting, then he raised his hand again, and struck her again.

I watched it all, standing stock-still. Not moving. Memorizing every painful slap he gave her. He hit her four times before he was done and he left the room. The window was empty now, only her bedroom walls visible.

Eerily I was very calm. Which was not a good sign. Any other person would've been phoning the cops, or kicking up a fuss, going around there to make sure was okay. But I wasn't going to do any of that.

I knew exactly what I was going to do… the same as I did the last time someone I loved got hurt.

I wasn't going to charge around to his house like a fool and beat him senseless for touching what was now mine. There would be time for that, of course. And even if he thought that because she was his daughter that he had the right to hit her, he didn't. He'd fucked up. Big time. And I'd make sure he'd pay.

It didn't matter anymore that I was his best friend, or his employee. All that had gone out of the window the minute he laid his hands on my baby girl.

Lola Ray was in pain, I knew that. No doubt she was in tears on the floor. But that was okay. She wouldn't be for long. She had me now. I wasn't going to let anything ever happen to her like that again.

And in a way I was glad that I'd finally seen him act. Now I could kill him without remorse.

DREAM DADDY

Chapter Fifteen
Lola Ray

I stayed down. My hands were over my head feebly trying to protect myself. But I knew if my father wanted to hurt me anymore he wouldn't let a couple of things like arms, or bones, to stand in his way. He would drag my arms away from my body, pin me down, his weight on top of me, until I couldn't move and continue with the onslaught. Thankfully, that time his anger was short-lived and I got away with only receiving four hits, mostly slaps to the face, backhands that stung my cheek as he demanded to know where my necklace was. I didn't know, I couldn't tell him. My hand went to my throat, it was definitely not there; the cheap clasp must have broke.

It felt like there were two fires burning on my face, furnaces stoked to the brim with coal, one on each side and I prayed that my face didn't swell up like a balloon. But I knew the next day for school I'd have to wear plenty of concealer and maybe some extra blush to cover up his actions. I wouldn't be able to stand people looking at me and wondering, pitying me. I told myself I could handle my father's rages. And while the last time he'd hit me had been only a few months ago, the unprovoked attacks were becoming more and more frequent.

It used to happen only once a year after my mom had gone, then when that didn't seem like enough, it became twice a year. *Like a substitute gift for Christmas and my birthday*, I thought bitterly. But in the last couple of years the rages had escalated to at least once every couple of months. I supposed with that timeline in mind I was overdue for my next one.

The scream that had shocked even me, the buzzing contraption at my crotch to blame, had gotten his attention, reminded him of his annoying daughter. The burden. He was probably more upset by the fact I hadn't stayed downstairs with him for dinner, waiting on him hand and foot while he ate, than the noise or the lost necklace.

But I'd given up trying to figure out exactly when the next outburst would come.

They were totally random. Sometimes I could be just standing there, quiet, doing nothing, and then *wham* I'd get shoved across the room and the shouting and hitting would begin. Or sometimes I would've done something wrong, known I'd had and felt the dread build in my belly as I waited for him to get it over and done with. Like the time when I loaded the dishwasher incorrectly and he trapped my fingers in the machine and closed the door on them. I had bruises on my hand for over a month from that, but luckily nothing had broken that time, and it wasn't my dominant hand. But he still expected me to cook, clean, and do everything else one-handed. God forbid I would do those chores any slower…

Staying low on my bedroom floor I let the tears escape. But I didn't sob. I'd been through it too many times that I was almost used to it. Instead the tears were a release, a trickle, a leaky faucet overcome with pressure—the rage bubbling upside forcing them out. I told myself I was strong, I'd gotten through worse. I thought of my mom. *But I wasn't going to put up with it forever*, I thought, as Mack's face flickered before my eyes.

I wondered if he'd seen anything? Had he seen my father beat me in front of the window? Would he even do anything if he had? He must have…

the buzzing had stopped almost immediately after I screamed. He must've seen it all from his chair. In a split-second of weakness I wanted him to rescue me, to turn up on our doorstep and return the favor for me, his fists pounding into my dad's face. The fantasy in my mind was so clear… and if he cared for me then surely he would do something? He would take care of me…

I listened intently for movements around the house, waiting for something to happen. Hoping. But also trying to keep track of my father's position after he'd gone back downstairs. There was always a chance he would come back, for round two—it had happened before when the rage hadn't billowed away and he still needed to take out his frustrations on me. I wanted to be ready in case either happened.

Thankfully the creaks of our stairs and the noise he'd made climbing them had alerted me to the danger before, and I'd managed to pull my clothes back on. Of course, I knew a split-second after the scream escaped my lips, making its way down to him, reverberating around the house, that he'd come to find out what I was doing. He probably felt put out, having to investigate, having to leave his meal, which would've only built up the irritation he felt for me. I supposed it probably wouldn't have made much of a difference if he'd found me half-naked in my room, he still would've hit me. Just maybe twice as hard.

But as I waited the feelings of hope withered away. Mack wasn't coming. I glanced longingly at the screen of my new phone. No new messages. Nothing from Mack to indicate he'd seen anything. I tried to convince myself that it meant nothing, him ignoring what had happened, that I shouldn't read into anything. Either he hadn't seen and therefore there wasn't going to be another text message... or he had and was deciding whether it was worth his time to intervene. Would it be worth the risk? Even I couldn't decide that. I knew what I wanted in my heart, though. But he would have to explain to my father how he saw what had happened in the first place...

But none of that mattered. Perhaps secretly I'd wanted him to see, and more importantly I wanted him to act. To save me.

I crawled along the carpet, away from the window, leaving the phone behind and slipped onto the bed under the covers.

He wasn't coming.

* * *

Before going down to make breakfast I double-checked my makeup in the bathroom mirror. The natural light was better in the main bathroom than my room and I studied my face. It would pass. I probably looked like I was overly warm, coming down with a cold, a little puffy around the nose. But overall my face looked relatively normal and didn't look like I'd been beaten the day before. At least not at first glance. But if anyone got closer, studied my face for a little more than a few seconds, maybe the developing bruises would give me away.

I put the coffee on to brew and went about pulling down the cereal boxes and bowls, then set the table.

As usual my father came into the room as if nothing had ever happened. He'd never, not once, after he'd hit me said sorry or acted like he'd been in the wrong. It was just a normal day to him. Like he didn't even have the capability to remember what happened or think about how I might have been feeling. I wished I could block out each beating, but each one stayed with me, dark little shadows following me everywhere I went.

I was already at the table eating my breakfast when he entered the room, took a bowl and filled it with his chosen cereal then poured the milk over it. No morning greeting, no small-talk—

which was a blessing really. I couldn't think of anything I ever wanted to say to him. He was a monster.

"I'll be away for a few days. Out of town," he announced as if that was all the information I was entitled to have.

"Okay," I replied, not wanting to push him into giving me more details and continued eating. Why should I care where he was going or what he was doing when he clearly didn't care one iota about me? He would volunteer more of his plans on his own terms, no amount of questioning from me would grease those wheels. Maybe he wouldn't come back this time…

I finished eating and rinsed my bowl and slipped it into the dishwasher, careful to stack it in the correct place. Absently as I lingered in the kitchen I grabbed my new phone and started to text Robin. She'd been giving me the silent treatment for a little while, mainly due to the borrowed dress I'd ruined. Several times I'd tried to tell her what had happened, but then thought better of it. If I'd told her about that night I wouldn't be able to stop myself from telling her everything… including what happened with Mack, ending up in his bed. It was too risky. Robin was a gossip, a queen among her peers for knowing the ins and outs of everyone's business practically before they knew it themselves, and before I knew it—if I did tell her, and regardless of us being besties—the whole school would know about my little incident and ending up in Mack's bed. Keeping her mouth shut just wasn't under Robin's control. It was like she had an innate need to tell the world all the stories, news, and tidbits she collected.

And if it did get out, no matter how I spun it, the details wouldn't matter, it never did with gossip and they'd make their own judgements. No doubt it would somehow get Mack into trouble, I just knew it would. So I kept my mouth shut and told her I'd been so drunk that I'd fallen and ripped it.

Thankfully she texted me back. I promised her that I'd make it up to her and she seemed happy enough with that.

Robin > Need a lift to class?

I looked up at my father. He'd managed to get his truck repaired and would normally drive me but with him going away I wasn't sure if that would still be the plan. And I didn't want to ask.

I bit my lip. But if I didn't find out one way or another it could be another excuse for him to get angry.

"Robin says she can pick me up. Is that okay?" I asked and held my breath.

My father grunted as if he didn't care, when I knew for a fact he did, and I repeated my question again cautiously. For whatever twisted reason he had, he liked to be in control of everything that concerned me. Where I went, whom I saw. It was a mind fuck if I was being honest, a paradox— he hated me and yet he needed to have constant control over my life. But I supposed he had a good reason why. Even though it was years ago now and no one would believe me, I was still a witness.

"Fine," he said and glanced back down to his food before his head snapped up again. "Where the hell did you get that phone?"

I froze and stopped typing the reply I was writing to Robin. How could I have been so stupid? I'd forgotten all about how new it was, how different it was to my old beat-up phone that I'd lost. The one that my dad had control over. The one on which he was able to monitor my calls and texts... even my browser history. *Fuck.* Flinching already, expecting a blow to come out of nowhere I started to back up, close the distance between me and the exit.

With the phone Mack had given me my father would no longer have the opportunity to oversee my usage, and I'd been stupid enough to parade around the house with it clutched in my hand, going about like normal, like it was no big deal.

I swallowed, he was waiting for an answer.

"Erm, it was a gift," I said and realized too late the mistake I'd made as I said it. My head tried to think two steps ahead but I'd been too slow. He would ask who it was from. And why. But I couldn't full well say it was from Mack, could I? Too many questions would come from that.

"Who from?"

I inwardly sighed. My mind scrambling for a way to spin the truth into something that he would find acceptable.

"A boy… just someone I'm seeing."

"Who?" my father growled, his insistent tone warning me I'd better answer, and I'd better answer quick.

The first name popped into my head. The college jock who'd been sniffing around me for weeks. He'd been persistent asking me out on dates, coming up to my locker trying to flirt with me.

"Samuel Black."

"The quarterback for the Weyworth Giants?"

I nodded and swallowed another thick lump in my throat waiting for his reaction. My father loved football, maybe he would think it was okay that I was dating a football player; and a quarterback at that, the top player.

"How long have you been seeing him? Why the hell have you not told me? And he's buying you a phone?" He paused to consider his train of thought and shook his head. Then he added, his voice low, as if he'd caught me in a trap, "What on earth are you trying to hide?" His eyes narrowed and I was lost for words. My hands were already trembling, but I clutched my phone tighter to stop them from shaking and tried to smile sweetly instead.

"Nothing, Daddy. I'm not hiding anything. I didn't want to bother you with it all, I know how busy you've been lately."

Thankfully I was saved when his eyes flickered to the kitchen clock mounted on the wall behind me.

"This isn't over. When I get back from my trip you will tell me everything. And I'd better meet this kid before I decide if you're allowed to see him."

He stalked away from me but before he could leave and I could breathe a sigh of relief he added one final thing, "And don't think you can bring him around here while I'm gone… you little slut," he said, adding that last bit for good measure. "I'll be asking Mack to keep an eye on you. No parties, and certainly no boys! Do you understand me? You know what will happen if you disobey me."

I nodded. *There would be no boys, that was for sure*, I thought with an inward defying smile. I was only interested in one guy, and he was a full-grown man who would protect me and give me more pleasure than any college quarterback could.

Chapter Sixteen
Mack

I decided to skip out of work early. It wasn't as if Will was there anyway to take notice of my absence. If the other crew members had a problem with it, they didn't mention it. And they could be relied on not to snitch. After all it was me they came to now when they needed time off. I was the one they could rely on to give them some slack when they needed it. Will was a hard-ass and it was no secret that most of his employees didn't respect him, they only tolerated him.

I hadn't thought I was one of them. I'd always stuck up for him, told the others he wasn't that bad, that he just had a business to run and they would do the same if they were in his position.

But that was all changing. Especially after what I'd seen him do.

It was a good thing he hadn't been in that day. He was off securing a new contract over in Eastdale. But if he'd shown his face in the office that morning, the day after I'd seen him relentlessly strike Lola Ray, I wouldn't have been responsible for what I would've done to him. I was still raw and pent up and frustrated. And I would've let it out all on him. Damn the job, damn the so-called friendship. That was dead to me now anyway. But mostly I was furious at myself. That I'd watched, that I'd done nothing. I was ashamed at myself for not getting in my truck the moment I saw him laying his hands on her, busting down the door of the house, and giving him what he deserved. I told myself that I would take care of it in due time… so I wouldn't get caught, not again… and I would eventually make him pay. But that didn't make the angsty adrenaline in my veins, full of regret, go away.

All day I hadn't been able to concentrate, my mind wandering, totally off the job wondering how she was, if she was okay. It was pointless me being there, so I jumped in my truck and left. The boys would be able to continue on without me for the last few hours of the day anyway.

I drove aimlessly at first, but my subconscious

seemingly had a plan of its own and I found myself getting closer and closer to the old community college. The same one Lola Ray now attended. The digital clock set in the console of the truck told me the last bell of the day would be ringing in a few minutes.

Had she gone in that morning? Even with what had happened the previous night would she have been able to face scores of questioning eyes? Of course she would've. Will wouldn't have let her skip. I just hoped he hadn't left a visible mark on her to cause her any problems. But I knew from the blows I saw, he'd hit her hard. There would be bruises, bad ones developing.

I managed to find an empty space close to the pick-up spot and shut off the engine.

Why on earth was I there? I asked myself.

It was crazy. If anyone saw me, questions would be asked. Of course I could easily shrug them away and give them an excuse—that I was there to pick her up... being a good friend to Will. Nothing untoward. And yet as I tried the lie out, speaking it out loud, practicing, my heart rate spiked and I could feel my hands become clammy.

I could lie to other people but I had to be honest with myself. I was there only for one reason.

To see her again, to make sure she was okay. To let her know, even if maybe I couldn't say it, that everything would be all right. That I'd make sure of it.

I glanced around the front of the school toward the stone steps. Already there were streams of kids spilling out the doors. If she didn't have any study sessions planned, she should be out soon too. I vaguely remembered her wanting to try out for the cheerleading squad at the start of the year but Will had put his foot down. But I expected it wasn't because of the skimpy outfits or the provocative dances the squads liked to perform in front of the football crowds, no, it had more to do with Will wanting Lola Ray to be at home, close by, under his control, waiting on him hand and foot. He couldn't allow her any freedom. He would be lost without her.

The seat under me squeaked as I shifted, waiting. It had been a few years since I was a senior but it all looked the same. Groups of kids pairing off and gathering into their little social groups, rehashing the day's events before heading home.

The jocks and their girlfriends were crowded around a battered picnic table near the student parking lot. I smiled, a little bit of nostalgia creeping into my thoughts.

Things definitely hadn't changed. That used to be our spot too. God forbid any other groups tried to claim that area for their own. They would've got the biggest beat-down of their lives.

But my smile died as I spotted a flash of blonde hair farther back from everyone else, in between two parked cars on the edge of the grass. Lola Ray stood with her hip cocked, as she tilted her head up to her companion. Her mouth was wide, laughing. Her hand casually moved to the guy's chest. But there was nothing really casual in that simple move. Even from that distance I could feel the waves of seduction flowing off her. Her target, a senior he looked like, smiled back. He was big and by the jacket he wore there was no doubting he was a part of the crowd of jocks. A football player, for certain.

Maybe I'd been foolish to be worried about her. She didn't seem to have been affected by either her father's brutal attack or whatever the fuck we'd been doing. There she was, happy as a clam, fawning all over some muscle-bound idiot. I'd obviously meant nothing to her. A plaything, a distraction. Nothing more. It was all just a game to her. Seeing how far she could get me to go, no doubt. And I'd been an idiot to fall for it. I shook my head and surprised myself as I let out a laugh.

The little minx had wrapped me around her

finger and I'd been foolish enough to think that I'd been the one in control.

I was about to start the truck and leave when I gave her one last glance. She was walking back toward the crowd of jocks, her hips swaying pleasingly as she left the guy behind her. He stood watching her a stupid grin on his face like he'd just won the fucking lottery. What had they been talking about? What had she promised him? Whatever it was his shit-eating grin pissed me off to no end.

Turn back the years and that could've been me, and how I wished in that moment I could've switched places with the kid. To be his age again, to have the chance to be with Lola Ray without all the fucking nonsense. Instead of years between us, there would've only been months. It wouldn't have been this big forbidden thing hanging over my head.

Fuck, she had done a number on me and it was time that I just let it be. If I let it go any further there was no telling how bad things could end up getting.

I turned away and started the truck. I was doing the right thing, I would drive away, mind my own business. I'd put up some fucking curtains, keep them drawn at all times and forget what I'd seen the other night. Forget what I'd done. I'd keep my job, keep myself out of prison… eventually I'd find a new job and perhaps even move away. Put some distance between myself and temptation. Hell I'd contemplated killing my best friend all because of her. Risking everything. It had to stop.

But before I could drive away and put my new plan into motion; the plan of doing nothing and pretty much staying away from Lola Ray and her father, the passenger door opened and Lola Ray heaved herself into the seat.

The door slammed shut and all my good intentions evaporated as I took her in beside me.

"Hello, Daddy," she stated, as if her being in my truck and saying hello to me was an everyday occurrence. The most normal thing in the world to happen. I continued to stare at her. Mostly in shock. But mostly I stared because I knew she was going to be my downfall. That this was the moment when everything was going to change. There would be no turning back. Had I decided a few minutes earlier to leave, to look away and not look back I could've prevented so much heartache, so much bloodshed. But I hadn't. I'd lingered too long and now, like a freight train barreling down on its unwavering tracks, we were stuck. It would be impossible to deviate now.

I studied her face. She stared back with cool calm eyes. Her makeup was a little heavier and

I could see the tinge of a muddy purple color that she'd tried to disguise with blusher on her cheekbone.

My hand reached out and I took her chin. She didn't flinch. She let me turn and tilt her head from side to side as I witnessed the hidden bruises that perhaps only she and I knew were there. As the light hit her face the marks shone through the attempted cover-up. My fury came back two-fold, the thought of her in pain made me insane with anger. Someone else had done this to her, and I couldn't let that stand.

From now on the only person who would be allowed to touch her would be me.

The only person who would be allowed to punish her, give her pain, then take it all away with pleasure, would be me.

I let go of her chin.

"You saw?" she asked, her voice soft, cautious, but she couldn't hide the eagerness of her question. She wanted to know precisely what I'd seen, and probably more importantly, why I hadn't acted. Why I hadn't come to her rescue. Why I'd stayed away, saving my own skin instead of hers.

I turned my attention to the passing cars, away from her inquisitive and penetrating stare.

God those eyes could make any man do anything she ever wanted.

The shame washed over me again. The thought that she'd been waiting for me to rescue her, huddled down low on the floor, not moving, not daring to call out for help—well it twisted my insides up. I was not one to regret shit that happened or didn't happen to me in my life, the could've beens or the what ifs, but on this one occasion I couldn't help thinking I could've been better. I could've done something. I could've made a difference.

But I did that once before and it all went to hell.

She shuffled in her seat as the silence suffocated us.

I couldn't change the past but I would change her future.

"He won't touch you ever again, I'll make sure of it," I said finally in reply. Under my breath I added, "and neither will anyone else."

She nodded, once. Content at my simple yet meaningful declaration. I meant every word. Not her father, not some drunken college shit-head, or jock would ever lay a finger on her porcelain skin. I wouldn't let them. Maybe she would've changed her mind had she known the full extent of my meaning if she knew what was to come, but she had to realize, even just a little bit, perhaps even subconsciously, that every little part of her belonged to me. Her life was no longer her own, I owned her now.

"You'd best drive, before anyone sees us and starts to ask questions."

"Let them see. Let them ask. I don't care anymore."

How things can suddenly change, I thought. Only five minutes ago I was ready to walk away from her, ready to give up. But by getting in my truck, voluntarily, and seeing her damaged face, she'd renewed the fight in me. Reinvigorated every single cell with a burning fire, stoked only for her.

Who was I kidding?

I wouldn't have been able to walk away from Lola Ray, no matter how hard I tried to convince or delude myself. Telling myself that was one big, fat lie. She was it, everything—my whole damn world. Could I even remember a time before I'd laid eyes on her? What had life been like before Lola Ray? I honestly couldn't remember. It had been dull, that was for sure.

Now there was color in my life, possibility, excitement... and my cock was so goddamn hard contemplating what I had in store for her.

I started the engine and the once turbulent air around us seemed to calm itself. Lola Ray crossed her legs and relaxed into the seat, her body deliberately angled in my direction.

Playing the innocent creature that she was, she tried to hide the small smile that spread across her lips by dipping her head low and staring into her lap. But I caught the tug at the edge of her mouth and the way her smooth cheeks rounded slightly, plumping up, with the action. She couldn't hide from me.

Whether she was continuing to play mind games, or if she was genuinely curious, or perhaps she just wanted me to admit it out loud, a moment later she lifted her head and made eye contact.

"What do you mean? You don't care anymore?"

"I mean things are going to be different from now on."

"Really? How so?"

"For one, you're going to stay away from that boy."

DREAM DADDY

Chapter Seventeen
Lola Ray

As soon as I spotted Mack's truck, Samuel Black, god's gift to college girls, was forgotten. I could hear his frustration as I began to walk away from him. He wasn't used to not getting his own way or girls turning him down or ignoring him. Especially not ones who got distracted and left him standing there like a fool, mid-sentence, after agreeing to go out on a date with him. Granted I'd approached him after class, initiating the whole thing, but talking to him and maybe even flirting a little didn't automatically mean I was his or that I had to wait to be dismissed once *he* was finished talking to me.

I mean okay, maybe I had led him on a bit and made it clear that if he was going to ask me out again that my answer would lean heavily toward a positive outcome. He'd been pleased by that. And I was too. After all I had to cover my ass, what with me putting my foot in my mouth and inventing a new boyfriend out of thin air to appease my dad and his questions about my new phone.

Samuel would be the perfect cover for what I had in mind. I'd let him take me on a couple of dates, give in to my father's request to meet him and then when the coast was clear and the lies were all tucked away nice and neat, I'd dump Samuel.

And just like I'd predicted Sam immediately asked me out on a date. He was as eager as they came. I could already see him envisaging how the night would go. He thought I would be easy, maybe even a cheap date. But after resisting his advances for so long he had to know I wasn't going to make it easy for him at all. Especially not when all I could think about was Mack.

Who was right there… My stomach flip-flopped and I stared off into the distance at his truck and wondered why he'd turned up. I didn't waste another moment finding out.

"So the coach said there'd be scouts… Are you listening to me? Where the hell are you going?" Samuel called after me. I didn't turn back and instead wiggled my ass a little more as I strode toward Mack's truck. "We still on for eight?" he shouted puzzled, trying not to sound desperate.

"You'll have to wait and see, Sam," I shouted over my shoulder as my response. Let him figure it out. No matter my teasing, I knew I would go, though. I had to lay the foundation in order for my plan to work and to get my father off my back. Then maybe my dreams would come true. I wasn't going to stand on ceremony and wait and see though, I was going to act and make sure they did come to fruition. I wanted Mack, and one way or another, I was going to get him. He was going to be mine.

The look on his face as I hopped in beside him was the best thing I'd seen all day. Mack looked equally confused, happy, and my favorite: guilty. Like he'd been caught doing something very naughty, and I supposed waiting around for me—cause what other reason was he at my school—could be considered that. He didn't have a kid taking classes at Weyworth Community, and he probably wouldn't be able to give an adequate excuse if anyone confronted him.

But him taking that risk, for me, made my heart sing.

He looked at me with hungry eyes, his gaze studying the contours of my face as we sat in silence.

I loved watching him and being able to do so openly, without having to sneak glances, was refreshing... and addictive. His thick brows creased and knitted together the longer he looked at me. His eyes narrowed and seem to get darker. For a moment I thought he was angry at me, for presuming too much, for getting into his truck without asking. But when he took hold of my chin and moved my head from side to side I knew what the source of the anger and his darkening mood was.

So he had seen.

A little of the confidence of being there with him right then drained away. He'd seen what my father had done but he hadn't done anything. Instead he'd waited until the next day to even come see me. I should've been angry, he was just another man in my life who wasn't going to protect me.

But then he said something that would change everything, that would seal my love for him. There was no doubt about it, my heart swelled, and right there I knew that I loved him with every part of me.

"He won't touch you ever again, I'll make sure of it."

Those few words meant the world to me. They

meant more to me than him perhaps even saying that he loved me… even I knew that it was way too early for that, regardless of my own feelings. But Mack declaring that I was essentially under his protection was everything I'd ever dreamed of; he was someone to go to bat for me, to think of me for a change and put me first. My mom had tried, but ultimately had failed.

After that he started the truck and drove. I had to laugh when he took the idea of my protection a little further. His tone even more serious, if that was even possible, when he declared that I had to stay away from "that boy."

"Don't laugh," he said, his face deadpan as he shifted his gaze from the road to me then back again.

I covered my mouth to hide my smile and the extra giggles that wanted to break free. But I was overjoyed.

"What boy?" I asked innocently, my voice thick with syrupy sweetness.

He shot me a dark but playful look that told me he would only tolerate only so much of my teasing.

"You know fine well what boy."

"Oh, you mean Sam? The one I was talking

to? …You were watching me," I said, the last bit a statement of fact rather than a question. From the side I saw a streak of red graze across Mack's cheek. "I get the feeling you like to watch me," I continued.

"Don't try to change the subject. But yes, the boy, Sam, whomever. The one who you had your hands all over and were flirting with."

"Are you jealous, Mack?" I asked, but he wouldn't admit to anything. He stayed silent, ignored my question, and continued to drive.

I sighed, content. He was jealous. That was clear to see. He wanted me all to himself and I wondered just how far that would go. He'd already revealed that he liked being in control and a part of me enjoyed his demands. I never expected to, not after what I had to put up with from my father, but somehow Mack was different…

I risked moving my hand across to his lap and began to lazily trail a finger up and down his thigh. His muscle tensed at my touch and he sat straighter in his seat. He was still trying to be cautious, but I think we both knew how this was going to end. And I had to prove to him I wasn't just some silly girl with a crush.

Quietly I said, "I'm doing it for us."

"Us?" he quirked an eyebrow as he turned his head to look at me. "You're flirting with some jock for us? What the hell does that mean?"

I was going to add that my father had found the phone he had given me. That it was my way of dealing with him and that by pretending to be with someone else it would completely keep Mack in the clear. After all, no matter how much I wanted Mack to make me his, I didn't want to be the cause of him losing his job... or his life. My father had a temper, an anger problem that was not rational at times, and god forbid what he would do to Mack if he ever found out about what we were becoming to each other. Because there was something, something huge. He wanted me as much as I wanted him. The slow burn of our budding relationship was intensifying and it was only a matter of time before Mack would take me. But before I could explain all this Mack held up a hand for me to stop what I was about to say. He pulled the truck to a stop outside my house, turned toward me, and retook a firm hold on my chin. He leaned forward, so close I could see the fire in eyes.

"You're not to see him again, do you hear me? Remember what I said, if we're going to do this we have to do it my way. You do what I say. You do what I want. Do you remember?"

I nodded and swallowed. But I wasn't scared, my heart beat in my chest wildly. Between my legs I clenched. God I was so turned on.

"And I don't want you to even glance at that jock. If he comes up to you around campus, you ignore him. You don't speak to him. You don't give him the time of day. And you certainly won't ever touch him again. Tell me you understand."

His low voice sent shivers all round my body, my skin buzzed with the aftershock of his words. Like cascading dominoes, word by word, one by one, as they fell, they shook the surface they landed on.

"I understand," I replied softly. I said the words but knew I couldn't abide by them, not because I didn't want to, but because otherwise if suddenly Sam was no longer in the picture, my dad would become even more suspicious.

"Don't play games with me, Lola Ray, okay?"

I don't know what made me say it. Maybe it was due to the fact he was so close to me, his lips only inches away, his fingers touching me, but he'd made me feel alive with mischief.

"I think you like games. I think you like to play… and I think," I said, my voice merely a whisper, "I think you want to play with me. And I want you to. So why are we waiting?

Why are you holding back?"

He seemed stunned by my sudden boldness and dropped his hand. Why indeed was he holding back? Resisting the temptation to take me. He could have everything he wanted right there and then.

"You and I both know my father is not home…"

"You're not ready," he replied.

I almost laughed, but I could tell he was serious. "I've never been more ready," I declared thinking I meant every word. I shrugged off the doubt and shuffled my butt off the seat so I could reach up my skirt.

"What are you doing?" he asked quickly as he scanned the street for anyone who might see. Luckily the houses in the area had been placed on plots far apart, so there was no one to see.

"You know what else I think? I think if I were any other girl, if I wasn't Will's daughter, you would've fucked me hard already," I said as I wiggled my panties down off my ass and down my thighs. I sat back down and pulled them off, stepping out of them, and then with an extended arm dangled my white underwear in front of his face. "How about you stop teasing me and give me what I want? What we both want."

His focus drifted from the swaying fabric to my eyes and down to my lap. I bit my lip, dropped my hand, my panties landing on his jeans and sank low into the seat. I could see him thinking about what he wanted to do, how he wanted to take me, thinking about how I was bare beneath my skirt… accessible. I moaned as I cupped my pussy, then through heavy eyelashes glanced back at him. "Touch me, Daddy."

He groaned and shifted closer. Cautiously he lay a hand on my thigh and started to scrape back my skirt, gathering up the material. Finally I was going to get what I wanted, and I didn't care that it was going to be right there on the street, in his car, out in the open. Exposed. It made it all the more tantalizing and exciting. I licked and nibbled at my lip again. How would he do it? Would he plunge right in and finger-fuck me for the first time in my life?

I felt the brush of his fingertips as they made contact with my bare thigh. The anticipation was killing me.

"Touch me," I whispered again, my tone demanding. I broke the spell. He snatched his hand back. And it was a good thing, too, because a second later, while I digested the action with my anger rising, a face loomed at the truck's window. A person tapped on the glass.

I sat rigid. Petrified we'd been caught but also furious that I'd been on the brink of having Mack's hands all over me, in me.

Mack buzzed down his window as he used his other hand to grasp and hide my panties in a closed fist. He pasted a smile on his face and greeted the man who had interrupted us. As the window made its slow crawl down I let out a small sigh of relief, remembering that Mack's truck was fitted with blacked-out privacy windows. Meaning no one could see in, but we could see out. But still it hadn't really diminished the shock or the panic.

"Thought that was you," a man in a worn denim jacket who I didn't recognize said in greeting to Mack.

"Hey, Ray. What you doing all the way out here?" There was a slight sheen of perspiration covering Mack's forehead but he managed to keep his voice even, nonchalant.

Somehow the two of them knew each other, maybe this Ray also worked at my father's construction firm, or maybe he was just an old buddy of Mack's. Mack was, after all, originally from Weyworth, had grown up here.

I sat silent wondering what I should do. Maybe if I stayed still enough I wouldn't give the other man cause to wonder why I was in Mack's truck.

"Just driving by. There's a property for sale I wanted to look at. We might be neighbors soon," the man said with a chuckle.

"Thanks for the ride, Mr. McClane," I said sweetly, interrupting the two men, and grabbed for the handle to let myself out as my addled brain finally started working again.

"No problem, anything for your dad," Mack replied without skipping a beat, then refocused his attention straight back to Ray as if I were inconsequential. I knew why he did that, of course, but it still didn't stop me from wishing his tone had been a bit warmer.

Chapter Eighteen
Mack

A few seconds later we would've been caught red-handed.

I hadn't intended for it to go that much further... no, I had plans for when I first touched her properly. I had it all laid out in my mind, the right moment, after I'd eased her into my unusual tastes. But she'd put me in a position where I couldn't resist anymore, said those words... Sat next to me in the truck, her legs wide and so fucking inviting, with her breathing out soft moans as she touched herself—I knew that all my plans were about to go out of the window. She was practically begging for it. And I didn't want to disappoint her. I never wanted to disappoint her again.

The look on her face when I examined where Will had hit her told me everything I needed to know. She'd needed me, and I'd let her down.

I wasn't going to let her down ever again. I would fuck her, as hard as she wanted, in my truck, on the street, wherever, for as long as she needed. Maybe I could even erase the buried scars she tried to hide, the haunted look she sometimes got when she didn't realize I was looking.

I could've helped with that. I could've had her right there and then... I would've dragged her into the back seat, pulled her skirt up, and attacked her pussy like I should've done a long time ago.

But that tap at the window brought me back to my senses. I could only imagine what would have happened if we'd already been fucking, the truck rocking to and fro with my unrelenting thrusts into her sweet virgin pussy... she would've been screaming, in pleasure and pain. Fuck, we'd been so close to being caught... so close to finally getting what I'd been dreaming about for so long.

Thankfully Ray didn't seem to notice a thing and I'd had the good sense to hide her panties from view. At least I'd come away with a bonus souvenir, but it wasn't enough. Not now. I'd almost tasted her and now I needed her even more.

That was one of the reasons I was back, hours later, in my truck, a ways down the street outside her house. I tried to excuse my behavior with some rational thinking. Will had asked me to keep an eye on her, to make sure that she didn't throw a wild party while he was away or invite boys around. But there I was with an ulterior motive running through my mind. I'd been sitting in the dark, cold truck for the best part of thirty minutes contemplating inviting myself into the house, surprising her and doing what she'd originally suggested.

There must've been some sense of self-preservation still clinging on inside me because I was still in the vehicle debating it all with myself. There would definitely be no going back if I got out of the truck and walked the short distance to the house. The shock on her face when she'd find me in the house after letting myself in would be exquisite, though. And I reminded myself again, I did know where the spare key was hidden.

But the decision was taken out of my hands when the lights in the house suddenly went out and it was plunged into darkness. A figure emerged on the porch, the glow of a mobile illuminating Lola Ray's face. She turned to quickly lock up then moved her gaze up and down the street as if she were waiting for someone. She didn't have to wait long as the glow of a pair of headlights shone behind me, reflecting in the mirrors.

The car sped past and screeched to a halt outside Lola Ray's house. I'd seen the sporty sedan before and tried to remember where. But I needn't have bothered wracking my brain, as the owner of the vehicle jumped out and waved at Lola Ray encouraging her to get in.

My blood boiled as soon as I saw his face. The fucking jock from the community college. The one I'd forbidden her from seeing. And yet hours later she'd already disobeyed me.

Lola Ray gave the boy a wave back and skipped down the steps and got into the passenger's side. The brake lights flashed once before he drove what was mine away from me.

Without thinking I started my truck and followed them. She would have to be punished for her defiance. She had to know that I was serious. That I wasn't playing games. She probably thought it was cute that I'd ordered her to stay away, thought that it was just something I said, a game to make whatever we were doing that little bit extra thrilling. But it wasn't a fucking game. I wasn't fucking around.

I'd been deadly serious. And it was about time she knew that.

* * *

The jock took her to the local diner. It wasn't a big surprise really, there were hardly any other place in Weyworth to take a date. I presumed it was a date, anyway. She'd made an effort in dressing up from what I was able to see from my view from the parking lot as she emerged from his car. Light from the pink neon sign splashed down onto the asphalt and over her. She wore a tight top, I couldn't tell what color because of the discoloration from the all the neon. But what held my attention as they walked side by side into the diner was the very short skirt she was wearing... it was much shorter than the one I'd nearly had my hand under earlier. I gritted my teeth. For some inexplicable reason that was what pissed me off the most and had me thinking of all the ways I could punish her. She would pay for her defiance.

I waited until they were seated at one of the booths before exiting my truck. I didn't head inside right away and instead I went to the flat bed, pulled down the gate and after a few minutes found what I was looking for. I stuffed the items into my back pocket, locked up the truck again, then casually went inside the diner.

She didn't notice me at first when I walked in and slipped into an empty booth on the other side of the diner, but when she did the momentary unease in her eyes had me rock hard in an instant. The smile on her face died and her attention wavered from the jock. Sam. That's what she'd called him earlier. And I'd seen enough of the college games over the last few months to be pretty sure that he was their quarterback... at least she aimed high. But after that night, the decision to go against me would never enter her mind again.

I ordered a coffee and whatever pie they had on hand and sipped it slowly as I stared across the room to where the two teenagers sat. Sam was oblivious to me, his back facing my direction. But Lola Ray who sat across from him couldn't help but keep glancing over. She'd recovered from the shock of seeing me there and the smile was back on her face as the two of them talked. Mostly though she was listening, only taking part in the conversation when necessary. Nodding her head when needed, letting her eyes wander over to my side of the room. She was more interested in why I was there. Even from across the room I could see the cogs of her mind whirring frantically as she tried to keep her composure.

I was halfway through my mug of coffee when she slipped from the red leather couch of her booth and to my amazement sat back down next to the jock, her back to me now. I couldn't believe her audacity, but then again I couldn't help but admire her boldness, either.

But it was what she did next that broke the camel's back. After I'd sat down, even with them across from me in the same room, I'd kinda cooled my jets and reevaluated my plan. I would've gone easy on her. But now after what she did, there was no chance of that.

She rested an arm on the ledge of the booth, turning her body toward Sam. Purposefully she caught my eye for a second, then turned back to Sam and kissed him on the cheek and let her lips linger there.

My grasp on the handle of the mug I held tightened. This girl was driving me insane. And she had absolutely no idea who she was messing with.

Sam was ecstatic with the result he was getting from his date and turned to properly face her. Since I was once his age I knew exactly what he was thinking. Wondering how far he could push her, what base he would get to that night, and whether he would have to work for it or if it would be a walk in the park. She obviously seemed eager.

Taking the chance, he leaned forward, moving

in for the kill. His lips getting nearer but at the last minute she turned her head, her eyes falling on me again momentarily. She grinned at Sam a little bashfully, then scooted backward in retreat, leaving the booth.

"I'll be right back," she said with a cock-teasing smile. *That poor kid*, I thought. If he felt half of what I did right then he was going to have a hard-on for a month. But I didn't feel too sorry for him. She was mine, after all. And I was about to make damn certain she knew it.

Lola Ray passed my own booth and the little minx didn't even look at me. She stared off into the distance, keeping her head fixed on her destination—the bathrooms round back, I assumed. I watched her go, disappearing down the long hallway that was cast in shadow. From being in the diner many times before I knew her route and that I had a few moments to spare.

I drained the last of my coffee, slipped a bill under the mug and followed Lola Ray.

She was bent over the metal sink washing her hands when I pushed open the bathroom door. She looked up but didn't seem surprised to see me. Without a word I pushed the door closed and snapped the lock into place. She couldn't help but smile as she watched me but I shook my head.

"What took you so long?"

"You're in so much trouble, baby girl," I said, my throat thick with the knowledge of what I was going to do to her. But she hadn't yet realized the danger she was in, she just kept smiling and pulling her bottom lip into her mouth. Nibbling on it.

"Me in trouble? You're the one following me," she said trying to stand tall. "You're the one in the ladies bathrooms—"

Before she could continue I'd closed the distance between us in a flash. I was behind her. My hand reached around her throat and I pressed her hard up against the sink. My other hand snaked around her tiny body so she couldn't escape.

I watched her eyes widen in the reflection of the mirror in front of us as I squeezed her neck.

"You've been a very bad girl," I whispered into her ear. "I told you not to play games with me. I told you not to go near that boy."

With my body pressed up against hers I could feel the frantic beat of her heart. She inclined her head and stared right back at me in the mirror. "It's not what you think," she urged.

"It's exactly what I think. You believe you can make me jealous."

"Well it's working, isn't it?" she shot back.

I let her throat go and wrenched her arms behind her and held them tight while I pulled the thick black zip-tie from my pocket.

"Hey, what are you doing?" she panted as I kept her pinned and slipped the tie around her wrists, securing her for the moment.

"Punishing you."

"But I'm doing this for us," she tried to explain, but her words fell on deaf ears. Blood was roaring around my head. I was there for one purpose only.

"Stop talking," I commanded and spun her around harshly. Her body mashed up against mine, her tits soft and warm pressed against my chest, which only made me harder.

"But—"

From my other pocket I pulled her white cotton panties she'd taken off in my truck earlier that day. I grabbed her chin, forced her mouth wide and stuffed the wadded-up material into her hole.

"I said be quiet."

Chapter Nineteen
Lola Ray

Panic filled me to the brim. That and overwhelming excitement. I couldn't seem to pin down my feelings. They teetered from one extreme to the other the longer Mack stood before me. One part of me was telling me to scream, to fight, but the other half of me was desperately wanting him to continue what he started.

Even if I wanted to shout, I couldn't.

I had no choice but to be quiet. The wad of cotton in my mouth rendered me speechless and even as I thought about spitting them out Mack tilted his head and said, "Don't even think about it." He'd also wedged them far enough into my mouth that I would be hard pressed to remove them.

My tongue felt trapped. My saliva was being soaked up by the fabric, mixing with my own juices that I knew were coated all over them from earlier that day. I could taste myself and at the same moment I realized this, Mack seemed to read my mind.

"I told you you tasted sweet. But you're not sweet, are you? Not as innocent as you'd like me to think you are."

I gave him a questioning look. To what was he referring?

"You tried to make me jealous. But more importantly you disobeyed me. Now it's time to pay."

I wanted to smile. But I didn't dare. At last he was going to take me. And while having my virginity taken in the bathroom of the local diner hadn't exactly been the place I thought I would lose it, I still couldn't wait. I'd been ready to give it to him hours before in his truck. I'd been ready for *months*.

He must've seen my relief, my impatience, and gave me the most delicious smile in return. But there was something cruel in that smile. Something dangerous. Was I making a mistake trusting him?

But he made my nipples hard. And with my

hands tied behind my back I pushed out my chest, forcing them up harder against Mack's body and wondered if he would be able to feel how aroused I was.

Over and over in the last few weeks I'd fantasized about how he would take me. Would I straddle him, or would he want to take me from behind? Either way I was about to find out.

"On your fucking knees," he growled out and pushed me down hard with a hand on my shoulders.

I practically fell to the dirty floor, unable to keep my balance. The force shocked me, but I managed to recover myself, and on my knees I looked up at him wondering what came next. This didn't seem like a good position to be in for what I had in mind.

But then again, I wasn't running this show.

I wasn't in control anymore.

He was.

"You look so beautiful on your knees. But just remember you wanted this," he continued. I frowned. Of course I wanted it, I wanted him. But then his fingers went to his jeans, popping the top button and sliding down his fly.

I couldn't help but stare at the monstrosity that sprang free. And if my mouth wasn't already dry from the panties, it was like a desert once I'd laid eyes on his mammoth cock.

Of course I'd seen penises on TV and in the movies, but never up close and personal. And my first time seeing one was shocking. There was no way that thing was going to fit where it was supposed to. It was huge. He was big with thick bumpy veins—a hulk cock.

Mack grinned at my terror.

"Now, are you going to be a good girl?" he said.

When I didn't reply he took hold of my breast again, like he had the time before, and tweaked my sensitive nipple.

I nodded. I would be good, for him I would do anything. But I had to wonder how on earth it would fit.

"Good. You're not going to utter a word, okay? Unless I tell you too, of course."

I nodded again before he could let loose another twist on my bud.

"That's my good girl. It's time for you to learn to never disobey your new daddy." He pushed a finger into my mouth and fish-hooked the wad of material out. Instinctively I began to lick my lips to moisten them and get rid of the dryness on my tongue, and then closed my mouth.

Mack shook his head and tutted. I didn't understand but I was going to be good, I was going to stay quiet.

"Open wide."

Confused, my brows knitted together. But I wasn't confused for long. Mack slipped his finger back inside my mouth forcing it open. Then he edged forward, his hard cock getting closer and then I realized what he wanted.

I shook my head. "I've never done that before," I said not thinking. It just slipped out.

"No talking! But there's a first time for everything. I'm going to torture that little virgin mouth of yours."

Without mercy he kept my mouth open and forced his cock inside. I had no idea what to do. I could feel him on my tongue as he plunged deeper inside. I resisted the temptation to close up or pull away and he groaned with pleasure. I guessed I must've done something right so I opened up wider, letting him fill my mouth.

On either side of my head his hands cradled me, his fingers threading through my hair keeping me in place. "That's it, open up for Daddy. Wider."

He thrust his hips forward.

"Now suck."

I pursed my lips trying to recall all the sex scenes I'd ever seen in my life in the movies but nothing had ever come close to this and I was momentarily at a loss. I didn't have to worry though, Mack began to lead the way.

"Good girl," he hissed, his movements becoming harder, faster. The realization that he was fucking my mouth suddenly occurred to me and I couldn't believe it. It felt like I was dreaming. Like I was watching myself from the corner of the bathroom, but more importantly like I had no control over anything. *But I liked it.*

I wanted more. I wanted him to hold my head firmer, to feel the rough thrust of his cock bump against the back of my throat. As if he read my mind he did just that. His grip tightened, and there were pinpricks of pain at my scalp. He'd wound his fingers through my hair and was inadvertently pulling on it. He bobbed my head back and forth on his cock. The pain made me clamp my eyes shut tight. But it also made the pulse between my legs thump even harder. If he could do this to my mouth I could only imagine what he would do to my pussy.

"Lola Ray, are you all right in there?" a voice

interrupted on the other side of the door. Thank god it was locked because I heard Sam's attempts to open it.

Mack lifted a finger to his lips and eased his cock from my mouth. My salvia trails coated it. He bent down and cupped my breast, rubbing it gently.

"Tell him you'll be right out," he whispered. "'Cause I'm not done with you yet."

I swallowed and nodded, then tried to find my voice.

"Lola Ray?"

"I'm fine," I called. My voice sounded strained, a little too high… and oh-so-breathless. This was the most exciting thing to happen to me… to nearly be caught again. I was loving it.

"What are you doing in there?" Sam asked impatiently. But I ignored him, looking at Mack then back at his hard cock stiff in front of me. I licked my lips. "I'll be out in a moment."

I wasn't sure if Sam left right away or if he was planning on waiting outside of the bathroom door for me, either way it didn't matter, I had bigger issues to worry about.

Mack ran his hands through my hair and clamped his hands around the side of my head again.

His hips tilted toward me, bringing his cock closer. I didn't have to be asked to open up again. I did it willingly… and eagerly.

"That's right," he whispered, his voice low with need. "Take what Daddy gives you. Lick me like a lollipop."

If I thought his thrusts were hard and intense before, they were nothing like what he was doing now. So rough, so delicious. I had no say on how fierce the continuing invasion in my mouth would be. Mack was unrelenting and I suspected that even if Sam tried to break down the door to get in, that he wouldn't stop making me suck his cock until he was done. My mouth was wide, my lips stretched so far around his shaft that I knew I would be needing some Chapstick later on.

"Open your eyes," he demanded.

I did even though I could feel, at the corners of them, the beginnings of tears. It hurt so much, but felt so good all at the same time. How was that possible? It didn't make sense. And yet I was alive, feeling every sensation and loving it.

"Look at me," Mack whispered as his cock slipped into my mouth. His movements had become a little gentler but like a good little girl I did what I was told and focused my gaze upwards at him.

He stared at me with wonder. A tear slipped free and then he smiled. Was he smiling because of the tear or because of something else?

All I knew was I wanted to please him. I didn't want this moment to stop, I wanted to hold on to these new feelings forever, but the urge to suck on him became too great to resist. It was as if I suddenly knew what to do and my tongue wrapped around his shaft, teasing him, licking him.

While I sucked, Mack groaned. Each moan sent me into overdrive. My body was becoming overwhelmed with all the new sensations, the taste of him, the way he felt in my mouth, hearing him want me. Not to mention how it felt good being bound up, at his mercy. It was all so confusing and yet clear too… but that didn't mean I wasn't a little scared at what it all meant.

"I could punish your mouth all day," I heard him say above me.

At that I renewed my attempt to please him with my newly acquired skill.

"Fuck… I'm gonna cum," he breathed. His cock slammed into the back of my throat, deeper than ever before and I wanted to gag but I didn't have the luxury of doing so. Again and again the onslaught continued. "Keep your eyes open," he said just as I was beginning to let them close.

I forced them wide. Forced myself to look up at him again. Then all of a sudden Mack growled, his grip tightened around my head, and my mouth was filled. For a second I couldn't figure out what had happened, my inexperience was getting the better of me. Of course, it finally dawned on me; he'd burst free and had cum in my mouth and all I wanted to do was spit it out.

Mack smiled down at me and stroked the side of my face. His cock was still in my mouth, my jaw ached. "You're going to swallow it. Do you understand?"

I nodded and his softening cock slipped free, though it was still fucking huge. It was a wonder I'd been able to wrap my lips around the thing.

"Go on," he encouraged. "Swallow."

Finally, knowing it would please him I did as I was told.

"There's my good girl."

I smiled. I liked the sound of that. I loved the idea of being his. Mack tucked himself away and took a step back from me. I was still on my knees, they felt scraped-up and my lips felt dry and maybe even cracked. The realization that I was still bound and the thought that he was just going to leave me there like that had me panicking again.

"Don't worry," he said and helped me to my feet, "I'm not that cruel." With an unseen implement that he must've pulled from his pocket he cut whatever he had tied me with and my hands sprang free. My knees and jaw weren't the only thing to ache, though I hadn't registered the pain around my wrists until then. I rubbed at them and looked questioningly at Mack.

"Now, let that be a lesson to you."

I went to reply, my mouth dropping open, but I stopped myself.

The grin that I was rewarded with let me know I'd done the right thing. His lips twitched, the corners pulling his mouth into a small smile. "You can speak."

I licked my lips. It was best to just tell him. "I wasn't actually here with Sam to make you jealous… My dad found the phone you gave me. I had to think of something."

"What did you tell him?" Mack said with a tone that could only be described as worry.

"That Sam gave it to me. It was the only thing I could think of. I thought he was going to hit me again. So I told him he was my boyfriend. I didn't want him to have any reason to think it was from you."

"Fuck…"

Mack surprised me and brought me into his arms. It was the last thing I was expecting after what he'd just done to me but it was welcome all the same. I wrapped my arms around him.

"You did the right thing… but you still disobeyed me."

"I know. I'm sorry."

"That's okay. You've been punished," he said with a glint in his eye. "I don't like it one little bit, but you being with Sam might be the best thing right now."

"I—" I began, but he cut me off.

"But, I swear to you, he's not to touch you. I mean it, Lola Ray. Lead him on all you want, but his hands do not touch what is mine. There's no doubt about it anymore. You're mine, do you understand? You belong to me. And I won't just punish you again—don't think that that's a good thing—I'll make sure he's dealt with too. I'll break every bone in his body, including his throwing arm, if he tries anything. So you best make sure he doesn't. Because remember I will be watching to make sure."

Chapter Twenty
Mack

"You'll be watching me?" she said with a hint of a smile. Her fingers trailed her sore red lips. I'd really done a number on them, but she didn't seem to regret it. She was maybe in a bit of shock, that was all. Some of her normal confidence had worn away and what was left standing before me was a pliable young woman who I had no doubt in my mind was now mine.

The seal had been broken and there was definitely no turning back now. In a way I was grateful that she'd disobeyed me. It had, after all, led us to this moment. Led me to action.

Fucking finally.

And while I hadn't yet reamed her pussy and stripped her of her virginity, that would come in time. Taking her mouth instead of bending her over in the bathroom and then sinking myself deep had been the better option. I wanted to at least try to savor her. Half the pleasure was the anticipation. And yeah I hadn't been able to control myself after seeing her being driven away by that jock, I was, however, pleased with myself that I'd resisted for so long.

"I'll always be watching from now on." I stroked her cheek and she let her head rest in my hand. "But you better go. Your *date* is waiting."

"When will I see you again?" she asked with desperation in her eyes.

"When I decide."

Her face fell and by god if that wasn't the most beautiful sight I'd seen all day. Not because she was sad, but because I knew right then she was hooked. She was mine to control.

Just to make her smile again I added, "Soon, I promise."

At that her face transformed and her eyes shone. "Go," I encouraged and unlatched the door. I held it open and with a last glance behind her, she left. I watched her for a second travel down the hallway toward the main part of the diner; she smoothed her hands over her clothes, making sure she was decent and fluffed her hair a little.

Staying in the bathroom I went to stand over by the sink and dropped the plastic zip tie in the trash. I kept her panties though and stuffed them back into my pocket.

As I looked up I caught my reflection in the mirror and contemplated what I'd just done. I hardly recognized the face peering back at me. There was an unusual light in my eyes, a small smile on my lips. Was I happy? I examined the warm glow in my chest that was the seemingly the origin of this weird unexpected feeling. I was. And it was all because of her. After all the years of feeling numb, somehow she'd managed to do this to me. Those eyes staring up at me while she took what I gave her had pushed me over the edge. No one had ever looked at me like that. She hadn't been faking... one couldn't fake that look. Honest, pure, and dare I say it, even with love?

Not once had I ever felt this extra need and desperation for someone after what I'd done. Normally, as expected, I'd feel good after having my cock sucked... but not this good. The longing I felt for her buzzed around my head like a gnat that just wouldn't quit. I couldn't stop thinking about her. She'd done something to me. Changed me. This was only supposed to have been a bit of fun... dangerous fun, but still only temporary.

And right then it felt like it was anything but temporary.

Wrestling with my thoughts I left the bathroom and immediately bumped into a middle-aged woman. She gave me a questioning look as she realized where I'd just come from. I gave her a shrug and a wicked smile, "Wrong door." She hurried away from me and darted into the bathroom I'd just vacated.

I wondered if she'd be able to smell the sex, the dirty sweet scent of Lola Ray's arousal.

As I made my way through, I noticed the diner had a few more customers than it had before I'd vacated my seat and most of them had their heads turned, their attention firmly upon the couple in the booth at the back. Lola Ray and Sam's booth. They were sat facing each other and Sam was shouting. Clearly not pleased that she'd practically ditch him on their date.

"—But you were gone for ages! What the hell were you doing?" Sam had his hand wrapped around Lola Ray's wrist, keeping her at the booth. I didn't stop, I kept walking. Her eyes saw the movement and flickered toward me.

She started to shake her head, trying to warn me away. But it was too late.

"What are you looking at now?" Sam yelled at her and her eyes snapped back to him.

I towered over the two of them in the booth, getting right up close to where Sam sat. My fingers twitched, they wanted to pick him up and drag him outside and beat the living hell out of the little shit, but what with the customers and staff behind me—witnesses—I had to be extremely careful and keep my anger in check.

"Is there a problem here?" I said coldly and pinned Sam with a deadly stare.

He had the courtesy of looking momentarily shit-scared once he turned his attention to me. But his bravado increased, bolstered no doubt by my girl who sat opposite him. He had the need to show off, to be the big man. He sat taller, his grasp tightening that little bit more on Lola Ray's wrist.

"This is none of your business," he replied in a dismissive tone. Like I was a servant, inconsequential, like he had authority over me. For a beat the kid impressed me. He had balls. Not many boys or even men would have the nerve to speak to me like that.

I placed my hand flat on the table—mostly so I couldn't bunch it up into a fist—and got up close and personal, leaning down, inches away from his face.

"Let go of her right now," I snarled, "before this gets messy. Before I drag your punk-ass outside and give you a beating of a lifetime."

His stare faltered and he looked away. He was trying to work out the best course of action. Could he back down and still save face? He had to know he would have no chance against me in a fist-fight.

"Who the fuck are you, her father?"

I tried to ignore the little gasp that came from Lola Ray's side of the table.

"Tonight, son, I'm your worst fucking nightmare. Now, I won't ask you again. Let her go, before I break your arm and every one of your fingers."

Finally coming to his senses he released his hold on her. I stood up, getting out of his face, and breathed a sigh of relief and turned to look at her.

"Lola Ray, are you okay?"

She nodded. That was my girl. So brave.

"Do you need a lift home?" I suggested, eager to have her far away from her date.

"No, I'm okay," she said, a smile reappearing on her face as if nothing had even happened. How many times has she had to put on a brave face after being assaulted? I didn't want to contemplate how often her father had beat her... but here she was again, another man thinking he could hurt her. It made me want to examine my own actions... but they were different, right? They weren't the same. I didn't want to hurt her for the sake of hurting her... it came bundled with pleasure. The difference was she was a willing participant. Right?

I had to get out of there before I convinced myself that I was just as bad as Will and Sam. It was selfish, but I didn't want to ruin the memory of her on her knees, her hands tied behind her back, looking at me with desperate eyes.

"Okay. You know how to contact me if you need me," I said and then suddenly dipped back down to Sam. He half sprang back in his seat, shock registering on his face. "Touch her again like that and your life won't be worth living, understand?"

"Yes, sir," Sam stuttered and I gave him a devilish grin.

"Good."

I left the diner and everyone went back to their food, the show was over. But I stayed, sat in my truck, to watch. Just in case there happened to be an encore.

DREAM DADDY

Chapter Twenty One
Lola Ray

He'd kept his word. I almost couldn't believe it. He protected me.

I thought it would've been best if I handled the situation. Sam had a bit of a temper, that was clear to see, and I was sure with a little bit of time, I could've calmed him down, made nice, and stopped the scene we were creating in the dinner. But Mack saved me instead.

His actions, not to mention the way he spoke to Sam, reinforcing his promise to protect me, made me fall for him even more. They hadn't been false words, he'd meant every one and was willing to act upon them too. It made me wonder how far he would actually go. But by the cold steel of his eyes when he looked at Sam I couldn't help but see he meant to do harm to anyone that hurt me.

The idea that he would go to such lengths for me was bizarrely comforting. And it made me feel powerful. It made me wish, for a split second, that we were the only ones in that diner, that there were no witnesses so I could see Mack rip Sam's hand from my wrist and make good on his promise to shatter every single bone in Sam's hand. All the pain I'd experienced I wanted to see reflected in Sam's eyes. For even daring to touch me like that. I wanted someone, for a change, to feel as helpless as I had. Even just for a moment. See how he liked it.

I shook my head to scatter the thoughts away. *I wasn't that person*, I told myself. I wasn't cruel.

After Mack left the diner it was a while before Sam got up the courage to talk again. He looked humiliated, but was putting a brave face on the whole thing. And I knew I had to make it up to him somehow because I still needed him to pull the wool over my father's eyes.

"Do you want to split a milkshake for dessert?" I asked, trying to recover the last of the evening.

He shrugged, but ordered a thick chocolate milkshake for the both of us anyway.

"Who was that guy? Do you know him?"

I didn't expect him to bring Mack up if I was being honest with myself. It seemed curiosity had gotten the better of Sam and he just couldn't forget.

I sucked on the straw taking a sip of the milkshake and nodded. "He's my dad's best friend."

"Oh," Sam said, the last of his bluster disappearing. "The way he looked at you I thought… Never mind."

That got my attention. "You thought what?"

"I thought maybe I had competition."

I wanted to let the smile I was hiding loose but I knew I couldn't and buried the feeling of elation deep down inside. On the one hand Mack looking like he had an interest in me was something to celebrate, but not if other people started to notice it too. I was beginning to realize the danger we were in. The danger Mack was in. Even though I was old enough, it would still cause one hell of a scandal in our small town. He would be labeled a monster… when he was far from one. He was the only one who actually cared about me.

I shook my head, denying everything I felt. "Nah, he's just my dad's friend. He works for him too."

"Ah, I see."

"He can be a little overprotective," I admitted, and gave Sam an apologetic smile.

"You don't say. I never would've guessed."

I played with the straw, swirling it around in the melting milkshake. "You would like him if you got to know him," I continued, loving the fact I could talk about Mack, even if it was in an indirect sort of way. "He's a good guy."

Sam was getting bored with me talking about another guy though, especially one who'd humiliated him and I changed the subject.

"So anyway. You were telling me the other day scouts will be coming to watch your home game next week?"

Sam's eyes brightened at the mention of football and he launched into a conversation that lasted practically the rest of the evening, all about his accomplishments and the football teams he thought might recruit him. I let him waffle on, and I admitted to myself that if I didn't already have eyes for Mack, Sam could've been a contender. But then as he grabbed me when we were leaving, his hand possessively wrapping around my sore wrist and leading me to his car, I remembered that looks could be deceiving. Sam opened the passenger-side door for me and waited for me to get in.

He was trying to make up for the evening's events too. But it was a pointless endeavor.

Out of the corner of my eye, in the back of the parking lot, a set of headlights shone brightly as they flickered on. The familiar outline of Mack's truck came into view.

I was already taken.

* * *

The next day after coming home from school I found my father waiting for me, back from his short trip. I wished he'd stayed away longer. It had been nice to have the house to myself, to experience a little bit of freedom. Not to feel so afraid anymore.

He sat rigid at the kitchen table, his face was unreadable. My guard went up. I knew instinctively to monitor what I said to him.

"You're late," he said and looked at his watch.

It was pointless to disagree with him. I was normally home a lot earlier than I was that day. And instead of coming straight home, I'd logged some time with Sam. He had football practice and though we weren't officially dating as of yet, he'd asked me to go and watch. So I did for an hour, building up some goodwill with him. If I'd said no and continued to play hard to get before my father met him, then all my plans would be ruined.

"Sam had practice, thought I'd offer him my support, he's got scouts coming to his next game," I replied with a smile, grateful that I didn't have to lie to him. Though I'd become skilled lying to my father, it always made me uneasy that he would catch me out or I'd end up tangling myself up with all the lies I'd spun.

My father inclined his head, thinking this over for a second. "Speaking of which, I want to meet him."

"Of course," I said sweetly. "I think you're really going to like him."

"We'll see about that."

"You already have so much in common. Weren't you a quarterback for the Weyworth Giants too?"

That seemed to bring a small smile to his face, but I wasn't quite off the hook yet and instead of him having to ask I thought it would be better to just get it out the way. I could invite Sam over, he could meet my father, and then I could get on pretending he was the one I was seeing when in fact I would be sneaking off to spend time with Mack. We hadn't really discussed what would happen but I knew we weren't going to just stop with what happened in the bathroom of the diner.

"Shall I invite Sam over for dinner tonight? That way you can meet him right away, properly?"

He frowned at me, his eyes narrowing but as he thought about it his head started to nod. "Fine. But I haven't forgotten about your phone. You know the rules. I need to know who you're calling. So something will have to be done about that."

I nodded and pinned a smile to my face. "Of course, no problem." All the while my stomach churned with dread. I had no idea how to fix that problem… and sooner or later he would find out that everything was a lie. That Sam hadn't been the one to give me the phone. And even if I did somehow manage to hand over the numbers of the people I contacted or who called me, surely he would recognize Mack's number?

"What are you waiting for? You better invite him over and start making the dinner."

"Oh, yes," I said with a shake of my head. *I could figure that out that later*, I thought. Quickly I let my fingers fly over the mobile and sent Sam an invitation. I prayed that he would say yes. Saying no right then, with my father in a temperamental mood, would be the worst.

Sam replied instantly saying yes and I blew out an uneasy breath then got to work figuring out what I could make for dinner.

Awkward was the word of the evening. Sam arrived promptly and I'd introduced him to my father but it was like there was something stopping the flow of conversation. Sam was eager to impress him, talking about football. But a few times he was forced to trail off when he got no response from him. It was uncomfortable and for once I was grateful that I could escape to the kitchen.

"Feel like helping me set the table?" I asked Sam. He gave me a grateful look like I'd just saved him from drowning. He nodded and followed me out, leaving my father to sit with his six-pack of beer watching the sports channel.

"He doesn't say much does he?" Sam remarked once we were safe in the kitchen.

"Not really. He's not exactly the warm-and-fuzzy kind of dad."

"That's an understatement. He looked like he wouldn't think twice about shooting me."

"I wouldn't put it past him," I said as I pulled the casserole from the oven. Sam's eyebrows rose but he recovered quickly.

"Parents love me, I'm sure he will too, eventually."

"Get him some free tickets to your games and that might do the trick."

"Good idea."

I took a deep breath before broaching the subject that was on my mind.

"Sam?" I said as I twirled a lock of hair around a finger.

He looked up from his task of setting the table. "Yeah?"

I moved toward him and bit my lip for good measure. "I have a teeny-tiny favor to ask of you."

"Oh, really?" he asked, intrigued.

"Yeah, just a little thing."

He pulled me toward him, capturing me in his arms. "And what will I get in return?"

"I'm sure I can think of something…" I dipped my head and looked away, letting my tongue run along my bottom lip.

"What's the favor?"

I pinned him with a soft stare and batted my eyelashes a couple of times. "If my father asks about my new phone, will you pretend that you got it for me?"

Clearly he was expecting me to ask him something quite different and he looked crestfallen. "Huh? Why?"

"Well I lost my other one and you've seen how strict he is. He'll kill me if he finds out I was so careless, and I kinda already said that you got me this new one to cover my ass." I tilted my head to the side and looked from his eyes to his lips and back again, my hands running up and down his back. "You don't mind do you?"

His Adam's apple bobbed and he shook his head and tightened his hold on me. "No, I don't mind."

"Thank you, you're my hero." I stood on tiptoes and rewarded him with a lingering peck on his cheek. "So, if he asks, you bought it okay?"

Sam nodded his head. He was securely wrapped around my little finger.

Later, my father seemed to warm up to Sam during dinner. Probably because he'd already drunk god knows how many beers, but regardless I wasn't going to look a gift horse in the mouth. My father seemed content, happy even. *His trip must've gone well*, I thought. And he even left me and Sam alone when we were finished with dessert.

Feeling my phone vibrate in my pocket I got up

from the table and excused myself. "I'll be right back," I said to Sam, wanting to check who the text was from. It was from either of two people. Mack or Robin. I was of course hoping for the former. My thoughts were constantly on him. So much so I'd daydreamed my way through my classes that day, earning myself dirty looks from one of my professors who wasn't amused by my lack of attention.

I skipped up the stairs to my bedroom and sat on the bed with the phone in my hand. I unlocked it and smiled at the text.

Daddy > Have you been a good girl?

Before I could send my reply another text came through.

Daddy > Because I can't wait to spank you if you've been naughty.

I could feel the blush rise on my cheeks. The image of Mack spanking me, bending me over his lap, his cock digging into my belly, and leaving red handprints on my bottom, had me grinning like a fool.

"Who are you texting?" Sam asked from the doorway.

Guiltily I put the phone away. "No one. Just Robin," I quickly added, hoping that would satisfy him. If it wasn't my father keeping an eye on me, now I had to worry about Sam too. Things were getting far too complicated for my liking. But I had to think it was all my own fault, really. I'd pulled Sam into my mess of a life. "She wanted to know how it was going with you meeting my dad, I mean."

He pushed off the frame and came into the room, closing the door behind him quietly.

"You shouldn't be up here, though," I warned him. "My father will kill you if he finds you in here."

"I'll take my chances," he said. He stood before me and pulled me to my feet off the bed. "Besides, you owe me."

"Huh?" I asked not knowing what he meant.

"I kept to my end of the bargain. I lied to your father at dinner when he asked about your phone. So now…"

"Oh." I hadn't expected him to cash in his favor right away. I thought he would give me some time, or secretly I hoped he would just forget all about it. But he had done what I'd asked of him. He'd lied like a trooper at the dinner table. Did it all with confidence and surety, which seemed to please my father.

"So now..." he said again, "I want something from you."

"What do you want?" I asked, my throat thick. He didn't think that I was going to have sex with him, did he? All in exchange for one tiny lie? He was out of his mind if he thought that. Especially when my virginity was no longer mine to give... it belonged to Mack.

With the thought of Mack, I prayed that he was true to his word and was always watching me, and stepped back closer to the window... From the look in Sam's eye, I needed saving again.

"I want you to take your top off, strip for me."

I shook my head. "I can't... my daddy, if he finds out."

"Fine, I'll just go tell him about your phone..."

I sighed.

"Just a little peek. Let me see your tits."

I bit my lip, what harm would there be? But I still didn't want to. Not on his command. Could I call his bluff? I didn't know Sam well enough yet to know if he would be that cruel.

"Okay," I said, "but no touching."

He grinned and settled himself on my bed. He laced his fingers together behind his head, and leaned back, waiting.

I turned away from him unsure even where to begin. But it was probably best to get it over and done with. Flash him and he would be satisfied.

Spinning back around I grabbed my shirt and pulled it upward, then just as quickly, pulled it back down again.

Sam frowned and shook his head, displeased.

"I didn't see a goddamn thing. Take your bra off this time."

He pulled at the tightness of his jeans, readjusting himself. But as he saw me watching he put his hand back and started to rub himself. Sam was hard, that was clear to see. "I'm waiting," he said in a singsong voice. "You don't want me to go tell your dad do you?"

Without any other choice I put my hands behind my back and fished to unhook my bra, then slipped it off while still keeping my shirt on. I let it drop to the floor. Sam was rubbing his crotch more vigorously now and the movement sent a wave of nausea to my stomach. I didn't want this boy to see me half-naked. I only wanted Mack to see me that way.

But beggars couldn't be choosers, I had to do this to keep Sam satisfied. To enable me to keep my secret.

I began to lift my shirt but before I could reveal my breasts the door burst open and my father, drunk and swaying, was there. Sam bolted up, his face reddening.

"What the fuck! He was right! Get out of here! Do you hear me? Now!" my father shouted at a startled Sam who wasn't moving a muscle. He looked too scared on the bed. "I've told you before, there are no boys allowed in this room."

Sam eased himself off the bed as I shrank back away from my father, one could never be too careful. He was like a bull that would instantly see red, no matter what the color.

"Sorry, sir. It was my idea... er, I asked Lola Ray to help me with some coursework."

"I don't care. Out!"

Sam gave me an apologetic shrug and managed to skirt past my father, then ran downstairs. My father followed him, shouting all the time and I went to close my door, hoping he would be content to drive Sam away and stay downstairs.

Something weird struck me though, niggled for my attention. What had my father said? I tried to remember his words. There was something odd about them. Before I could figure it out, my phone buzzed.

A shiver ran down my spine as I read the message.

Daddy > Seems you have been very naughty indeed.

Chapter Twenty Two
Mack

Sam blew past me just as I reached their gate. His face was a picture and I couldn't help but grin as he fled from Will's house, like he was running from the scene of a crime. He jumped in his car and sped off. I turned back to the house. Will was standing at the door. He gave me a nod and motioned for me to come in. As I made my way up the steps to the porch, I fired off a quick text to Lola Ray upstairs.

"Thanks," he said, slurring his words a little.

"No problem. I had a feeling you'd want to know what I saw."

"Lucky you did. The little slut." I bristled at his words but tried not to let it show. She was anything but a slut. Even from the distance in my den, looking up and out toward her window, I saw the reluctance on her face. She didn't want to strip for Sam. And I wasn't going to let her down again. I'd picked up my phone and given Will the heads up, thankfully he was already back, but I'd still made my way around to their house just in case.

"You didn't have to come around, though," he said and closed the front door.

"Thought you might've needed some backup," I joked. "Nah, was wondering how you got on. Did we win the bid for the contract?"

Will grinned. "We did. Come on, you're here now. Let's celebrate. Better than drinking alone."

We sank into the chairs and he handed me a cold one. Empties littered the small coffee table, and as I looked around the room seeing how much he'd already downed an idea began to form in my mind.

"Got anything stronger? We should celebrate properly. This is, after all, a big win, right?"

Will thought about this for a second. "You're absolutely fucking right. I've got some whiskey around here somewhere." He hunted in the liquor cabinet then pulled out a half bottle of Jim Beam.

"That'll work," I said.

We cheered to his good fortune. I wasn't just blowing smoke, either. Winning the bid was a huge deal not only for Will and the health of his company, but it meant his crew had secure jobs, and would be able to feed their families for at least another few months. And in this day and age in Weyworth, that meant a fucking lot.

I sipped on the whiskey while Will began to knock them back. We chatted and talked about the future, well Will mostly did the talking. I sat back and watched him get drunk. And it wasn't long before he became incoherent and he struggled to keep his head up as it lolled from side to side.

Finally my patience was rewarded and he passed out.

While I watched him, his mouth dropping open, and starting to snore, I counted the seconds, then the minutes. I wanted to make sure he was completely out of it before I did anything. But already my blood was pumping, just waiting for the moment when I'd stand and work my way up those stairs to Lola Ray's bedroom.

Above me I heard the rattle of the pipes. She was moving about, in the shower. Naked and dripping wet. The idea of surprising her in there was appealing… the look on her face would be almost worth it. But I had a better idea.

Slowly I got to my feet and moved past Will who was still fast asleep, making the noise of a freight train. He wouldn't be waking up till the morning.

In the hallway at the bottom of the stairs I looked up into the darkness and as I listened to the sound of the water running I started my ascent.

I was at the top when the water was shut off, the sounds of the shower dying. I didn't have much time and darted into Will's bedroom, flicked the light on for a second and grabbed what I needed from his closet.

Before Lola Ray could emerge from the bathroom across the hallway and find me standing there, I exited Will's bedroom, and as quietly as I could, padded into her room, dodging the squeaky worn floorboards that I knew from experience were there.

Without a moment to spare I found my hiding spot and settled in for another wait. My hands trembled with excitement and I had to force myself to count my breaths to keep myself under control.

I'd never done anything like that before…

I'd always wanted to. And it was like the opportunity had landed in my lap and I wasn't going to pass it up.

Her door creaked open, then softly thudded closed. I closed my eyes and willed my heart to stop banging so fucking loudly. I didn't want to give the game away right from the start. She moved about her room and I imagined her toweling her body dry. The scent of her, clean and floral, drifted to my hidden position and I took a deep but silent breath. She was intoxicating.

I wondered how long I would have to wait before she would climb into bed and turn off the lights. The anticipation was almost killing me and my dick was thrumming. He wanted to come out and play. And maybe, just maybe, I was going to let him.

Thankfully, my Lola Ray wasn't a night owl and thirty minutes or so later the bedsprings above me sank down a little. Then the room was plunged into darkness.

The house settled around us and she shifted a few times above me. Turning to get comfortable. Was she thinking about me? Wondering when the next time would come when I would tie her up and make her suck my cock?

I listened to the sounds of her breath, slowing, relaxing. She was drifting off and I began to make my move. Trying as best I could to not make a sound I slid partially out from under her bed. My jeans rustled against the carpet fibers, they sounded so loud, and I winced, pausing to listen to her again. Her breath was even. She hadn't heard me. But just as I was out, lying right next to her bed, with nothing above me, she called out, "Who's there?"

I imagined her eyes springing open. Panic laced her words and the bed shifted with her weight as she sat up, straining to listen no doubt. "Dad, is that you?"

I kept totally still and held my breath. Not yet. Not just yet. I had to wait a little bit longer in the shadows.

After a few moments she eased back down and turned over.

In my head I started to count again. I made it all the way to five hundred before my impatience got the better of me and I shuffled to my knees. I unfolded myself out of the crouch and towered over her bed. With a little light coming through her window I could see she was laying on her side, her cheek shining, a pale moonlight blue in the dark.

My cock pressed against my jeans as I reached out my hand and curled it around her mouth.

The moment contact was made I felt her lips part, moving to scream. But I clamped down hard and sprang on top of her on the bed. She was pinned, struggling, wriggling beneath me but she had nowhere to go. Her eyes were wild. The whites of them so bright, so wide with fear so delicious and palpable, as she bucked to try and get me off.

I began to lean forward, satisfied with her reaction but not wanting to completely terrorize her. There was only so much pain I wanted to put her through, after all.

Her body immediately stopped, going rigid as I loomed over her. Her eyes were full of tears and she quickly blinked them away, as if trying to understand why, trying to make sure she wasn't imagining that I was actually there.

"Shh, baby girl," I whispered. "Daddy's here to make the scary nightmare go away…" I let my words sink in for a moment and after a second her eyes, no longer filled with tears, shined with something other than fear. Instead, there was pure need.

"Were you dreaming of me? I bet you were. Wondering when I would come for you."

She gave me a little nod and shifted beneath me, arching her back. She was like a cat in heat now the fear had subsided.

"You're not going to scream are you if I take my hand away?" I said keeping my voice low, barely audible.

She shook her head and I dropped my hand. She gasped, her chest rising and falling fast with the exertion.

"What are you doing here?" she asked, the fear was back. "My father… shit, seriously if he finds you…" She trailed off and I bent to silence her worries.

Our first kiss. I couldn't believe I'd waited so long to kiss her. I should've received some kind of an award for my abstinence. I should've done it so much sooner.

I thought nothing would be able to top the fantasy of her mouth, of how it would feel against my own… but the reality was oh so much more. My lips touched hers, soft and supple, and within my chest my heart sang for more.

I ran my tongue over her lips encouraging her to part them. She moaned as I entered her, letting my tongue explore her mouth slowly. Taking my time before pulling back.

"Mack you can't be here."

I shook my head. I wasn't going anywhere. "I've taken care of your dad, don't worry."

She tried to sit up but my weight upon her wouldn't allow it. "What? You've killed him?" she said a little louder than I would've liked and instinctively reached to silence her, my hand over her mouth again.

"No, of course not," I hissed. Granted the thought had run through my mind more than once over the past few weeks… but that was just another fantasy. One that could never come true. Yet what on earth made her think that? Did she secretly want him dead?

"Shh, now. Let me play. I'm going to take what I came for."

With that I restrained her, grabbing her wrists before she realized what was going on and tied her arms to the headboard of her bed. She lay helpless her arms spread wide, looking up at me, her mouth slightly parted as if she couldn't believe what was happening. Lola Ray tested her bonds, her father's silk ties that I'd lifted from his closet dug into her skin as she tried to pull away.

"What are you going to do to me?" she asked, breathless with anticipation.

I ignored her question and ran my hands over her shoulders and down, pulling the cover off from her body as I shuffled down the bed. A light pink camisole was revealed and as I went further, her legs unable to move beneath my weight, a pair of cotton pajama shorts came into view, her smooth, long legs sticking out of them. God I would have to be careful to resist just devouring her. I told myself to go slowly, to enjoy every inch of her. Make the moment last.

She sucked her stomach in as my hands trailed down her waist, doing my best to barely touch her. I paused at the waistband of her shorts. Ripping them off should've been my next move, and even Lola Ray tilted her hips up a fraction as if she wanted me to do just that. But again, I resisted.

Continuing down I stroked the tops of her thighs and as I eased off the bed I took the weight of her leg in my hand, her calf muscle tensing beneath my touch. She moaned as I reached her foot, her toes tightening, curling. I pulled the third tie from my pocket and looped it around her ankle and yanked it tight, closing the knot. She gasped at the sudden roughness. The other end of the tie I wrapped around the end of the bed. There was only one other limb left to be secured. When it was done I stood back, by the side of her bed, and admired at my handy work.

Lola Ray was stripped of her covers, her arms up wide, her legs spread open. She was in the form of an X. Again she tried to move, seeing exactly how well the knots were formed. I didn't have to worry, she wasn't going anywhere. She could wriggle and pull, twist and try to set herself free but there was no use. In fact I wanted her to try a little. To tire herself out, weaken herself. It would make the rest of the evening more fun.

"Mack?" she muttered.

"I'm not Mack," I replied as I kneeled beside the bed next to her head. "Call me Daddy."

"Daddy," she breathed as she made eye contact. "Daddy, I want you to fuck me."

I arched an eyebrow at this sudden demand.

"You don't get to decide that," I said and stroked her cheek. "Now, where did you put the present I gave you? Somewhere hidden, secret?" I started my search before she could reply, tugging on drawers and delving into them. I pulled out bras, underwear, tights, and socks before my hand found what it was looking for.

"Here we go."

With the vibrating panties in my hand I got back on the bed and knelt in between her splayed legs.

"Daddy, are you going to touch me?"

"Baby girl, I'm going to do more than touch you. I'm going to make you scream."

Delving into my pocket I found the little remote control I'd attached to my keyring and pressed the button. The panties began to vibrate in my hand. Turning the material inside out, so the little buzzing mechanism was facing outward I hovered it at the crotch of her pajama shorts. Her head lifted, straining to see what I was doing.

I watched her eyes go incredibly wide as I let the vibration make contact with her mound. Her hips jolted and she gasped as if there was no air in the room. She tried to dodge away from the buzzing sensation, but with her legs bound tight, there was nowhere to go.

I pressed the vibrator closer, harder up against her. This time she began to moan.

"Oh, god. I don't think I can take much more," she begged, desperately searching my eyes, pleading for me to take away the vibrator.

For a second I removed the device and she looked at me, grateful. But then wickedly I pulled her pajama bottoms down, and plunged the device upon her clit. It was the first time I was seeing her naked up close and god was it a sight to behold. My mouth filled with hot saliva at the thought of parting her pussy lips and licking her. But first thing's first.

I held the vibrator in place and leaned over her as she writhed beneath me.

"Stop, oh god, stop."

"I don't think you want me to stop, do you?"

She didn't have much time to think as I began my assault again. Buzzing her clit into submission.

Her mouth fell open and I slipped a finger into her mouth. "Suck," I demanded as she continued to wriggle, doing her best to break the contact from the unrelenting buzzing.

She tried her best to suck on my thick finger, but the sensations must have been too overwhelming for her because every few seconds she would stop, her mouth widening, her eyes closing.

"Something'a happening," she cried, her body arching up, tense. "Oh fuck, I think I'm cumming…"

I wickedly removed the vibrator and she flopped back down on the bed, her muscles relaxing.

"Not until I let you," I said, whispering in her ear.

"Please."

"Please, what?"

"Please, Daddy, let me cum."

I smiled. She was a quick study. "Good girl… but nope. Not yet."

I slid my hands down her body, pulling on her camisole to free her tits, as I got into position again between her legs. But this time I was crouched low, on my elbows and knees, my mouth barely a whisper away from her pussy.

From above I let the vibrating part of the panties drape across her clit, not exactly touching, but close enough and doing enough to keep her breathless. She jolted again but with strong hands I kept her in place. She relaxed, beginning to enjoy how helpless she was, and I with long fingers began to reach out to part the lips of her sweet virgin cunt.

"You're so wet for me, dripping. You dirty girl," I said unable to stop the smile. Even in the dark, she glistened. I let only the tip on my finger run the length of her, feeling her slippery juices. She smelled divine, like forbidden juicy fruit, that would be all mine. I would devour her and I couldn't resist a sneak preview and popped my finger into my mouth.

Once that happened, I became a man on a mission. My tastebuds lit up like a Christmas tree and my tongue darted out for more. I held her firmly, parting her wide and lapped at her pussy.

She was moaning constantly now, getting louder and I knew I would have to be careful not to really let her scream the house down, but I was too preoccupied licking her cunt, sucking her flaps, and letting the tip of my finger tease her entrance.

"Put it inside me," she whispered from above me. "Daddy, I can't wait any more."

For a second the lines were blurred and I did what she asked. I breached her entrance. Up to the first knuckle of my index finger. It slipped inside her. I wanted to thrust the rest of it in, put two or maybe three fingers inside her and spread her so wide... maybe even my whole fucking hand, fisting her 'til there's no tomorrow, 'til she screamed my name and her juices trickle down my arm. But no, the first time I was going to really fuck her would be with my cock. I just hadn't decided whether it would be that night or not.

Chapter Twenty Three
Lola Ray

I was having trouble processing what was happening to me. I was bound to my own bed, unable to move and every part of me felt like it was going to explode. Like I was going to shatter into a million pieces and never be the same ever again. But as I was teetering on the edge, barely holding on, the sensations stopped. My once-blurred vision became crystal clear with the absence of everything.

Mack stopped touching me, his thick tongue no longer at my entrance and the buzzing ceased. I almost cried out to beg him to continue, but knowing that will displease him, I bit my tongue. Hard.

But just as I decided I shouldn't say anything, I couldn't help myself. The words slipped from my mouth. I wanted him to touch me again, I needed him to.

"Fuck me," I pleaded, "I saved myself for you. Please…"

In the dark I couldn't be sure but I had a feeling he was smiling. At the foot of my bed he was still, unmoving. Perhaps debating what to do with me. And I hoped for my own sake he was just doing it to tease me. That he'd continue like he did before, but this time instead of teasing me with his tongue and finger, I was desperate for something more. I wanted him to pull down his zipper again and let me catch a glance of his cock before he put it in me.

When he didn't answer I tried again. "Mack?" I whispered.

If I weren't tied up I would've thought I had dreamed the whole thing. He was as quiet and as still as a statue. If it weren't for the smell of his aftershave and the subtle shifting of the bedsprings under his weight I would've thought he wasn't there at all. He was a shadow in my room, a ghost that I so desperately needed to turn into a substantial being, to finish what he started.

"Not tonight, princess," he finally said.

My head whirled with disappointment. Surely not. Surely this was another game. He was only messing with me, right? He wouldn't sneak into my room, somehow get by my father, and then tie me up if he wasn't planning on fucking me and stripping me of my virginity.

"But… I'm ready. I want you inside me."

"And one day I will be inside you. I will stretch your tight little pussy and pound into you until you beg me to stop, and even then I won't. I'll fill you up completely and it'll feel like you won't be able to breathe without me." His hands ran the length of my body, skimming over my breasts, hardening my nipples as the ripples of his touch cascaded down my skin. "But not now. You, my dirty little girl, will have to wait. This is your punishment for almost letting him see you."

"Who?" I spat out, already forgetting the events earlier in the evening. They had been obliterated away as soon as Mack appeared in my room.

Mack moved off the bed and stood a foot away, keeping his distance perhaps… trying not to give into temptation.

"Mack, please," I said again, "I'm sorry, but please don't leave me like this. I need you. I'll do anything you want. Spread me wide and make love to me…"

The words were out of my mouth before I could stop them and I hoped that he hadn't heard them. My cheeks flushed with embarrassment.

He took a step and was by my bedside table, looking down at me. "No."

I wanted to cry. And scream and call him every name under the sun for torturing me like this.

"If you don't fuck me, I'll tell my father what you've done!" I said shocking even myself as I tried to blackmail him. I couldn't think of anything else; I didn't want him to leave. My skin was cooling, but I already knew it was no use. Once Mack made his mind up about something, he followed through with it. Stubborn as an ox.

The silence in the room scared me. And I worried that I'd just ruined everything. Mack leaned down, his face inches away from mine.

Tears sprang to my eyes. "I'm sorry, I didn't mean it."

A sudden pain, sharp and fierce, shot through my left breast, my nipple was being squeezed.

"If you ever say anything like that ever again, I will never touch you again. That's a promise. Besides… it would be your word against mine. And who do you think he'll believe?"

"I'm sorry,' I said again, "Please don't go."

What could I say to make him stay?

He took hold of my chin, roughly. And a flood of relief battered down upon me as he kissed me hard. I kissed him back with everything I had, my neck straining, putting all my mixed-up feelings—love, need, passion—into that kiss. Hoping he'd realize how much I wanted him. He took my breath away and I almost didn't care if he never gave it back.

Then just as suddenly he stopped, pulling back. There was a violent tug at my left wrist and my arm flopped down, free. I was so surprised by it, flexing and bringing my hand to my chest that I didn't see that Mack had left my room.

* * *

After I eventually released myself from my bonds—which must've taken me the best part of twenty minutes, undoing the tight knots, and hid the neckties deep in my closet—all I could do was sit on my bed, in the dark, and replay everything about that evening in my mind.

It had not ended the way I wanted it to, far from it. Partly I was angry about that. Although I certainly hadn't planned for Mack to turn up in my bedroom that night, once he had, I envisaged it going so differently. I told him I was ready… I knew I was. Couldn't he see that? So why would he torture me? Why would he leave me naked, still *untouched* and intact, when he could've had me? It was indeed punishment... and it certainly was cruel. And I wanted payback.

It was about time I stopped letting men control me and took the lead myself, I thought. And if I wanted to get out of my father's house for good, out from under his authority and menace, I'd decided there was only one way to do that. I had to seduce Mack once and for all.

However that was going to prove difficult. For the next few days he was nowhere to be found. I'd texted him but there'd been no response. I'd even risked going around to his house, knocking on the door, with an excuse already formed in my head just in case someone, a neighbor or even my father, caught me. But nobody answered.

If he was doing this on purpose, wanting me to go insane with worry and lust... then he was doing a very good job of it.

"What is wrong with you?" Robin said, interrupting my thoughts as she pulled her car up against the curb outside my house. "You haven't said practically one word to me all day."

I turned to her and shook my head, forcing an easy smile on my face. "Nothing's wrong."

"Is it Sam? I overheard some of the players you

know… You can talk to me if you want about it."

"What? What were they saying?"

"Oh you don't have to be embarrassed."

"I'm not," I said, getting worried and defensive. I had a feeling it wasn't going to be good. "I just don't know what you're talking about. Tell me."

"Well, and remember I only heard it from a third party…"

"Just spit it out, Robin."

"There was talk that you and Sam tried to, you know… have sex. And you froze on him."

"What? That's so not true! He's really saying that?"

She shrugged and patted my hand. "You don't have to deny it to me."

"I'm not, seriously, I'm not. Nothing even happened. Not really," I muttered remembering that night.

"What did happen?" she asked, her voice soft.

"It really was nothing. I asked him to do something for me, and in return he wanted a little striptease. But before he got to see anything my father busted in the door and chased him from the house. That was it. I swear."

Robin sighed.

"I can't believe he's saying those things."

"Maybe there was some misunderstanding? You know how the rumor mill goes. Things get twisted all out of proportion. You should ask him."

I shook my head defiantly. This was the perfect opportunity to get rid of Sam, cut ties, so I would never have to see him again. But I knew he was my best shot at keeping my relationship with Mack secret. I still wanted to kill him though, for spreading rumors about me. He must've been really pissed at me. Cause Mack wasn't the only one avoiding my calls and dodging me, Sam was too. And now I knew why.

The thought had me clenching my fists with rage.

"Hey, before you go, Sam and I bumped into your neighbor the other day at the diner. It kinda got heated."

"What?" I asked, my jealous hackles rising. Surely she didn't mean Mack? And what was she doing with Sam?

"Yeah, the one who was in prison. The hot one? The one Sam's really taken a dislike to. Didn't he tell you?"

I frowned and shook my head trying to figure out who she was talking about. Mack hadn't been to prison.

"Who are you on about?"

"Sam said he was your dad's friend, lived close by?"

My head buzzed, not understanding. "Mack? Maddox McClane?"

"Yeah, that's him. Sam Googled him afterward."

"But Mack's not been to jail… And what were you doing with Sam?" I asked turning to her.

"Don't look at me like that. First of all, he so has… look it up yourself. You should stay away from him just in case, Lola Ray. Even if he is your dad's friend, he's dangerous. And second I was helping your dumbass boyfriend with his college assignments so he doesn't flunk out."

"Oh, okay." I let it drop. But I still couldn't figure out why she would lie to me about Mack being in prison… it didn't make any sense. Unless she wasn't. I quickly said goodbye to Robin, thanked her for the ride, and went into the house. I couldn't sit around and wait for Mack to decide when would be the next time he would pay me a visit—I needed answers. Besides, I was getting sick of the constant waiting, the sick anticipation that was settled low in my stomach, like butterflies that were too heavy to fly, yet still managed to bump around.

I dropped my bag in my room and marched through the house to the yard. My father wouldn't be home for an hour or so, and I'd got to the point where I didn't care if I wasn't there when he got back. He could make his own damn dinner. I was done with him. Instead I would be waiting for Mack.

Using the boost from a large stone that was against the fence, I managed to scramble over it and thudded down in a crouch on the other side, in Mack's yard. Remaining low, with my heart doing double-time, I sprinted to the back door. I'd never broken into someone's house before, never even stolen a lipstick from the cosmetics counter, and yet there I was jiggling the handle praying it would open.

It didn't.

Scanning the yard, I whirled around, looking for something that could help me either jimmy the lock or bust the door down completely. There was no way I was going to give up or turn back. I was doing it. I was getting in there so I could be waiting for Mack when he got home. I would make him tell me everything. The truth. He wouldn't be able to resist me... I wouldn't let him.

Over in the corner, in a makeshift storage container, I smiled as I spotted a small sledgehammer. *That would do the trick*, I thought.

It would make some noise, but I doubted anyone would be able to hear it, and I was sure that Mack didn't have any kind of alarm system.

At least I hoped not.

It hadn't actually occurred to me, until then. And I'd only been inside Mack's place that one time. He'd always been the one to come over to my father's. *Come to think of it*, I pondered, *he'd never even invited his best friend over*. At least not that I knew about. Why was that? What did he have to hide? Did my father know that Mack had been to prison? And what was it for? My Internet searches hadn't exactly yielded any forthcoming results on that score, not yet at least. Though I had to admit I didn't dig too much. Maybe deep down I didn't want to know? But if it came to it I would ask the man himself.

The hammer was heavy, hefty even, and lugging it toward the door was a workout in itself. But I managed it. I even managed to lift it, doing my best to stay balanced as I aimed and swung the head toward the doorjamb. The hammer bounced feebly, then ricocheted against the glass panel of the door. It cracked. I winced. I hadn't meant to break the glass, just force the door open. But I gave a little shrug and tried again. This time, the same thing happened, except the hammer flew out of my hands hammer and went through the glass completely. The panel came down like a sparkling waterfall, and dangerous shards splashed on the ground around my feet.

At least I was in, I thought, and reached inside and unlatched the lock. I would make it up to Mack. He would forgive me… *or he would punish me*, I thought with a wicked smile. Either way was good. I liked it when he felt the need to punish me. *Maybe this time he would spank me*, I thought. All questions about what kind of man he actually was, what he'd done to go to jail, forgotten.

I considered what he would do to me as I explored his house. I was under no delusion that what I was doing was a violation… but like I'd told myself earlier, I wanted payback. He'd come into my bedroom, tied me up, and then just left me laying there, totally unsatisfied.

I moved deeper in the house, searching for Mack's bedroom—thinking I could prepare myself for when he arrived home. I couldn't quite remember which door was the main bedroom, there were four to choose from. So I tried them all.

The first looked like a small guest room. I closed the door and continued my search. It was when I opened the second one, a dark room that was lined with wood paneling and no windows, I thought perhaps I'd made a serious mistake in going there.

I could hardly believe my eyes.

His words from long ago came back to haunt me.

Had this been what he'd meant when he said I wasn't ready?

DREAM DADDY

Chapter Twenty Four
Mack

My cell phone dinged as I parked the truck in my driveway. I didn't have to look at the screen to know it was from Lola Ray. For days I'd been ignoring her… an extra extension to her punishment and for what she'd said to me. Threatening to tell Will about us. It was low but I could see she was desperate. It also meant she was nearly ready for the next step. I knew she would have never gone through with telling Will. She just didn't want me to leave. Wanted me to keep touching her. And by god I'd almost relented and stayed.

My cock had throbbed for hours afterwards. I cursed myself for not taking her when I had the chance, but there was a method to my madness and I kept telling myself it would all be worth the wait, especially because she was on the brink. She'd enjoyed being tied up even if she had struggled initially.

Shoving my phone in my pocket, ignoring it, I let myself in. It didn't take a genius to realize that as soon as I walked through my front door that there was something *off*. The feeling of the small house had changed. For one it was a lot colder than expected. Had the boiler blown itself out?

I eased the door shut behind me and moved deeper inside. There was a breeze coming from the back and my guard instantly went up. A break-in? Who in their right minds would try to rob my place? If they knew me, as most people in the town did, they knew I didn't have anything worth stealing, except maybe my truck. My money was secure in savings. And there was only one other thing that I spent it on and I was sure they weren't after that and wouldn't have known about it in any case.

From the kitchen entrance I spotted immediately the cause of the breeze and sudden drop in temperature. Glass from the rear down coated the tiled floor. The door had been opened and closed again, though, as there was a void where the glass had been brushed back by the bottom of the door.

So either they'd come and left… or they were

still in the house.

Movement upstairs, from above, had me looking up. That answered that question then. My hand drew a chef's knife from the butcher's block. I wished I had a gun; I hated knives. But I didn't have one in the house. Wasn't allowed one. Not anymore. The only person close enough who did was Will and there was no time to go get it. They were in the house now.

I thought about calling the cops. Thought about the time it would take them to get there, what they would do… traipsing around my house. Nosing about my things. Looking into places and seeing things they shouldn't. Not that I was ashamed, I just didn't want my life spread all about the town, I'd already had to put up with that for the best part of a few months once I got back. It was better to deal with the fuckers who thought it was okay to break into my house myself.

As quietly as I could I made my way up the stairs, breathing hard through my nose, my hand tight around the knife's handle.

My ears pricked up, tracking the noise. It was coming from the end of the hall. It was insanity to deal with an intruder by myself but I was by the door now, and I wasn't about to turn back. I took a deep breath and gently put my hand on the wood of the door and pushed.

Never in a thousand years would I have predicted what I would see when the door swung open right then. I almost dropped the knife in shock. But god was it a sight to see.

The room was a collection of equipment I'd recently taken out of storage. Seeing them wasn't the surprise, though.

It was the sight of Lola Ray stripped down to absolutely nothing strapped into what I liked to call my fuck table. A heavy wooden contraption, like a pommel horse, but thinner and instead of being completely flat, it tilted downward. It also had four small additions to the side, little wooden-like shelves, one for each limb. And at the end of each of them were leather straps with buckles.

She was facing away from me, bent at the perfect angle and position, at the perfect height, the table forcing her ass in the air. Her legs were spread, open and wide, resting on the plinths at the back. Her ripe virgin pussy in my direct line of sight… just waiting there. Ready for cock.

Somehow she'd managed to climb onto it and single-handedly used the leg straps and buckled herself in. She'd also done the same to one of her wrists. Her left was bound, and though the right arm was free she was still holding onto the strap, keeping herself in position.

"Fucking hell, Lola Ray," I breathed. I knew this girl was special but I truly didn't expect this. She'd actually broken into my house, found this room, and taken it upon herself to get ready for me. She wiggled her ass at me.

"Like what you see?"

Fuck, did I ever. I could've stared at her all day. In fact that's what I was thinking of doing. She obviously wanted me to lose control, give in and fuck her, but I could've easily sat down—after securing the last bond, of course—and stared at her dripping pussy for as long as I wanted. She would've been furious. A smile crept over my face.

"Of course you do," she said, straining to see over her shoulder as she glanced back me. "Mack, I'm not sure how many times I have to say it, I don't care what you've done, or what I need to do to convince you, but I'm ready." Her voice was firm, no-nonsense, and dare I say it, a little more grown-up.

"I'm convinced," I breathed, and stepped closer, moving around the table, like I was taking a tour of a museum piece. She was breathtaking. But I didn't chance touching her, not yet. My will would crumble, and I wanted this to last. There would be only one time that I would get to be her first.

I did however point the knife at her and allowed the blunt edge of the blade to skirt over her skin. She shuddered from the cold steel.

"What are you waiting for?" she demanded, her voice tight.

"If you think I'm not going to savor this moment, then you have another thing coming."

I put the knife down as I reached her right side and helped fasten the remaining bond. She was stuck for sure now. At my mercy. I wondered if she was going to panic and change her mind. Instead she stared at me with a furious glare, but not because she was trapped, because I still hadn't laid a finger on her.

"What are you doing?" she asked as I took a step back and reached into my pocket, pulling out my phone. I held it up and swiped a couple of times until I found the right app. "Mack?" Her eyes widened as the automatic flash went off in the dim room, her pale skin shining.

"Hey! I didn't agree to you taking photos."

"Too late," I said with a smile. "I want to remember this moment forever." I took more, some from far away, some up close. She fumed in her restraints. "Don't worry, you look absolutely stunning and they're just for me."

She relaxed a little the more I took, even gave me a cheeky smile from down low as I moved in for a close up, framing her bent over, her pussy the focal point.

"See how beautiful you are?" I said as I showed her one of the photos, strapped in, helpless.

My next tour around the table I put the camera away and let my hands trail down her sides. She moaned, little impatient breaths. I tested how far she wanted me to go and began to squeeze her dangling breasts. Her little nipples were hard and she gasped when I tweaked them.

"You like that, don't you?"

She nodded. Her hair slipped forward and covered her face. While she was unable to see I dug into a nearby drawer and pulled out two clamps. The next time I touched her breasts I was gentle, caressing them first, but then quickly I put the two clamps on her nipples and stood back to watch her reaction. Her head shot up, searching for my eyes, as she sucked in a breath. She bent back down to witness what on earth was causing the pain.

"Oh god, it hurts," she hissed.

While she was distracted I loosened my belt and brought out my cock. Pumping my fist a couple of times. I stepped forward just as she looked up again and she came face to face with my hard meat stick.

"This will make it better," I promised and urged her to take me in her mouth.

She licked her lips once and smiled through the pain. Her lips wrapped around me without any further prompting. I grabbed a handful of her hair and slipped in deeper.

"That's my good little girl, take it all." She sucked and pursed her lips, tightening them around my shaft, god she was good. A beginner, but a natural. She tilted her head to the side. I played with her hair, stroking it, while her tongue licked up and down my shaft.

She paused at the tip, then began again swirling her hot tongue around my head. Beads of pre-cum emerged and she lapped them up. But then infuriatingly she stopped again.

From her position she looked up at me, with those perfect innocent doe eyes. I knew what she was going to ask before she even opened her mouth.

"Daddy, will you play will my pussy, please?"

"Soon, but if you want me to stop, at any time, just say the word," I said.

"Like a safe word? What word?"

"You decide." She thought for a moment.

"Okay, erm, strawberry?"

"Are you sure?"

She nodded.

"Okay then." I pushed my cock back into her mouth roughly, surprising her. Her long hair draped forward and I grabbed hold of it, it was like I was holding onto pigtails. I yanked and thrust forward and she gobbled me up.

With a pop, my cock springing free from her mouth, I suddenly released my hold and stood back. Lola Ray nibbled at her lip as she glanced up at me, eager, barely able to contain herself as she imagined what was to come.

I kicked off my work boots, stripped my jeans away and peeled off my shirt. It was the first time I'd been naked before her and I could see the hunger in her eyes as she took in every inch of me.

She was in an awkward position but I crouched down so she no longer had to strain her neck upward to see me. My eyes were level with hers and I searched them for a second to make sure

I was going to do the right thing. To make sure that *she* was truly ready.

"There's no going back after this," I warned her. "I might not be able to stop once I start. Your virginity will be gone forever, are you sure you want me to take you this way?"

"Yes," she breathed without hesitation. "I've been ready for you for months. I've wanted this more than you can even imagine. Besides, I have my safe word now, don't I? Don't make me beg again."

"But I like it when you beg."

She blinked and her eyes began to sparkle. She didn't miss a beat. "Please, Daddy, fuck me raw with your cock… I want your cum inside me. Make me your little girl."

I leaned forward and kissed her dirty, foul mouth, loving and tasting every word. Then left her side and got to work.

She couldn't help but wiggle her cute, teen bubble-butt at me as I stood behind her. My cock so fucking close to her pussy I could've just dived right in there.

But she was in for a rude awakening.

First I ran my hands up her thighs and pulled her cheeks apart and bent to lick her from behind. Sweet as ever. Her juices danced on my tongue and her moans were like music to my ears. Knowing what I was about to do, I squirted some lube into my hand and palmed her pussy, getting her even more slippery. She leaned back as far as she could, increasing the pressure, clearly enjoying my hand on her sex. I gave her pussy a little slap for being so naughty and she sprang away, but she was back for more and I slapped her again, getting her pussy lips nice and red.

It was time.

I covered her pussy with a clear plastic cup and gave the rubber bulb in my hand, which was connected to the cup, a single squeeze to form the seal. At the foreign touch she turned to look, trying anxiously to find out what I was doing. I began to pump at the bulb again, little by little, and the rim of the pussy pumper made a soft seal against her, creating a vacuum.

The more I pressed, the more her cunt began to swell up, thickening.

"What are you doing to me?" she cried, moaning a bit.

"Getting you ready," I whispered, marveling at how her little pussy was becoming engorged the more the air was sucked out around the cup. "How does it feel?"

By her hesitation I knew she was unsure. "I don't know, I've never done this…" She was finding it hard to choose her words. "It feels good but intense. Like you're sucking on me."

I grinned, just what I wanted.

I let the bulb go for a moment, the suction cup firmly stuck in place for the moment and went to remove the clamps from her nipples. Her face fell as I removed them and I gave her breasts a reassuring squeeze. "Don't you worry your pretty little head… there's better things to come."

With that I placed the first nipple pump on her. Once it was secure I put the other one on. She hissed and squirmed as her buds became hardened, like little bullets trapped in a see-through tube.

She kept saying, "Oh god, oh god, oh god," over and over again. But she didn't tell me to stop and at that I was proud of her.

A couple more squeezes of the bulb attached to the pussy pump later and she was getting antsy. She was on the verge of telling me no. Every once in a while I'd glance over to see how she was doing, strapped at my mercy, her head bent forward. A few times she turned to look at me, making eye contact and she would give me a slight nod to tell me she was okay.

"You're doing so well," I crooned to her as I came round to the front. For a lack of anything better to do her mouth sought my cock and I let her suck on it like a pacifier for a few seconds.

She seemed to calm after that and I wiped at the tear that rolled down her cheek. She wasn't crying, just overwhelmed and bombarded with a ton of new sensations.

Much to her dismay I left her again anxious to see her fat, swollen pussy again—the vacuum had done its work—her little entrance was so pink and visible now.

Her asshole puckered as I circled it with my finger. She clenched but I kept one hand on her cheek pulling her open. My tongue darted out and swam around her ring, she began her mantra again and I had the wicked thought of gagging her. But for her first time I was going to be nice, I'd let her scream as much as she wanted.

DREAM DADDY

Chapter Twenty Five
Lola Ray

He was going to fuck my ass. The notion suddenly popped into my head. It hadn't been one that I'd considered. Not at all. It wasn't something I'd agreed to, but then again, I hadn't really agreed to anything.

I'd brought it upon myself to strap myself onto the table I'd found, shedding my clothes, so he would have no choice but to be turned on when he saw me. Feeling helpless, unable to move properly, and him taking my virginity was what I was prepared for. Not that. Him shoving his penis into my ass was not what I had in mind. Panic began to rise in my throat and I let out a tiny squeak, that was supposed to be a scream, as I felt his slippery finger press down on my anus.

Did I dare say the safe word? I could feel the tip of him enter me and I gasped, shutting my eyes tightly. I wanted to please him, I so wanted to… but this I couldn't. *No…*

Before I could form the word the pressure was gone, his finger no longer probing. "We'll leave that for another day, I think. But no doubt about it, I will be taking your virgin ass someday."

He brought his hand down on my butt, a quick hard slap that made me suck in a harsh breath. He did it again on the other cheek, then squeezed the flesh, grabbing a good handful playfully.

There was another satisfying crack as he slapped me again. The flesh of hand deliciously smacking against my bottom, causing it to go red, sent throbs of desire to my pussy. I felt even more sensitive down there, with what I could only describe as some kind of pump making me swell and puff up. It felt amazing and with each squeeze, I felt a tug, my clit pulsing outwards, even more prominently than before. I couldn't wait for him to remove the thing and put his mouth on me again.

But as I was thinking about his tongue sucking on my pussy, a new, sharp, and extreme pain hit me. There was a crack in the air and I screamed. My throat opened and out came a wail I could not control.

He was spanking me, with what I could not tell. It was definitely not his hand anymore. Whatever it was, it hurt and it brought tears to my eyes. Seconds passed and I thought that was the end of it, a reprieve, the worst of it over. The pain started to dissipate, turning into something else—a yearning, a fever for more.

"Daddy, I've been naughty, spank me again," I said with a throaty voice, hardly believing I was asking for more.

I got what I wanted and managed to get a glimpse of what Mack held in his hand.

Leather tassels hit me again and again until I could barely breathe. Strapped in, part of me tried to dodge the blows, but another part of me was grateful that I was secure in place, unable to get away from what I craved.

"Had enough?" he asked roughly, though beneath the surface I sensed a hint of adoration.

"Yes, Daddy," I responded, getting my breath back.

He hit me again, my ass wobbling as I screamed.

I should've known to expect it. But I didn't, not then.

He patted my rump, smoothing my hot, sore skin with the coolness of his palm.

But he didn't stop.

The sucking began again in earnest, the edges of the cup dug into the sides of my pussy and I winced. But then just as I thought I couldn't bear it any longer, the vacuum was released—a tiny hiss—and the object removed.

I felt deliciously sore and full.

Mack moaned. Glancing over my shoulder as much as I could I saw him staring at my enlarged pussy. His lips were wet, and he had a sheen of sweat on his forehead.

"Amazing," he breathed.

I dipped as low as I could go, arching my back to an extreme angle, so it pushed my booty out farther, my sex fully on display for him. He let out another primal moan and was unable to resist touching me. My eyes rolled back as his finger slipped between my puffy folds, rubbing and hitting upon my clit. I dripped with need. He was so close to being inside me and I thought I was going to pass out if he didn't finally make a move to enter me.

His fingers left me. Saddened by this I let out a heavy impatient moan. Thankfully he ignored my annoyance and rewarded me with the slap of his cock. There were thick wet smacks against my pussy. I ducked my head down, to watch from under me, eager to see. Between my swinging breasts, framing the view, Mack rubbed his cock against me. I was shocked to see how large my pussy had actually become, my flaps much bigger that I remembered. But they were nothing in comparison to the monster of Mack's penis.

As if he was thinking the same, his voice rumbled out a question that I didn't expect him of all people to ask, "Are you sure about this, baby girl? Are you sure you want me to take you like this... your first time?"

Nothing could've made me say no at that point. I'd been waiting for what seemed like forever for this. And I wasn't going to turn back at the last hurdle.

I strained my head to the side, to make sure he understood I was for real. He was positioned directly behind me, his cock at the ready, his hands on my hips. I knew if I told him no, uttered the safe word I'd chosen, that he would back away. But I didn't want that.

"Fuck me, Daddy. Make me yours."

He raked me with his blue eyes for a long second. What was he waiting for? Was he deciding whether he could trust my words or not?

As I regarded him, I frowned. He wasn't going

to do it. He was going to leave me high and dry again.

Then he slammed into me.

I let loose the loudest scream I'd ever expelled in my entire life.

He didn't take me slow. He didn't ease himself in.

All at once he was inside.

He grabbed and dug his fingers into my hips for leverage and in no uncertain terms fucked me.

My legs felt like jelly as he speared me. I felt like I was being battered with every conflicting emotion I'd ever experienced, and some that I'd never encountered before too.

"Scream for me," he grunted, never letting up. He split me wide and it was the most amazing feeling ever.

He filled me like I never thought possible.

The skin on my knees and elbows chafed, and became sore under the constant friction, but somehow I managed to keep myself partly up, supported by the beams.

Mack's hands moved up to my waist, squeezing, getting a better hold. His strokes getting deeper and deeper as he got better leverage. The wooden legs squeaked with the force of his thrusts, moving across the floor.

There was a slapping noise I managed to focus on in between the moans, the pain, the cries, and feelings of complete and utter ecstasy. Like the beat of a clock it was keeping time. *Slap, slap, slap.* I tried to figure out what it was through my delirious state. By that point it felt like I'd burst open a million times. Each rush of pleasure more intense than the last. Then it hit me, no pun intended. His balls smacked against my engorged pussy and made a pleasing soft crack.

My walls clenched, at least that's what it felt like, my insides tightening… and when they did I realized I hadn't even begun to cum yet. The small waves I thought were orgasms were only ripples…

"Not yet, baby girl," Mack called, his hand tugging on and removing the tube that had been attached to my nipple. He massaged my tit as he removed his cock. The void was heartbreaking. The absence of him inside me almost made me weep.

The build up I'd been feeling only moments ago in my center was ebbing away, letting me catch my breath again. And though I was pissed that he'd stopped, I had to trust that he knew what he was doing. I had to trust he wasn't just going to leave me feeling so unfulfilled.

I lifted my head and he was there looking directly into my eyes. His own shone, creasing at the edges as he smiled. "You okay, my darling?" He stroked my face and kissed my lips. I nodded my reply. Though if I were being honest with myself I was absolutely exhausted, I had barely moved and yet I trembled with fatigue. My legs were weak, my arms could barely support my upper body.

To my surprise he reached for my wrists and unbuckled the restraints, unlatching them one at a time. He did the same with the ones around my ankles, and just before I was about to flop down onto the table he scooped me up into his arms and kissed me.

"Put your arms around my neck," he encouraged. I did. Looped them around and he carried me out of his playroom.

I hadn't had time to explore the rest of the upstairs after I'd found the room that was full of sex toys but it seemed like Mack was taking me back to his actual bedroom.

He pushed a door open with his foot and took a few strides before we were near the end of a bed. With gentleness he put me down on top of the cool, soft, and silky sheets. My body began to tremble again.

He took a moment to stare at me, then kneeled to get on the bed, joining me. He didn't waste any more time. He pulled at my legs, wrapped them around his neck, my bottom and lower back lifting off the bed a little, and then he buried his face into my cunt. He kissed me delicately at first, teasing my clit with the flick of his tongue and I could feel the pressure begin to mount again.

Thick and meaty, his muscle drove into me. Of course it wasn't as big as his cock but it felt good.

"I could lick you like this forever," he claimed, his words partially muffled. His breath tickled me and I let out a short giggle, thoroughly enjoying this side of him too.

He lapped at me and my laughter died, replaced by a shortness of breath. The air in the room seemed too thin, I couldn't get enough. My heart seemed to register the lack of oxygen and picked up the pace, hammering hard.

My hands reached out, grasping on to anything I could. The sheets wadded in my fists as I became dazed, overcome. I heaved and thrashed as he held onto my thighs that had become pressed around his head, keeping me in place, his tongue buried deep, never giving up. Not giving me a moment to compose myself. But then that was the whole point, this was the ultimate goal, to lose myself and become undone, and by god was he doing just that.

I was coming… coming apart.

My throat was sore as I cried out.

Fuck, fuck, fuck. Was I speaking the words out loud or was the mantra playing over in my head? I had no clue. I couldn't tell what was real anymore as sparks before my eyes erupted. Were they even open? He was sending me to whole new heights… ones I'd never even knew existed.

"I'm cumming," I whispered, shocked that I finally knew it was true. Mack was making me cum. And like a stack of unstable dynamite I exploded.

The wetness between my legs doubled and once my vision returned and I looked up I saw the juice glistening on Mack's lips. "So fucking sweet," he said grinning.

With both hands he hoisted my legs off his shoulders and down around his waist. Roughly bringing me to his crotch. My ass rested on his thighs and I thought maybe he was going to give me a moment to recover as he wrapped his fist around his rigid cock. But he was merely getting it ready, wiping some of my earlier juices upon it and angling it to meet my entrance again.

All it took was one single hard thrust for him to be inside me again. He grunted greedily as he filled me. And my breasts jiggled at the movement. Long, lengthy strokes in and out had me short on air again. If I was sensitive before, I was even more so now. The raw pain of my overworked clit mixed with need for more… to cum again.

He lifted me up, cradling me, bringing me closer than I ever thought possible. I was practically on top of him now, our faces inches apart, but he was still in control. He sought my mouth on the next stroke, his tongue going inside me just as his cock did down below. I moaned with pleasure. Nothing could ever top this night…

"You want my cum in you, don't you?"

I squeezed my legs around him. "Yes, Daddy. Cum in me, fill me up." I let the dirty words fall from my mouth.

"Say you want it. Say you want me to fill your little pussy."

"Yes!" I screamed. "Give it to me. Yes, yes, yes!"

His arms tightened around me, his head dropped down close to my ear. The ripples of his labored breath sent shivers down my spine. And with a few lasting powerful thrusts, feeling like he was splitting me in two, he spurted his seed within me.

He roared as he came and held on to me as if it were the only thing tying him to this world.

At the thought of what was happening my mind went into overload, my body following closely behind as I joined him, digging my nails in, my toes curling, every muscle tensing… then erupting again. Raining down with cum.

Chapter Twenty Six
Mack

Lola Ray was asleep in my arms and I didn't dare move. She was perfect. Everything was perfect. I shut out the rest of world and was content to just stare at her, ignoring what we would have to eventually face.

A few strands of her hair fell across her face but I knew if I swiped them away she would stir. And I wanted the moment to last just a little bit longer. But I already knew it couldn't last. I didn't know what the time was but it was late. I spent hours worshiping her body, sweat dripping off the both of us as we moaned and came in unison. She smiled and giggled each time we flopped down back onto the sheets. Unable to believe that it was real. Even I was having trouble believing she was there and this whole night hadn't been a dream.

I certainly hadn't expected to come home to find her in my house, strapped up and ready for me to fuck the virginity right out of her. But I did, and I had. And it'd been glorious.

There was a soft thud downstairs.

At first I wasn't alarmed but I did try to remember if I'd latched the door properly after Lola Ray's little break-in. Then there was another thud, a crash of some sort. I told myself it was just the wind. With the glass shattered, the wind would be streaming through, blowing items over, sending things crashing to the floor. Yet I couldn't shake the feeling that it was not just the wind. There was no rhythm to the thuds, they weren't consistent.

The third noise woke Lola Ray and I sat up, my muscles tense. Someone was definitely in the house.

"What is it—" she started to say.

I put my finger to my lips to silence her and shook my head. Her mouth slammed shut with a soft click.

Similar thoughts from earlier ran again through my mind. Who in their right minds would break into my house? I was just about to get off the bed and leave Lola Ray when my name was called.

"Mack? Mack, you here?"

Lola Ray took a sudden intake of air when we both recognized the voice.

"Oh my god, he can't find me here. He'll kill me. He'll kill us both!"

I launched myself back onto the bed and put my hand hard against her mouth to shut her up. She was trembling like a leaf, absolutely terrified of her father and what he might do.

"Lola Ray, I'll take care of it, I promise. Stay here. Do not move. And keep quiet," I hissed.

"You up there, Mack? Whoever you are, I have a gun!"

The whites of her eyes were startlingly bright as they widened.

I shushed her trying to calm her and eased my hand from her lips. Thankfully she had the good sense keep her mouth shut.

"Will, is that you?" I called out, feigning grogginess, as if I'd been asleep. "What you doing, man?"

I stepped out in the hallway pulling on a pair

of shorts as I went and closed my bedroom door behind me. I prayed that he'd heard me and wasn't about to shoot me right there, mistaking me for an intruder. But he was at the bottom of the steps.

"Hey, Mack. Sorry did I wake you?"

"Yeah, what the hell? What's going on?" I asked as I started to descend, wanting to put some healthy distance between his daughter, naked in my bed, and Will.

"Fuck, man, your back door is busted in. Your house was dark and I thought some fuckers had broken in. I came to check on you."

"Ah, yeah. That. It was too late to call anyone to come get it fixed. I'll probably just do it myself in the morning. Thanks for checking, though. Nice to have a good neighbor," I said, my tone equal parts friendly and annoyed. Instead of calling the cops or phoning he'd taken it upon himself to let himself in… There was something off about that, and I couldn't work out what it was.

I was in the middle of escorting him to the front door, motioning with my hand when he stopped and studied me. In the partial darkness, with his eyes on me, it felt like I was under a microscope. His stares were like hard pinpricks. He knew I was hiding something from him.

And I began to tense up, ready to spring into action in case he decided, for whatever reason, to charge up the stairs and bust through the door. I couldn't let that happen, I would stop him before he even got close.

But then he grinned, a snake-like, conspiratorial smile. "You've got a girl up there, don't ya?"

I gave him a small shrug. But then checked myself and returned his smile. It would've been suspicious if I didn't play the guy who was getting lucky.

"All right for some. Hey, remind me when is your sister coming around again, she's single still, right? Hasn't found a new husband yet?"

"Yeah right, you think you can date my sister… you'd have to go through me first," I said easing into the banter.

"I never said anything about dating her…"

"Uh, gross man." I pulled the front door open, wanting the conversation to be over, and a rush of night air slipped past us. I needed him to get the hell out of my house. "Anyway, I better get back."

"Of course, can't keep the lady waiting. Who is she anyway?" he said, lingering in the doorway. Couldn't he take a hint and leave?

"No one you know," I replied, keeping my answer brief. I certainly didn't want to give anything away, not right then at any rate. Not when he was armed.

He put up his hands in surrender. "I can take a hint, I'll go. Hey, before I do. I don't suppose you've seen Lola Ray around, have you?"

I studied him before answering, pretending to be thinking if I had. Was he fishing? Was this all just an excuse to see if I would tell him the truth, or trap myself in a lie?

"Nah, can't say that I have." I shook my head for good measure. I should've kept my mouth shut, but stupidly trying to cover my nerves I added, "Isn't she seeing that kid, the football player? Maybe she's with him?"

"Maybe."

He paused running this thought over in his mind, I could see the cogs turning, but all the while he was staring intently at me. Like he was accusing me with his eyes. Or that could've just been my guilt projecting.

"You see, the thing is, her cell keeps going to voicemail," he said and dug his own mobile out of his pocket. Before I could stop him he swiped his thumb across the screen and dialed Lola Ray's number.

I tensed. This was it, I thought. Her phone, wherever it was, upstairs amongst the piles of her clothing she'd taken off in my playroom, would start to ring. The little tone would cry out for attention and Will would hear it through the thin walls and floorboards of my house. He would know the instant it rang on the other end that she was in there. Inside my house… upstairs.

He would know I'd been fucking his little girl. Doing unspeakable things to her.

He would reach for his gun and I'd be forced to do something I hadn't done in a very long time.

I would have to kill again.

Was she worth it?

There was no doubt in my mind that she was. She was everything I never knew I'd been searching for. Though she'd been the one brave enough to seek me out. She'd found me, and I wasn't going to just let her go.

My jaw was tight as all this went through my head in a split second. I'd come to a decision. Will had to die.

But just as I was waiting for Lola Ray's phone to sing out from above, there was just silence.

Will held up his as the call cut out. "See? No answer."

I nodded. Because what else was I to do? I couldn't reassure him that she was okay, safe. Not that he normally cared.

"I have a good mind to find that Sam kid, go round to his house, and drag her home by her hair. I had to fucking fix my own dinner tonight. The ungrateful little cunt."

I bit my tongue and let the bluster in him play out.

"Probably not a good idea. Besides isn't Sam's dad a cop? He won't take kindly if you show up in a rage," I said after a moment of silence. Bluffing. I had no idea if the kid's father was in law enforcement, but it was something that could prevent Will from doing something stupid. "She might not even be there. She's probably fine, maybe having a sleepover? Did she leave you a note? Anyway, I'm sure she'll come home when she's ready. She's a big girl. But I better go…" I said and pointed to the ceiling.

Will nodded and stepped out onto the porch. "Yeah, of course. See you later."

I thanked him again for checking in on the house and closed the door, feeling extremely grateful when I was able to click the lock in place.

For a second I leaned against it, my head pressed hard against the wood. That was too close.

***

"Is he gone?" she asked from the bed, the sheet wrapped around her supple body.

I entered the room fully and went to her. "He's gone."

Slipping beneath the covers I replaced the sheets around her with my arms and pulled her against me. She was smooth and warm and I just wanted to forget the little interruption and sink back into her. But my mind was annoyingly preoccupied. How could this, whatever this was between us, develop into anything more when her father would be a constant source of worry?

She took my head in her hands, her fingertips resting on my temples. "What did he say?"

I shook my head. "It wasn't what he said that's the problem."

"What do you mean?"

"It was the way he looked at me. As if I knew something… like I was hiding something."

She smiled tightly. "Well, you kinda were…"

"That's not the point. He came in here to sniff around. I'm sure of it."

"You're being paranoid. He knows nothing. He's a drunk. A fool. He was probably just worried who's going to cook his next meal."

"Yeah, he was pissed about that. You should've left a note or something…"

"Well I didn't exactly plan tonight."

"We have to be careful in the future."

She nibbled on her lip and I was about to take possession of it when her eyes lit up. "The future?" she broached. "You think we have a future?"

I wasn't one to normally declare my love, or feelings for that matter, after one night of passion, but it was Lola Ray. She was the sunshine in my life, the light I never knew I needed. She gave meaning to it all, and for the second time that evening I knew I never wanted to be without her.

"Mack?"

"We do. But we have to figure out how it's going to work. We really do need to be careful."

"You know we could just kill him," she said, her tone flippant. I stared at her. Was she serious? But then she started to laugh, her face creasing up with a broad smile.

"Your face!" she said, struggling to get her breath back.

"It wasn't funny."

"Oh it was."

I retook hold of her and we lay back on the bed, her head on my chest. "You know, that did actually cross my mind once," I admitted. Truth be told, it was more than once, but I didn't want to scare her.

"Really?" she asked and propped herself up, intrigued.

"Only for a moment," I replied and stroked her face. "After, you know…"

She nodded, her tone turning somber. "When he hit me."

"Yeah. I wanted to kill him for hurting you like that."

She lay back down, her fingers playing on my chest, absently exploring. The room went quiet, as if it were taking a much-needed breath. Then her voice cut through the night, clear as a bell. "I wish you had."

DREAM DADDY

Chapter Twenty Seven
Lola Ray

For the next few weeks I was on an insane high. And it wasn't because of the Christmas holidays, either. The after-effects of being with Mack were beyond what I could have ever expected. I had to be careful though when I was around my father, and for the most part I managed to curb my happiness. He did look at me across the dinner table funny once, staring longer than usual. But even his cold lingering gaze couldn't penetrate and dim what I was feeling. I practically sang, humming to and fro rooms.

And though my father had been watching me more than usual, I had to admit he'd relaxed his stance on my supposed boyfriend, Sam, letting me leave the house more often to go see "him."

Of course, instead of going across town, I was only walking the short distance around the block to spend my evenings with Mack. Sometimes just to make sure that my father was not getting suspicious I batted my eyes at Sam, arranged a date, and had him pick me up at the door. Mack was not entirely pleased with that workaround but if it let us continue seeing each other without his best friend finding out that he was fucking his teenage daughter, then he knew to let it happen. Of course I didn't tell him about the few times that Sam had tried to advance his way along the bases.

It was a necessary evil, and all the while when Sam was kissing me, I was thinking of the next time I'd see Mack.

"You know, there's something really different about you lately," Robin said as she put a French fry into her mouth. She began to chew. She'd been sneaking glances at me all lunch as we ate. She swallowed and continued, "It's like you're a totally new person. You're not a pod person are you? Have aliens taken over your body and you just didn't see fit to tell me?"

I lifted my shoulders in a shrug. "Nothing's changed, not really."

"But it has. I don't know what but it has!" she said insisting on probing me and my life further.

At Mack's command he'd forbidden me from telling her, and I couldn't say that I blamed him. Before, when I was crushing hard on Mack, it might've been safe to let her know, she would've teased me and maybe joined in with my lusting, but telling her about that first night at the club and then what followed shortly after was way off-limits.

However keeping silent hadn't prevented her from speculating and guessing what was up with me every so often. We'd had this same conversation so many times over the last few weeks since I'd lost my virginity… another thing she had no clue about.

"Maybe I'm just maturing," I said, sticking my tongue out.

"As if!"

She went silent, turning her attention to her fries. But I could see she was still trying to puzzle it out. It must have been infuriating for her to sense something was going on and not know what it was. Especially for her, the queen of the rumor mill.

Robin straightened in her chair suddenly, her chest billowing out, putting her best assets forward as a loud cluster of students came in to the cafeteria. It was some of the football team.

And soon enough, as I predicted, Sam was wrapping himself around me, nuzzling into my neck. I let him and pretended he was Mack, transplanting his face onto Sam's in my imagination. It was the only way I got through the times I spent with him.

"There's my girl," he said, finally letting go and sitting down, helping himself to some of my leftovers. I wasn't that hungry anyway. "Are you coming around tonight?"

I turned to him and gave him a saucy smile. I found it was best to always make him think he was on the verge of getting lucky; just one more date, or kiss, or compliment, he would think, before I would give it up to him. He didn't have a chance in hell though. But I still needed to keep him securely on the hook. Especially if I wanted my semi-concocted plan to work. I'd gone over it in my head so many times, keeping it to myself. I just had to hang on a little longer before I could implement it.

"I might be, I haven't decided yet."

"Aww, come on. You promised."

"No I didn't."

"Yeah, last week you did. You haven't been around in ages."

"You're exaggerating, it's only been a few days," I said mentally trying to remember the last time I'd gone on a date with him. But he was right, it had been nearly a week. The previous time I was meant to be with him, I just couldn't stomach it and had given him the excuse that I hadn't been feeling well and instead slinked into Mack's house and had some fun in the playroom.

Sam gave me the sweetest impression of a puppy that he could muster and I was almost tempted to pat him on the head. "Okay, you're right. Can you pick me up later then? I won't be able to stay long, though."

"I won't need long," he replied waggling his eyebrows.

"Dude, that's not something you should brag about," one of his buddies said behind him.

"Shut up, you know what I mean."

Robin's eyes widened and she tried to give me a meaningful look, but I skillfully glanced away. I knew exactly what she was thinking. And I was okay with her thinking it but I knew I wouldn't hear the end of it, either.

She caught my eye, beaming with a huge smile. "You little slut!" she mouthed, then started to laugh. She leaned closer so no one could hear us, "Well, it's about damn time! You're so going to tell me everything later."

I nodded and didn't feel the need to correct her assumption.

The team decided to stay and soon took over our table, the noise escalated but it was a good distraction from my constant thoughts, longing after Mack, letting my imagination run wild.

Everything else, college included, seemed so pointless now that I was with him. I felt like I could probably stay tied up in his playroom forever and be perfectly content.

While Robin was busy flirting with the team's running back and Sam was preoccupied with stuffing his face, finally getting his own tray, I risked putting my plan in motion. "Hey, Sammie," I crooned sweetly in his ear.

"Yeah, baby?"

"Can I borrow your cell for a moment? Mine died."

"Sure, here you go." He didn't give the question a second thought, unlocked it, and handed it over. He turned back to his buddies and I, while under the cover of the table, got to work.

* * *

After spending some time with Sam at his house he dropped me off at home. He was disappointed, of course, like he always was, that the hours never amounted to much of anything. A few kisses here and there, some subtle hints that maybe next time I would be ready. And every single time he fell for it.

As I reached the front porch I turned to wave goodbye. When I spun back around to go into the house I was confronted with a solid wall of muscle. My father was standing, blocking the way inside.

The moment he spoke I knew he was drunk. When he was like that he was my worst nightmare. I never knew what he was going to do.

"What the hell are you so happy about?" he asked as I tried to get by him. But he put up his arm immediately, the doorway completely filled with him now.

"Nothing, Daddy," I said as neutrally as I could. I'd been planning on dumping my things and then making an excuse to pretend to go to Robin's… when instead of course I'd go to Mack's. *But now, with him like this, I may need to change my plans*, I thought.

He let his arm drop and I quickly scooted by. If I made it upstairs, out of his sight before he could start up again, there was a possibility he would forget whatever was bugging him. That he'd forget that I irritated him so much, reminded him of darker times.

But as the door slammed shut and I passed by, there was a sudden painful yank I wasn't expecting. He had hold of my wrist and was keeping me in place.

"You're sleeping with him, aren't you?"

For a split-second Mack's face danced across my vision. My mouth opened to speak but no words came. How had he found out? I'd been so careful, we both had. We both knew what kind of man my father was, the temper he had.

"Answer me! You are aren't you? Just like your mother. A tramp."

What did my mom have to do with this?

"You're sleeping with that kid… you little slut. Don't even think about denying it."

I was careful not to let my relief show, thank god he meant Sam. I could deal with that, or at least I hoped I could.

"I'm not. I promise you, I'm not sleeping with him."

He shook me as if he were trying to rattle the truth from me.

"Don't lie to me! You're always with him! You're going to end up just like her you know. Knocked up… always spreading her legs. Mark my words though, I'll kill you if you get pregnant.

I'm not working my ass off to support and feed another mouth! You ungrateful little bitch. You don't know how lucky you are!"

He grabbed me around the throat and pressed me hard against the wall. "Say something, deny it. I fucking dare you."

I gasped for air. I had no thoughts of telling him he was wrong, not when I had more important things to worry about like breathing. I batted at his hands. "Let me go. You're hurting me."

"I'll fucking break you if you're not careful. Don't make me regret keeping you." He shook his head. His lip curled with distaste and finally he let me go. I fell like a stone to the floor. "Shame me, girl, and I will make you pay. I have a reputation to uphold in this town. You being the town slut won't do you or me any good."

I nodded, showing him that I understood. Tears streamed down my cheeks and I waited for him to retreat into his den before getting up and escaping upstairs to my bedroom.

I fought the urge to tear my whole room apart. The rage that was desperate to be set free was clawing for an outlet. But I knew it would've done no good. Acting out would only get me in more trouble.

I had to be smart.

I had to stick to the plan. And if that meant bringing it forward then that was what I was going to do.

* * *

That night I let Mack know that I wasn't able to get out to see him, and instead would be around the following day. With it being Saturday I was able to spend the whole afternoon and evening with him, and sometimes stayed over too, pretending to be at Robin's for a sleepover. Those times, though, were few and far between, especially if my father had recently blown up, like he had the previous night.

But regardless I was in Mack's arms again. Grateful that I didn't have to pretend at all when I was with him.

"You're quiet today," he said. "I didn't go too far this time, did I?"

I remembered the pleasurable torture he'd performed on me earlier that afternoon. Strapped into thigh cuffs and hoisted up into the air, suspended from the ceiling, he'd reamed me hard, surprising me as well when he slipped a buttplug up my ass without telling me about it first. He said he was getting me ready for when he brought out the big guns. Whatever that meant. But I shook my head.

"No, it's not that. Today was wonderful, *Daddy*," I said smiling and raising my eyebrows at him suggestively. Little did he know that word meant more than ever now. I continued to lazily stroke his arm, dreaming of a future with him. I didn't want to think of the past anymore, and though I thought to ask him so many times about his own past, what he'd done, I'd kept my mouth shut. The past was better left there, but I knew knowing what I did about him would help me. It would help us become free. It was a calculated risk, but I was betting on it working.

"You have to tell me if you ever want to stop…" he said with a hint of worry in his voice.

"And I will if it comes to that. But I haven't so far. I love everything you do to me."

He bent his head and found my lips. Every kiss with him felt like the first. And I had to believe that this was what it meant to be in love. I didn't dare say the words yet though.

"Then what is it? What's wrong?"

He sat up and snapped on the nightstand lamp and really looked at me as I remained silent. *Should I tell him?* I fought the instinct to let it all out.

His eyes narrowed and for a moment I thought he was mad that I was holding out on him but he was not looking in my eyes, his gaze had travelled down to my neck. My hand reached to cover the place he was inspecting.

His fists bunched up into hard lumps and his jaw became rigid. "Who did that to you?" he managed to growl. "That bruise wasn't there the other day. And I know I didn't do it."

I let my head fall forward but he lifted it back up and peeled away my hand that tried to hide the developing marks on my neck.

"Lola Ray," he said his voice turning soft, "Baby girl, tell me. Was it Sam?" He said Sam's name in hope, as if Sam would be the easier of the two to deal with but I think he already knew who had squeezed my neck almost to the point where I couldn't breathe. Mack knew who was responsible. He waited a beat then tried again. "Will?"

I nodded, confirming his suspicions.

He got up from the bed and I watched as he paced around the room. "I'm going to kill him… I have to," he muttered. I quickly got out of bed and went to him, wrapped my arms around him, and made him stop moving.

"You can't. I can't lose you," I said, knowing it would be the end of us if he murdered my father in cold blood. He didn't know that I knew about his past. He didn't know that I'd Googled his name, curiosity getting the best of me after a while, and finally found out the reason why he'd suddenly turned up back in his hometown.

His eyes found mine and perhaps he was wondering if I did indeed know about what he'd done more than five years ago, all to protect his sister.

"Okay, you're right. That doesn't mean we have to stay. We can leave. We can run away. I will take you anywhere, wherever you want to go. I have enough saved now that I won't have to find work for a little while… Lola, baby, we could be on the road tomorrow. Away from him, away from everything. Together."

He smiled, so full of hope that I would say yes. But I shook my head. It was everything I wanted him to say, and it was my dream to leave, to get away from my father. But it would only be temporary.

"No. He'll find us."

His beautiful face fell, crushed that this was the one time when I would say no to him. I took his large, rough hand in mine and led him back to the bed in which we'd shared so many nights.

"He won't."

"He will, trust me. I don't know how but he always does. He found me the last time I tried to run away… before I met you."

"I didn't know you—"

"Why would you? You weren't here. It was years ago, I was fifteen the last time I tried."

He swallowed and held me in his arms. "How many times have you tried?"

"Alone? Three."

"And each time he brought you back?"

I nodded. "And each time that he did, he beat me harder for it."

Mack's eyes lit up with renewed fury again. "This time will be different. I'll be with you. We'll have money."

"It didn't work for my mom…"

He frowned and tried to understand my meaning. "But he didn't bring her back, he didn't find her?"

I took a deep breath and struggled to keep the tears at bay. It had been a while since I recalled the exact events that took place what seemed a lifetime ago.

"She left with a man called Stewart Wicks."

"I thought she left alone, abandoned you both?

At least that's what Will said," Mack interrupted.

"No, there was Stewart, my mom… And me. She took me with her too. She didn't leave me behind. She never would've left me."

"Okay so, he found you?"

I nodded.

"He found us all."

"I don't understand. If he found all of you, why did he only bring you back? Where's your mom?"

I nodded again and wiped away the tears.

"She never would've left me," I repeated. "She would've come back for me at the motel… and that's why I know she's dead. He killed them. Both of them. That's how I know we can't run. He'll find us, he'll kill me this time. Most of all he'll kill you. And you can't kill him because then I'll lose you too. You'll go back to prison. No we have to do this my way. You have to trust me."

DREAM DADDY

Chapter Twenty Eight
Mack

It was hard to concentrate on work when all I could think about was what Lola Ray had revealed the night before. Had Will truly killed his wife and the man with whom she tried to run away with? And how on earth did Lola Ray know about me and my past?

I wondered what it would've taken for Lola Ray's mom to decide to leave. But if the bruises that occasionally appeared on her daughter's skin were anything to go by, I didn't have to imagine too hard. There was something not quite right with Will and for Lola Ray's sake I wished I'd spotted it sooner. But he'd fooled me, just like he had the rest of the town.

Most of them worshiped him, except maybe

his crew who he worked to the bone. But overall he was a businessman who bent over backward to make sure his men had enough work. Many felt sorry for him, believing he was unnecessarily abandoned by his wife. I could see it now, the whole town rallying around the one-time golden boy who'd driven us to two state championships. But it just went to show that one never knew what truly went on behind closed doors.

A man like me, with his own secrets, should've appreciated that. I should've picked up on it sooner. But instead I'd taken him at face value like everyone else. He was an old friend… And yet there I was working for a ruthless killer.

In some ways we were the same, we both craved control and I had to wonder where the line was. I too had killed… gone to prison for it, did my time. But the circumstances were different. I'd been protecting someone I loved… I hadn't meant for it to go so far. One wrong punch and my sister's abusive husband never woke up again.

But Will had yet to pay for what he'd done, and for everything he'd put Lola Ray through. I could barely contemplate what she'd had to endure living alone in the same house as that monster. And no matter what she said, there was only one way we'd be able to secure our future together. And that was with him gone.

I was fully prepared to make him disappear. But for some reason she was reluctant about making that happen as well. I couldn't understand why.

"You joining us for Christmas Eve, Mack?"

"What?" I asked, startled. Will had managed to creep up on me while I'd been deep in thought.

"Saturday. The game. And Lola Ray will be making a fine spread."

You would be forcing her to, you mean, I wanted to spit at him. But I reeled in my desire to smash his face in right there on the construction site. It would be the ideal place to do it, of course. Most of the men had already clocked off, the pits were already dug. All it would take would be some fresh concrete and a bit of time…

"Mack? I need to know if she has to make more."

"Oh right. Then yeah I'll be there."

"Good stuff, I might need backup besides," he said with an amiable chuckle. Was his persona all just a farce? I found myself scrutinizing his every word, movement, and facial expression. All of it had to be fake, an act.

"Backup?"

"Yeah, I've invited that little piss-ant of hers over too."

I frowned, unable to believe my ears. After Lola Ray had recounted what Will had said to her, accusing of her of sleeping with Sam Black, this was the last thing I expected of him. Putting his foot down and forbidding her to see him (and blowing what little cover we had) would've been my first thought. But inviting her pseudo-boyfriend around to the house to spend time with him, eat, and watch the game with him was just peculiar. Out of character, one could say. He had to be up to something.

"Her boyfriend? How come?"

"Gotta keep an eye on them somehow," he said with an indifferent shrug. "Maybe even put the fear of god into him too."

"Yeah I guess," I replied. But if Will was up to something then I had to look out for the kid who'd inadvertently helped keep my relationship with Lola Ray a secret. "You should just tell her to break up with him. Be done with it."

He raised his eyebrow at me. "Why do you say that?"

I shrugged as if it meant nothing to me what he did either way. "Dunno, there's something off about the kid is all. She's better off without him. Concentrate on her studies, you know? Besides it'll mean more hot wings for me on Saturday."

I grinned, hoping that would do the trick. Sam Black didn't deserve whatever Will had planned for him, especially not now that I knew what kind of man Will actually was, and if that meant that Lola Ray and I would have to be more careful, find a new patsy as it were, then so be it. Will didn't look too convinced and his continuing stares began to make me uneasy.

But then just as I was about to open my mouth again, add to my argument, try to bolster it up a bit, he thankfully clapped me on the back. "You might be right. But might as well give him a chance, though. He's a Weyworth QB… he can't be all bad."

I wondered if he recognized the irony of his own words. He was just like Sam as a kid, held his position as team captain too, and look how he turned out—a sadistic wife- and child-beater.

After that conversation I was more driven than ever to come up with a foolproof plan that would put us in the clear. The New Year was looming, *I could wait 'til then*, I thought. I knew Will had more out-of-town trips he had to take after the holidays were over and everyone was properly back at work. It would be the perfect opportunity for him to just disappear.

There would be a nice kind of symmetry to it as well. Just as he'd made his wife, Lola Ray's mom, vanish without a trace, I'd do the same to him. Lola Ray wouldn't even have to know. She was adamant that it was the wrong move. She didn't want me to get involved, or at least that's how it seemed. But once it was done, I was sure she would be relieved. Then again, I didn't need to tell her it'd been me. The less people who knew, the better, the more I could protect her.

I mused about it more on the drive home from work. I could even make it look like an accident so she wouldn't be suspicious. Of course she would have an inkling that I'd done it. What with our conversations on the subject. In hindsight, it may have been a mistake to reveal to her my desire to kill Will, but there was no taking it back now. Besides I'd wanted us to be honest with each other… she'd been honest with me. And that was the way I liked it.

Speak of the devil, I thought as my phone buzzed. A message from my girl. She was definitely mine now, that was for sure. I waited until I was inside to respond.

Baby Girl > Heard you're coming to dinner on Christmas Eve ;)

Mack > Yeah, but don't you get any ideas. We'll have to be even more careful. He's going to be watching you like a hawk.

Baby Girl > Spoil sport. Can't wait to see you though.

Mack > Not coming around tonight? I was thinking of tying you up and seeing how much cock you could swallow.

Baby Girl > Would love to. Can't. He's got me on lockdown. Literally.

Mack > ?

Baby Girl > If I tell you, you can't get mad.

Mack > ???!

Baby Girl > He's installed a padlock on my door. I can't get out.

Mack > WTF…

I squeezed the delicate phone made of glass and metal in my hand.

Baby Girl > It's ok… don't do anything stupid. Promise me?

Mack > This has to stop.

Baby Girl > Mack, promise me.

In the middle of my living room I roared until my throat hurt. I was tempted to throw the cell as hard as I could. Instead I grabbed hold of the nearest lamp and threw that against the wall. "Motherfucker!"

It took me a moment or two to calm down. By then I'd received a few more texts, pleas really, from her.

Baby Girl > Promise me!

Baby Girl > We have to be patient.

Baby Girl > He's only doing this because Sam turned up the other day and he thinks he losing control over me. He knew grounding me wouldn't work. But I'm okay. Really. At least in here he can't hit me.

Baby Girl > Tell me you're not thinking about doing anything stupid.

I gritted my teeth and let my fingers tap out a response.

Mack > Of course I am! I'm thinking about all the ways I'm going to kill him.

And I was too. I'd only killed one man… and really that was an accident. But now I was contemplating all the ways I could end Will Saxton's life right then, that night, without any planning, and get away with it. I could make it look like a suicide. Get him drunk… borrow his gun. It wouldn't take long. Or I could fix the breaks on his truck. That thing had seen better days. It wouldn't come as a shock if the break line deteriorated and failed one day. Or even better,

I could make it look like a break-in. I could be violent then. Make him scream. Make sure I left no trace or evidence behind. My fingerprints were already all around his house. I'd pretend I'd heard the noise from my own house and came over to see what had happened. But I would of course have been too late. *Will would've, by then, sadly bled out on the floor*, I thought sarcastically.

Baby Girl > Mack…

But no, I couldn't do that. Could I? It would look too suspicious surely? Especially with my record. I sighed.

Mack > Fine. You win. I'll rescue you from this nightmare one day soon, though. Mark my words.

The New Year couldn't come soon enough.

DREAM DADDY

Chapter Twenty Nine
Lola Ray

The kitchen was stifling. I'd been up since the early hours of the morning getting all the dishes for the day prepared. Chopping vegetables, baking all manner of goodies, and not to mention roasting the turkey, making sure it was basted on the hour every hour.

I'd made good progress before my father had even gotten out of bed and came down for his first coffee of the day. But did he even praise me on what a good job I was doing? Nope.

And instead of offering to help—god forbid he lifted a finger on this special day—he grabbed what he could for breakfast and moved into the den, ready for a day in front of the TV, getting drunk, and watching football.

As I looked around the kitchen—there were bowls and food everywhere, which of course I would have to clean up too—I sighed. All this effort was in vain. It would all go to waste. But at least it looked good.

Going through the motions was a necessary evil, though; I had to look like I was doing my part. I had the day all planned and I wasn't going to let the lack of a Christmas dinner stand in the way of getting my way.

I was surprised at how calm I was too. I was expecting to feel all kinds of nerves, but my hands were rock solid. It was as if they were determined not to let me down.

"Sam's here," my father called from the other room. And for a moment I didn't recognize his voice. He sounded happy for once. *It had to do with the time of year*, I told myself. Christmases for my father were always a big thing, so much so it had become a tradition to celebrate it a day early. Like he just couldn't wait. But though it was a big deal for him, it had always been a holiday I dreaded, what with my mom not being there anymore. She'd been the one to make it special for me... not him.

Sam entered the kitchen and shrugged off his thick jacket, then peeled off his beanie. He was a little early, but I could deal with that.

It could even be a good thing, I thought. Bring up the timetable and get it all over and done with before the game even started perhaps.

Sam grinned at all the food.

"Hope you brought an appetite," I said with a coy smile, then licked the spoon I'd just used to stir some cake batter.

"Oh you know I did."

He crossed the kitchen and wrapped his arms around me from behind. I feigned a little squirm, protesting at his intimacy, in case my father came in and saw, but in fact my real intention was to do the complete opposite. I let my ass brush against his crotch. I needed him worked up into a frenzy, pliable…

I let my spoon drop into the bowl and turned to face him. My arms hooked around his neck and I looked at him. I could see I wouldn't have much of a problem, his eyes betrayed how much he wanted to fuck me.

"Hey," I protested as his hands began to explore further down the sides of my waist and then spreading across the tops of my cheeks. "We have to be careful," I said in a breathy whisper, but didn't attempt to move away from his grasp.

"I know," he replied, with a groan, "but I haven't

seen you for days. Besides there's something I want to give you for Christmas…"

"Oh really?" I tilted my head to the side and looked at him through come-hither eyes. I lowered my voice and let my finger caress the back of his neck. "Is it something big?" If that wasn't enough to get him all hot and bothered, I didn't know what else would.

"God, you drive me crazy…"

He leaned in for a kiss and I opened up ready for him.

"Oh, sorry…" a voice behind us apologized. I recognized it at once and my heart sank. It was one thing to have to pretend that Sam was my boyfriend, with all the privileges that that entailed, but to have Mack see what I was forced to do was another matter. I turned to look at him but he'd already left the room.

"You don't think he'll say anything, do you?

"Who? Mack? I doubt it…"

Sam grinned again. "Okay then, where were we?" Sam quickly glanced toward the door behind me, making sure the coast was totally clear this time, then gave me a hard squeeze, bringing my body up close with his. Sam lowered his head and I had no other choice but to kiss him again.

I had to play along. Even if it was the last thing in the world I wanted... I just had to remember I was doing this all for me and Mack.

I let myself get lost in the kiss, pretending that it would be over soon.

Sam's hands snaked up my waist, to my blouse, searching for an entry point. I thought he was never going to find one, but finally his fingers skimmed my torso and proceeded higher. Clumsy. Too impatient. Totally different to how Mack handled me. His touch was nothing like Mack's experienced caresses but I found myself moaning to encourage him along.

"We shouldn't," I said, but I didn't push him away. I wanted him to continue...

"Shh. But maybe we should go to your room?"

I shook my head. "No, you're banned from my room, remember."

Sam locked his lips on my neck, he was trying his best, but it was a far cry from what I felt when Mack and I made out. Roughly, as if he couldn't wait anymore—he had, after all, been waiting months to get to where he wanted to be—he grabbed hold of my breasts from beneath my shirt and mashed them together.

I gasped and though it wasn't exactly the right

time, he'd surprised me and my elbow knocked the bowl off the counter.

"Shit," Sam cried as it landed with a thud and sent batter everywhere. Unfortunately it didn't smash, but I hoped it'd made a loud enough noise to get the attention of my father in the other room.

"Doesn't matter, don't stop," I said, pretending that it was inconsequential. But Sam was frozen in place, waiting to see if anyone was going to come and see what was happening. When he was satisfied my father wasn't coming to investigate, he gave me a wolfish grin.

My heart sank.

The whole point of this little exercise was to break my father's good mood, to get him angry...

Sam pulled me to him again and I was forced to continue where we'd left off. He spun me around and pushed me against the wall. I hadn't expected him to become this insistent. A little kissing, some fondling, I thought would be all that would happen. But I'd pushed him too far, held out too long, and now he was determined to get his hands in my pants.

They were already between my thighs, trying to pry them apart. He thought I was playing, making it difficult for him. But the last thing I wanted was him anywhere near me.

Suddenly the pressure of his hands and his body were gone and I opened my eyes to see Sam being shoved across to the other side of the room. I expected to see my father's face glaring back at me, but instead it was Mack.

"What the hell!" Sam foolishly cried out.

"What's going on in here?" my father said, finally making an appearance. He looked from me, to Sam, then to Mack for answers. But it was clear he understood. He didn't need Mack to explain.

"He was getting a little handsy with your daughter, Will," Mack said through gritted teeth. I could barely look at him, partly ashamed, partly playing a role. But I could feel him glaring at me and I urged him to stop. He couldn't act like a jealous boyfriend, he couldn't give my father a reason to be suspicious.

"Was he now?" my father said, his tone menacing. "Think we need to have a little talk, boy." He grabbed Sam by the back of the neck and pushed him out of the kitchen. "I invite you over for Christmas dinner and you disrespect me… I should throw you out, but I guess it is Christmas…"

Their conversation faded out as they moved into the den. My father would probably give him a good talking to, lay some ground rules for now. Scare him a little. It was perfect.

But Mack hadn't moved a muscle. He stayed in the kitchen, stuck like glue in the middle of the room and simply stared at me without saying a word.

"Mack," I whispered, pleading with him to understand. But I hadn't told him about any of my plans so he had no reason to.

He shook his head and put his hand over his mouth, stroking his beard as if debating whether or not to let out exactly what he wanted to say.

But he lowered his hand in defeat and headed for the back door to go outside.

I let him go. He would cool down. While he was away I left the kitchen, skirting past my father and Sam, who gave me a miserable shrug, and headed upstairs to the bathroom.

It was now or never, I thought, as I recovered what I'd hidden in there earlier. Once I did this last thing, there would be no going back. I paused to look at myself in the mirror. The person who was reflected back looked older, worn out. But determined. I had to be strong. I was doing the right thing, for all of us. I wouldn't end up like my mom, she had the right idea to try and get out. But unlike her I was going to be successful.

Instead of staying upstairs and hiding, I forced myself to go back down into the kitchen and let out a heavy breath, then started to clean up the mess on the floor. The bowl made a solid clink as I put it in the sink and I was just about to get back on track, listing all the things I needed to do and still get finished before the turkey was done, when a hand captured my neck, fingers dug into my flesh, squeezing and almost cutting off my oxygen. Keeping me in place. I was unable to move.

"You and me we need to talk now..." His tone was furious. Livid and beyond consoling. He pushed my body hard against the edge of the counter. Trapping me between it and his equally rigid frame, the outline of his cock hard and unyielding against my ass. "Actually, it's probably best if you don't speak." His other hand dug its way up and between my thighs, under my skirt, and tried to force my legs open. With the nudge of his foot at my ankle, almost kicking me, I had to take a step apart.

His hand left my neck and travelled up my throat to my mouth.

Just before he clamped his fingers across my lips, I whispered, "*Daddy.*"

Chapter Thirty
Mack

Something had snapped in me and I couldn't control myself. I thought taking some air would've helped but it merely made it worse. It was like stepping into a freezing ice bath. The shock of it woke me up and I knew I was done; I'd had enough pretending. I didn't want to hide anymore.

She was humming as I came back inside, and it tipped me over the edge. She had to know she was mine, and flaunting her pretend little relationship with *him*, right in front of my face… well she had to know she would be punished for it. And there was no time like the present.

She cried out a little, a whimper that tried to escape through the fingers I held over her mouth, as I yanked her panties to the side. I wasn't gentle, far from it. I pushed her against the sink, my hips pinning her in place and sought the entrance of her cunt. She squirmed but knew it was no use. In a matter of seconds I thrust two fingers inside her and her head tilted back, pressing against my chest.

"I don't know what the fuck you're playing at, but it has to stop," I grunted as I drove my fingers deeper inside her. Her eyes were wild, darting back and forth between me and the door.

She tried to speak but I wouldn't let her. I gave her a shake of my head and pressed harder on her mouth. "I don't care if they hear or see. I'm done hiding, Lola Ray. You're mine, no one else's. Do you hear me?"

She nodded and swallowed.

For a second I dropped my hand from her mouth and moved her to the island counter, spinning her around and then slammed her chest down onto its surface so she was nice and bent over. Her arms went wide upon it, and she turned her head so her cheek pressed up against it too.

With fast fingers I unbuckled my belt and pulled my cock out. I didn't think I'd ever been so hard in my life. Not even our first time together when she was tied up. That time she knew in a way what she was getting herself into, she'd put herself on that table. But now, this hadn't been her idea, she hadn't prepared herself for it.

Finding her sweet hole again, I made sure her panties wouldn't get in the way and were pulled to the side, no doubt digging into her the more I held onto them.

I leaned over her. "You've made Daddy angry," I said, trying to rein in the force of my tone. "Don't you ever do that again. You're going to break up with him. Today. Or else…"

She dared to open her mouth. "Or else what?" she gasped defiantly.

My cock rammed into her and I just managed to cover her mouth as she cried out. I rocked back and forth furiously, fucking her with every inch I had. Her moans were low and I was worried that maybe they could be heard from the den, but the game had started earlier so perhaps the sound from the TV would cover the noise. But then again, I almost wished Will walked in and saw me spearing his daughter from behind. At least then it would be over, we'd be able to move forward. Because for the last few months, as wonderful as my time with Lola Ray had been, I felt stuck in time. With her I suddenly saw a new future. No longer was it bleak, but full of possibility. And I wanted it so badly I'd dreamed of killing Will to make it a possibility.

I clawed my fingers through her hair and I felt all my muscles begin to tighten. She let out a forced exhale with each violent thrust. Surprising me, she reached for my hand, pulling it down from her head and putting one of my fingers into her mouth and began to suck.

It's that last image that made me come undone. I bit my tongue, containing the growl I wanted to emit, and continued to fuck her as I unloaded inside her sweet little pussy.

The sweat dripped off me when I was done and I eased from her.

She was limp and almost slumped to the floor, but I took her in my arms and kept her upright. The way she looked at me then it made me want to take her again and again.

"You're jealous," she whispered, then added, "I didn't mean for you to see that."

"But I did, and I can't ever again. I think we should leave. Tonight. I'm done hiding what I feel for you. And I'll do anything to keep you safe. He won't find us if we leave the country."

She patted my chest, contemplating my words. A sliver of hope peeked through, *she's thinking about it.*

"You don't want to be here, I know you don't,"

I said pushing the issue further. She bowed her head, then after a second of thought, lifted it up to catch my eye.

"What is it?" I asked and smoothed my thumb over her cheek. She wasn't normally this quiet. "What are you hiding?"

"Mack!" Will's voice boomed around the house and for a delirious second I thought he was just celebrating a touchdown or something. But when he shouted for the second time I could feel the blood drain from my face. The moment I'd been waiting for had arrived. Somehow, even though he sounded like he was upstairs, calling my name, he knew about me and Lola Ray.

As if on cue, Lola Ray stepped away from my side and before I could wonder why I heard loud thuds, the house began to shake, as Will—at least I thought it was him—ran down the stairs. From the kitchen the noise was partially muffled and I went toward Will's continuing yells. It probably wasn't the best idea, I should've been turning and fleeing in the other direction, but I was a fighter and I was going to make sure I fought for Lola Ray.

But as I was just about to step through into the dining room that led to the den, Sam came bolting through and nearly knocked me over.

"Grab him! Grab the little son of bitch!" Will shouted, following shortly after. "Mack, grab him!"

I blinked trying to process what was happening. Will wasn't accusing me, he wasn't after *me*. And without thinking, my meaty arm shot out and caught Sam before he could reach the back door of the kitchen.

I held him in place as he struggled against me. "He's crazy! Let me go!"

"Will, what the fuck is going on?" I said, ignoring Sam's attempts to throw me off. I didn't register it then, but later as I replayed the scene back in my head, I remembered Lola Ray on the other side of the kitchen against the wall. I thought she was trying to stay out of the way, making herself small. But she had been smiling. Pleased at what was happening.

"That's what I'd like to know," Sam said, but though he tried to say it with confidence, his words were quiet.

"Just keep him there!" Will said as he strode over to Lola Ray. He slapped her hard. The smile was no longer there. He had her by the throat.

"Will, what the fuck are you doing? Stop it!" I was about to let Sam go and go to her rescue. I would've done anything to make him stop squeezing her neck like that.

Without missing a beat, or removing his hand, he turned to me and Sam and pointed what I thought was his finger. "That little fucker has got her pregnant!"

"What?" Sam said.

From Will's outstretched hand he launched something that spun in the air and clattered to the floor.

He turned back to Lola Ray. "You just couldn't keep your legs together could you, you piece of trash. You slut! You're as stupid as your mother."

In shock, I watched as the long, thin, plastic pregnancy test that had been in Will's hand only moments before slide toward me. It was positive.

Lola Ray was pregnant?

"So fucking stupid, you didn't think I would find out did you? But you're an idiot, you left it in the trash." Will laughed cruelly.

I tried to take in the news but it was like trying to fit a square peg into a round hole. It just wouldn't fit or line up properly. *She's pregnant?* How could I not have known? And if she was… after what I'd seen earlier that day, how could I even know it was mine. I looked to Sam. I still maintained my hold on him and it would've been easy to snap his neck. Had he fucked what was mine? Had she lied to me all this time?

None of it was making any sense. And for a second another possibility entered my muddled head. Maybe it was all a ruse… was the test fake? Was this what she meant when she'd said to trust her?

Will still had Lola Ray in a tight grasp and I tried to catch her eye. I needed to know what the hell all this was about. I needed to know she hadn't pulled the wool over my eyes.

Did I even know her at all? Had I been about to risk everything for a girl who had been deceiving me all along? I couldn't understand her motives… if only Will would let her go and we could talk.

"Will, let her go. We can figure this out."

"I didn't touch her!" Sam claimed and began to struggle again. He must've been in as much shock as I was.

"Will, I won't tell you again, let her go." He turned to look at me, astonished that I would tell him what to do.

"Not until I'm finished with the whore."

Chapter Thirty One
Lola Ray

His hands around my throat were so different from the feeling I experienced when Mack had his around me. My father seemed intent on squeezing the life out of me. He wanted to see me in pain, to cry... and in a way Mack had wanted the same too, but there was a big difference between them. In Mack's eyes I saw adoration, affection, maybe even love, while in contrast as I stared helplessly at the man who raised me, all I saw was hate. He wanted to kill me. He wanted me to die. But a part of me didn't understand why he didn't just let me go when he clearly didn't want me. He could've been rid of me years ago. He didn't need to come after me when I'd tried to run away. No, instead he'd felt the need to bring me back again and again and essentially torture me. Why?

The question withered away as I began to feel lightheaded. I couldn't breathe and while it was tempting to let go, there was someone else I lived for. My eyes swiveled to Mack, his face unreadable for a change. Maybe my whole plan had been a mistake. I hadn't really expected my father to go off the deep end at me and not Sam… but now that he had, I had no other choice but to fight back.

I had my baby to protect.

Mine and Mack's love child. A baby who would never know the evils of his or her grandfather. My baby would be loved, loved by the daddy of my dreams. But as I continued to stare at Mack, my confidence began to falter. He'd heard that I was pregnant, hadn't he? And yet his eyes were sad. That hadn't exactly been the way I'd wanted to announce it to him, but now that it was out in the open, where were the smiles? Where was the joy? He was supposed to be happy, over the moon.

Instead, as he looked back at me, his gaze was cold. There was no love in those eyes.

Regardless, I wasn't going to let my father kill me without a fight. I began to claw at the arm he had locked onto my neck, raking my nails down his flesh, scoring deep red marks into it. He winced but held on.

"Stop that," he warned snarling so close to my face I could smell the stale beer he'd been drinking since the morning. Not to mention the vodka I'd slipped into it, spiking the bottles I brought him. His voice went low so only I could hear, and he smiled. "I should've killed you when I had the chance, all those years ago." But then he leaned back and looked to the other two people in the room and laughed. "And she's not even mine."

With everything that was happening I was hardly able to digest this new information.

He grinned and bellowed out a laugh.

"Your face," he said, "you actually look disappointed."

"I don't understand—" I managed to squeak out and for a moment he eased up his hold. Mack and Sam's stunned faces disappeared into the distance as I tried to wrap my head around what my father—or was he?—had revealed.

"You silly bitch. Are you that stupid? Do I have to spell it out for you?"

"You're not my father?"

"Oh look, I think she's finally getting it."

"Then why…"

My head was buzzing with conflicting thoughts, as well as the throbbing pain.

"You're not her father?" Mack chimed in, but Will ignored him.

I couldn't think of him as my dad anymore, and in a way it all began to make sense.

"A missing wife is one thing. That could easily be explained away. And really I didn't even have to lie that much. She did run off with that schmuck. But a missing kid? A kid who was supposed to be my daughter? It would've looked odd, don't you think, if you hadn't returned and I hadn't kicked up a fuss to find you? Missing kids always got attention… too much. I couldn't risk it."

"So you—"

"Yeah so I brought you back. But how do you repay me? You turn into a fucking slut just like her!" With his last words he shoved me against the wall like a rag doll. "If you think you're going to keep that baby and make a mockery out of me and what I've done for you, you have another thing coming."

I stared at him defiantly and clenched my fists. He wasn't going to touch the life growing inside me and just as I was about to fight back, Will was pushed back away from me. Mack's broad back was in front of me, shielding me from Will's anger.

"You don't want to do this, Will," Mack said as he blocked every attempt Will made to get at me, pushing him back again and again. Not being overly aggressive, instead acting like a deflector.

"Move god damn it, this has nothing to do with you!"

"You're drunk, Will. You're not thinking straight."

For a tense moment I thought that maybe Will might actually back down—break a habit of a lifetime—but thankfully his anger was renewed when Sam, full of confusion, interrupted Mack's attempts to calm Will.

"But I never touched her… I mean we kissed, but I never… She can't be pregnant. We never slept together. The baby can't be mine."

We all turned to stare at him. Sam shook his head as if that would help convince Will and Mack. And I couldn't let him say much more without ruining the powder keg that was about to blow.

"You liar!" I shouted.

DREAM DADDY

Chapter Thirty Two
Mack

Will and I both turned to look at Lola Ray. She'd just gone and landed poor Sam in it. There was no way Will was going to stand down without a fight. But at the same time, my heart shattered into a million pieces. She betrayed me, tore down everything I thought we'd built up together—the trust, the love. It was all gone now. Behind my back, whether she was doing it to keep our relationship a secret or not, she'd slept with Sam. Made a baby…

Yet still there was a part of me that didn't want to believe it. Clung to the hope that it was all a big misunderstanding. That if there was a baby, it was mine. Mine to love, and protect, and cherish. There was something so exciting about that thought. A baby with her represented a new fresh start, but if it wasn't mine, what then? If she'd slept with someone else… surely it was over.

She wouldn't meet my gaze as I stared openly at her.

Will chuckled. "See, even the little slut admits it! Are you going to deny it now, huh?"

Will got round me, I was too preoccupied sorting through my thoughts and sending questioning glances at Lola Ray. He advanced across the room to where Sam was standing. Sam should've cut his losses and ran out the door the moment I let go of him, but for some inexplicable reason the fool had stayed.

"I promise you, Mr. Saxton, it's not true. I wouldn't lie to you. Not after what you said before."

The poor kid was shaking like a leaf, but he managed to stand tall and stick to his convictions.

"So you deny it?"

"Of course I do!"

I was too late to notice the gun Will had pulled from behind his back, it must've been tucked into his waistband. But now it was pointed directly at Sam's head. Granted Will was swaying a bit, his drunken ass not able to hold the gun as steady as he would've liked. But it still tracked Sam's movements.

"Fuck!"

"Are you going to fucking deny it now?"

"Oh god, oh god," Sam muttered, his hands up as if that would help him.

"Will, put the gun down," I said slowly, trying to get close to him. But he wasn't having any of that. For as drunk as he was he knew where I was too. He pointed a finger in my direction without taking his eyes off Sam.

"Don't even think about it, Mack. This won't take a minute."

Lola Ray shuffled behind me, edging around so she could watch what was happening. I turned to her. "What the hell have you done?" I hissed.

"Even with a gun to your head you're going to stand there and lie to me?" Will shouted, continuing on his crusade. He was out of his mind, why on earth did he care when it was clear to everyone that he couldn't give two shits about Lola Ray?

"It's not true," Sam wept.

"It is," Lola Ray announced, twisting the knife, "check his phone. All the proof you need is on there!"

"What?" Sam cried.

"Fuck," I muttered and ran a hand over my face. This was a nightmare. How had this day gotten so out of control?

"Mack, check his pockets and grab his phone. I wanna see if the slut is telling the truth."

Will swung the gun on me when I didn't move. "Now!"

I had no choice but to sidle up to Sam, reach into his back pocket to retrieve his cell, then used his thumb to unlock it since it had one of those fancy fingerprint scanners.

As I scrolled to the photo app, my stomach dropped as I began to piece it all together. I knew exactly what I was going to find.

"Hurry up! We don't have all day!" Will insisted.

Sam peered over my shoulder, his eyes tracking the movement of each photo as it zoomed by.

As soon as I hit upon the pay dirt he let out a desperate whimper.

"I swear to god, I did not take those!"

"Show me," Will called a few paces away, the gun had obviously gotten a little harder to keep level and had dipped down a fraction. But it was still pointed at Sam and his chest.

I shook my head in disbelief. Why had she done this? Why had she taken the photos I'd snapped of her and planted them on Sam's phone? Granted they were some of the tamer shots of our activities—her naked, spread-eagle on my bed, her on all fours looking seductively over her shoulder—but her face was clearly visible in every single one of them. There was no doubt it was her.

"Show me!"

With the threat of the gun on us, I lifted the phone so Will could see the screen. He let out a bark of surprise.

"She's a slut, but at least she's not a liar," he said.

"But I didn't…"

"Are you still going to deny it?" Will asked interrupting Sam, his tone full of menace and I wanted to urge Sam to choose his next words carefully. But it wouldn't have mattered either way. He kept quiet. It was Will who continued to speak. "I didn't think so."

The sound of the gun going off was practically deafening in the kitchen. The ceramic of the tile reverberated the sound back and forth, multiple times over. It was as if more than one shot had been fired, and perhaps there had been.

I was too busy trying to figure it out. And Lola Ray's screams, accompanying the madness, certainly didn't help either.

Without thinking I charged at Will and knocked the gun out of his hand. But I was far, far too late. Sam was already down. Blood was seeping from him. As I wrestled with Will, trying to get control and subdue him, I shouted at Lola Ray to call the cops, an ambulance… anyone.

Will was strong, even when he was drunk, a wild animal, and managed to land a few punches that had me dazed. I started to believe my only real chance of getting out of there alive was that gun. But I couldn't spot where it had skidded. Instead I was forced to lay into my best friend. We traded countless punches and it was only when Lola Ray stepped forward that we were forced to take a breath and drop our fists.

"Stop it, or I will shoot you," she said, her little voice trembling. For a moment I thought she was directing her command at me, but as my vision cleared I saw her shaky arm was angled a little to my right. Pointed at Will.

"You won't shoot," he said and laughed at her.

But he couldn't see the seriousness in her eyes. Her once bright eyes had faded, twisted… she was ready to pull the trigger.

"Lola Ray," I whispered, trying to get her attention, and scrambled to my feet. And I almost cheered with relief when she looked at me, a single tear making its way down her cheek. She wasn't completely gone. She was still in there. And I couldn't let her lose herself. I couldn't allow her to do an unspeakable thing and pull that trigger, no matter how much he'd hurt her or put her through over the years. No matter what he'd done to her mother, I couldn't let her take a life.

"I'll do it! I will!" she yelled, the gun shaking even more now. Will merely laughed again. He wasn't helping. She already had some weight on the trigger, any more and it would fire.

"Baby, don't do this," I tried again. "Look at me. Give me the gun. You don't have to do this. He's not worth it."

"Baby?" Will questioned. "What the hell?"

I ignored him. Not daring to take my eyes off her. I could see she was having second thoughts.

"I just wanted to be free of him," she said, her bottom lip trembling.

"And you will be. I promise. From the bottom of my heart if you give me the gun right now I promise you, you will never have to look at him again. We'll go away, we'll leave together. We'll raise the baby together. We'll have the family you deserve."

"You and her? Are you fucking kidding me? You're fucking my daughter?"

Without breaking eye contact with Lola Ray I shouted, reminding him of his own admission, "She's not your fucking daughter! She's all mine now. You don't deserve her."

Will made the mistake of stepping forward, perhaps he was about to launch himself at me for betraying him. I guess it really didn't matter the nuances of our relationship, the betrayal was still there. But Lola Ray swung the gun onto him and through bleary eyes told him not to move.

"Lola Ray, baby, please, no. Don't do it. Your mom wouldn't want this for you. Let me protect you. I love you… please. Give me the gun."

Finally her eyes softened and she stepped into my arms and handed over the gun in the process. I held onto her like she was my lifeline and let her weep into my chest. I stared right at Will as I hugged her and I could see the fury build up inside him, his face going red in the process.

I kissed the top of Lola Ray's head. "I was just trying to look after myself and the baby…" she said in between sobs.

"But now you don't have to, you have me," I replied and levied the gun at Will's chest.

I squeezed her against me the same time I pulled the trigger.

DREAM DADDY

Chapter Thirty Three
Lola Ray

I sat shivering opposite the silent police station on a hard, low wall as the sun started to peek over the horizon. It was a beautiful crisp Christmas morning and I couldn't help but feel like a weight had been lifted from my shoulders. In a way the events of the previous day was the best present I could have ever received. Will, my pseudo father, stepdad—I didn't know what to call him—was gone. Forever. And I was glad.

He bled out on the kitchen floor. A heavy metallic tang in the air, the smell of gun smoke combining with the stink of the forgotten turkey overcooking in the oven.

Mack held me for a short while after he'd fired the gun. For the most part I was relieved that I didn't go through with killing Will myself. Grateful that Mack was able to take on that burden. In a way it showed me how much he actually cared for me. However there was a small part of me that was mad at myself for not having the strength to pull the trigger. I wanted to do it for my mom. After all those years, I wanted him to feel pain at my hand. But I also knew Mack was right. I wouldn't have been able to live with myself… as much as I tried to portray how strong I was, when it came to it, I needed to let myself lean on Mack one more time and let him protect me.

But after I got my breath back and reviewed the mess in the kitchen, I was adamant that Mack do exactly what I say. He had to stick to my plan. Yet whether or not he did what I told him was a different matter.

I was beginning to get a bad feeling the longer I sat and watched the sun rise. If he was telling the police what I told him to say, that I shot Will after he went into a rage as the result of finding out I was pregnant, then why on earth were they still keeping him in there, questioning him? They'd let me go after only a few hours, and I'd been the one to tell that I'd done it, that it had been me wielding the gun and who'd killed Will. Maybe they hadn't believed I was capable of doing it, and with Mack's previous record he was the more likely candidate. Convicted of manslaughter after protecting his sister from her husband, the cases, I had to admit, from an outsider's point of view, had their similarities.

The door opened and blinded me for a moment as it reflected the orange sky. I sat up longing to see Mack's face. I couldn't see who was coming out and blinked to restore my vision.

The man was wearing a thick coat over his uniform. Just another officer leaving after a long shift, I assumed. More officers left the building over the next few minutes and others took their places as they arrived for the morning shift. I zoned out as I watched them go in and out.

"God, you must be freezing, how long have you been sitting there?" Robin asked as she startled me from the sidewalk. I looked up at her with big question marks in my eyes. She took off her own coat and slung it around my shoulders and joined me on the wall. "I only just heard… and I've spent the last thirty minutes looking for you, worried sick. Are you okay?"

I nodded and longed for her not to ask what happened. I'd already spent half the night recounting the particulars of the previous day, going over every detail again and again. But she was too curious, and what was one more time?

It probably wouldn't be the last either. Yet, I had no delusions about telling her the truth.

"What on earth happened?" she asked predictably.

"I shot him, I killed my father," I replied absently, numb to the reality. Maybe if I said it enough times I would be able to convince myself that it was true.

"Oh god, why?" She tried to hide the eagerness to find out in voice, but even though she asked the question with a slight whisper and squeezed my hand, she wasn't able to completely hide her curiosity.

"The short story? He went after Sam. He shot him. I can't believe he shot him… and somehow I got hold of the gun…"

"Why on earth would he do that? I don't understand."

I took a breath, she was going to find out sooner or later… besides it was part of the official story. Or at least I hoped it would be.

"I'm pregnant."

"Holy crap. It's Sam's?"

I couldn't say the words. I didn't want to admit to that part. Instead I shrugged, giving her a noncommittal answer.

"God, this is insane." She paused for a moment suddenly coming to a realization. "What I don't get is why you're here, though. They let you go right? Let me take you home... or I mean to mine. You probably don't want to go home."

"I can't, I have to stay. I have to wait for..." my voice cracked as he stood before me, the door slowly closing behind him. I got to my feet and locked eyes with Mack across the street. They'd let him go!

I was about to run across the road, wanting nothing more than to jump into his arms, but with an almost imperceptible shake of his head, my steps faltered and I stopped moving.

"Who's that?" she asked squinting.

The love of my life, the man of my dreams, the father of my baby...

But I didn't say any of that.

"Oh, your neighbor was there too?"

I ignored her.

Robin stood with me as Mack made his way toward me. He looked like he'd just been through the ringer. But he was out... that had to be a good sign, right? I wasn't sure whom I was trying to convince... I felt like if I lost him then all of it had been for nothing.

He dug his hands deep into his pockets, but not before I noticed the slight redness around his wrists from where the harsh cuffs had been. "Are you okay?" he said breaking the silence, while shifting his gaze to Robin.

"Can we have a moment?" I said to her, ignoring his question. I would be fine if we were in the clear, but I could no longer read his face. Robin's brows knitted together but soon smoothed out again. I knew exactly what she was thinking though: who was this guy, how was he involved, and what was he to me? Some day I guessed I would tell her… maybe. Or she would eventually figure it out.

"Sure, of course. I'll let you two talk… I'll be right over there if you need me." She pointed to her car.

Mack stepped forward as close as he could without it looking suspicious or weird. I had to continue the pretense; he was just a neighbor, my dead dad's best friend. A witness to what had gone down, nothing more.

"Why did they keep you so long?"

"Just making sure I guess. And they had to get my parole officer to come down."

"But you stuck to the story? That it was me? That I shot him?"

"Against my better judgement, but yes," he said and nodded.

"Thank god…" I closed my eyes. My body suddenly wanted to let go of all the worry it had been holding in; tears wanting to escape. "It's over."

He took a step toward me, the sound of the movement making me open my eyes and look at him. "It is… at least for now. I'm sure there will be more questions. But I think they're happy enough to let it go down as self-defense."

"And you're safe? You're not going to prison… you're not going to leave me?"

His Adam's apple jutted down, then back up in his throat. Had this all been for nothing? Was I going to lose him now? He had to know that I was only doing it for us, didn't he?

"Lola Ray… I need you to answer me one question."

"Anything."

"Two, actually." He paused as if everything weighed on what he was about to say. "Is there a baby? And if there is, whose is it?"

My shoulders were tense in preparation but I let them drop softening, and dangerously closed the gap between us. I took his hand, then stared directly into his wanting blue eyes. "It's yours, it's always been yours. Sam never laid a finger on me."

The reaction I'd been waiting for, the one I'd been expecting the previous night when the truth had come out, was now evident on Mack's face. It was as if the last few hours had never even happened and I was telling him for the first time. I was pregnant and it was his. He stood taller, his eyes crinkling with happiness.

"You're going to be a daddy," I whispered.

He struggled to keep his emotions in check as we stood awkwardly outside the Weyworth police station, and before I could stop him, he pulled me to him, wrapped his arms around me, and held me tight.

"I can't wait. Let's go home, okay?"

"Home, where's that now?" I said with a slight wince. Will's house had never felt like a home, not since my mom was gone, and I didn't feel like I could ever step foot into that place ever again.

"With me, of course. Where you belong. The both of you," he said and eased his large hand upon my stomach. "I'm never letting either of you out of my sight."

Epilogue
Mack

I did a double-take when I saw a flash of pink speed by the open doorway of my office. We'd moved into the new house and were nicely settling into a town a few states away from "home." But this was our home now. Where no one knew us, where we could be ourselves. And it seemed my new bride was making herself very comfortable.

She was glowing, gorgeous as ever, her belly beautifully ripe with my child, her neck adorned with the diamond pendant she deserved... and she was naked. Walking past my office door nude, in the middle of the day, like it was the most natural thing in the world.

Lola Ray had been pouting earlier, complaining I was working too much. And in a way I supposed

I had been. There'd been a lot on my plate since the move.

After a few months, things had begun to settle down in Weyworth and though we were still being very cautious, we'd decided it was best to leave it all behind. Sam was finally let out of the hospital, having made a full recovery—he'd lost a lot of blood and bumped his head, but he was alive—and though he didn't exactly remember everything from that night, he remembered enough to back up part of our story and help get the case officially closed. Later, to tie up loose ends, Lola Ray admitted to Sam that the test had been a false positive, though she hadn't known it at the time. But for all intents and purposes there wasn't a baby. At least not one that was Sam's.

After that no one really paid us any attention or looked in our direction, but we were surprised when Will's estate, including his business and house were all awarded automatically to her, because she was technically—on paper—his next of kin.

At first she was reluctant to accept the windfall. Lola Ray had little interest in running a construction company and all that it entailed. But she soon realized with practically no persuasion on my part—I wanted it to be her decision—she figured a lot of good could come out of taking the money and starting a new life elsewhere. So she passed the business side of things to me. We sold Will's house, left my rented one, and moved ourselves and the company across state lines to begin anew, but not before donating a large portion of her inheritance to a battered women's shelter in memory of her mom.

Taking on the business had been a big undertaking, one I wasn't fully sure about, but Lola Ray said she had the utmost confidence in me to make it work so we could support our family and have a fresh start. Of course, that didn't stop her from grumbling when I had to work late to get up to speed and make sure the business was running smoothly.

I closed the lid of my laptop and watched the door intently. I didn't think I'd imagined her walking past and if I knew my baby girl, it wouldn't be long before she walked past the other way, in case I hadn't seen the first time.

A moment later I heard her pad down the hallway barefoot, then she was framed deliciously in the open doorway. She slowed down and turned her head only a little, maybe just to see if I was paying attention. Our eyes locked and she giggled, running away.

"You have my attention now!" I bolted to my feet and was around my desk in a flash, my dick hardening, pointing the way to her, like a missile seeker.

She was still laughing, but the bubbling giggles were muffled.

"You can't hide from me," I called, blood rushing through my veins, pounding around my body as I thought of what I was going to do to her once I caught her. "Daddy's going to find you!"

I didn't have to look far, stripping my clothes off as I searched, but she still took my breath away when I lay my eyes on her again. It was like I'd been transported back in time, back to all those months ago, to the day I'd come home to find that she'd broken in to my house and had positioned herself just so, ready for me.

She licked her lips as I entered our new playroom, casting a wanting glance at me over her shoulder. Straddling the table she was bent over, spread and partially on her knees, her ass in the air, presenting her wet pussy to me. But I had something else in mind instead.

I gave her an initial slap on her round bottom and got a pleasing gasp in response. "Harder, Daddy," she moaned. I knew exactly what she wanted me to do, but this time I was going to have my own way. I'd been patient long enough, and though I hadn't planned for it to happen right then, now was the perfect opportunity. She was relaxed and begging for it.

"Not this time, baby girl. Daddy has other ideas," I said as I grabbed her cheek, softly kneading my fingers into her soft ass and tugging her to the side a bit. I kicked off the last of my clothes and reached for the bottle of special lube we kept nearby. I glanced at the mechanical fucking machine for a second debating whether or not to set it up, but I was too eager, too needy and impatient… maybe next time. Instead I pulled a thick dildo from our collection, one that matched me in girth and size, almost a replica of my cock, and set it down on the table ready, out of sight.

"What are you going to do to me?" she breathed, adding in a playful hint of apprehension. She was a good little actress when she wanted to be, and it made our lovemaking sessions all the more enjoyable. I couldn't have dreamed up a better partner, if I was being honest with myself.

"Wouldn't you like to know," I replied, wanting to keep her in suspense for as long as possible.

"I want you to take me like our first time," Lola Ray said locking eyes with me.

"You'll get what you're given little girl…"

I teased her pussy with my tongue, lapping her up and sucking on her lips, getting her good and excited. She was so succulent. But with my finger on her clit, continuing the build up I began to move my tongue a little higher, exploring and letting the tip of my tongue flick over her rim. Her little asshole puckered but she panted and touched herself, squeezing her breasts that had practically doubled in size during her pregnancy. Carefully, taking my time, I deepened my touch, pushing my tongue a tiny way into her tight hole. It had been the one place that was left unexplored, her virgin little asshole. That I promised one day I would make mine. And today was going to be that day.

She squirmed a little getting used to the sensation. I trickled a few drops of lube onto her, aiming them so they would splash down onto her ass. With the tip of my finger I spread the lube and boldly teased her hole again, easing my finger into her.

It hadn't exactly been the first time I'd done this to her. I'd been slowly building her up, training her little asshole with ever increasing buttplugs, getting her ready for this special day. But she clenched a fraction nonetheless as it perhaps began to sink in what I had in mind.

"Relax, baby." I switched focus and went back

to playing with her pussy, rubbing the head of my cock against her. She arched back, desperate for me to slip inside her.

She cried out with surprise as I rocked into her cunt, hard. In the past I'd always resisted filling her up when she did that, so it was no wonder that it came as a shock when suddenly I was balls deep within her.

It didn't last long though. I pulled myself out straight away, and she moaned in frustration. "Put it back," she demanded like a petulant child, as if her favorite toy had been taken away from her.

"I'll give you something better…"

My cock nudged her virgin asshole, slippery with lube. Instinctively instead of arching against me she leaned increasingly forward, forcing me to grab her around her waist and keep her place. I leaned over her, my chest touching her back and whispered into her ear, "Let me fill you like you've never been filled before, I promise I'll be gentle. Let me feel how tight you are."

I could feel her heart pounding against me, mouth open, breathing hard. "I'm yours to take, Daddy."

My fingers trailed down her spine, kissing her back, as I got back into position, and slowly spread her cheeks wide and began to take her, inch by inch.

She hissed like a cat but with a constant stream of loving words she began to relax, easing into the new feeling. It was almost too much for me, and I found myself having to pause every few seconds for fear of exploding. She was incredibly tight.

"You feel so good, baby," I moaned to her, and was surprised to feel her push back for more. It seemed I'd awoken a need within her.

"Faster, please... I like it," she uttered, and I could tell by her soft voice she was close to cumming.

"Not yet," I replied. Still trying to acclimate myself. But as I did, I remembered the dildo I'd gotten out. Keeping her stationary and making sure I wasn't going to move either, my hand found what it was looking for on the table and brought its tip to her pussy's entrance.

"Oh god," she breathed as I stimulated her with the hard dildo, wiggling it into her and she begged for more. Soon enough, with my arm aching, I was screwing her hard with the thing, ramming it in and out. And slowly as if on her own accord she began to rock back against my cock, deepening it inside her ass. I pushed forward cautiously, tilting my hips all at the same time as I operated the thick dildo inside her cunt.

I wanted to let go of it, so I could grab hold of her hips and drive myself even farther into her. "Hold it," I commanded breathing hard, "Fuck your sweet cunt." We were so in sync she understood immediately and snaked her arm beneath herself and claimed the dildo.

I was like a dog without a leash now, uncontrollable, free. My fingers dug into her waist and yanked her closer. Her moans echoed around the room as I shifted deeper inside her. Without a doubt I could feel the intense tightening of her walls as they contracted around my cock, starting to squeeze me and I thought I was going to go insane with the bliss I was experiencing.

"Harder, Daddy, harder!" she yelled as two cocks simultaneously filled her up. The only thing that could've made it more delicious was having a third fill her mouth... but perhaps we'd save that for another time, I considered, as I imagine a mechanical fucking machine filling her asshole, the dildo in her cunt and my cock finally in her mouth. *Maybe for her birthday*, I thought with a smile.

My plan though right then was to pull out of her and cum on her ass but I was too far gone, and she'd already began to keen, dripping her juices onto the table. I thrust inside her once more, so hard I thought I was going to split her in two. Instead I let loose a wild cry, my eyes scrunched up hard, my balls writhing, and emptied myself with such force I could've sworn it was enough to propel her forward.

Spent, we let our moans die down for a second and regained our breath. And though my legs shook, after I eased myself slowly out of her, I picked up my pregnant wife and carried her to our bed. She turned to me with lazy, dreamy eyes and managed to muster enough energy to shake her pretty little head.

"That was amazing. I'm a little sore, but I never knew how intense it could be…"

"*You* were amazing," I countered, stroking her hair and face, then letting my hands trail down to her belly.

She blushed, two bright pinks spots appearing on her cheeks. "You are," I continued. "You're everything I thought I never needed. You, Lola Ray, are my sunshine, my moon, my all. You've made me the happiest man alive. Don't you realize that?"

"Even in spite of everything that happened? Even after I practically forced and manipulated you to kill your best friend?"

I paused to consider this, but chose to be honest with her. "Darling, I would kill a thousand times over for you. Nothing and no one will ever hurt you again, I'm just disappointed with myself that I didn't do it sooner. Can you ever forgive me?"

"There's nothing to forgive," she said and tightened her hold on me. "You're everything I ever dreamed of too. And you're going to be a wonderful father."

"I'll never let you down again… I'll protect you and our baby with every fiber of my being. That's for damned sure, Lola Ray."

"I know you will, Daddy," she said beaming at me. The glint in her eye telling me she'd recovered enough and was ready for another pleasurable dream wrapped safe in my arms.

The End

All about Emilia Beaumont

Emilia Beaumont is a full-time writer, originally hailing from England, living in the South of Ireland with her husband and a house full of cats. Surrounded by peaceful emerald fields she always has a pen and notebook to hand ready for when the next saucy idea strikes. Emilia is also an avid comic-book reader, and a wildlife advocate.

www.facebook.com/authoremiliabeaumont

emilia@emiliabeaumont.com

DREAM DADDY

Also by Emilia

BILLIONIARE STEPBROTHER
KISS ME AGAIN
HITMAN'S REVENGE

Expecting Stepbrother series:

EXPECTING MY BILLIONAIRE STEPBROTHER'S BABY
LOVING MY BILLIONIARE STEPBROTHER'S BABY

Forbidden Desires Series:

SNAKE
VULTURE
SHARK

DREAM DADDY

Made in the USA
Columbia, SC
23 April 2017